IN IT TO WIN IT

WYNN HOCKEY

KELLY JAMIESON

CONTENT NOTES

Content notes for this book and all my books are available
on my website at
https://www.kellyjamieson.com/content-notes

THE WYNN DYNASTY

Bob Wynn, owner of the California Condors. Originally married to Grace Rogers (deceased), parents to Mark and Matthew with Grace. Parents to Everly, Asher, Harrison, and Noah with Chelsea Wynn. Grandfather to Jean Paul (JP), Théo, Jackson, and Riley.

Chelsea Wynn (formerly Clark), married to Bob Wynn, mother of Everly, Asher, Harrison, and Noah.

Matthew Wynn, owner of the Long Beach Golden Eagles. Son of Bob Wynn. Married to Aline Gagnon. Father of Théo and Jean Paul (JP).

Mark Wynn, coach of the Long Beach Golden Eagles. Son of Bob Wynn. Divorced from Victoria (Tori) Kendall. Father of Jackson and Riley.

Théo Wynn, general manager of the California Condors. Son of Matthew Wynn and Aline Gagnon. Grandson of Bob Wynn (with Grace).

Jean Paul (JP) Wynn, son of Matthew Wynn and Aline Gagnon. Grandson of Bob Wynn (with Grace). Plays for the Long Beach Golden Eagles.

Jackson Wynn, son of Mark Wynn and Victoria (Tori)

Kendall. Grandson of Bob Wynn (with Grace). Plays for the Chicago Aces.

Riley Wynn, daughter of Mark Wynn and Victoria (Tori) Kendall. Granddaughter of Bob Wynn (with Grace). Goalie coach for the San Diego Hawks, affiliate team of the Long Beach Golden Eagles.

Everly Wynn, daughter of Bob and Chelsea Wynn. Executive director of the Condors Foundation.

Asher Wynn, son of Bob and Chelsea Wynn. Sports reporter for *Playmaker* (hockey blog).

Harrison Wynn, son of Bob and Chelsea Wynn. Plays for the Pasadena Condors, affiliate team of the California Condors.

Noah Wynn, son of Bob and Chelsea Wynn. Plays for the San Diego Hawks.

1

JP

I should have known a Wynn family wedding wasn't going to go off without drama.

Didn't think it would be me in the middle of it, though.

Then again, it totally makes sense, because apparently, I can never be trusted to do the right thing.

Let's go back to last night . . .

My brother Théo is getting married, but this isn't a typical wedding (it's the Wynn family, need I say more?) because Théo and Lacey are already married, after a quickie Vegas wedding a few months ago. My mom was so disappointed about not being at their wedding, she wanted another one, and shockingly, Théo agreed.

So there haven't been bridal showers or bachelor and bachelorette parties. Tonight is the first time the wedding party and family are getting together for the rehearsal at the Shore Hotel in Santa Monica, where the wedding will be held tomorrow.

I'm standing next to Théo where the ceremony will take

place. Right now the arch next to us is bare, but tomorrow it'll be decked with flowers and bows and shit. We're outside on a raised terrace, the beach right behind us.

I'm the best man. Except I'm most definitely *not* the best man. A year ago I fucked up and screwed over Théo, my own brother. It's taking some time for our relationship to recover, but he says he's forgiven me.

I haven't forgiven myself.

And the rest of our family hasn't forgiven me either.

I've had dirty looks, subtle shade, and outright hostility from my cousins, my aunt and uncles, and especially from my grandfather.

Which sucks, because Grandpa is my idol.

Bob Wynn, the King of Hockey. The man I looked up to my whole life. Until the last couple of years. He's made some . . . um, interesting decisions lately. To be honest, I'm not sure what's really going on, except I know my dad and my uncle Mark are pissed as hell at him, so much that they're actually suing him, claiming he stole money from them.

This makes family gatherings—like this wedding—a tad uncomfortable.

But never mind all that . . . my attention is on the hot bridesmaid.

Taylor Hart.

I keep looking at her over on the other side of Lacey, the bride. Taylor's gorgeous—perfect oval face, long dark hair, toffee-colored eyes, and a full mouth that's perpetually curved into a smile. For the rehearsal, she's wearing a burgundy dress that wraps around her body and stops just above her knees, and suede heels that match the dress.

I catch her eye and grin, and she smiles back . . . a wide, glowing smile that lights up her face. She has a great smile. It's like sunshine. Warm. Bright.

She also has a great rack.

She's not here with a date. She's not wearing a ring. Fuck yeah.

I can't wait for this formal stuff to be done so we can party. Everyone knows what's supposed to happen and when. I have to hand over the ring, Lacey's best friend takes her bouquet, blah blah blah. Now let's have some fun.

There are about twenty of us who move to the private room after the rehearsal, and I see there are three round tables set up. Place cards identify who sits where, and since I'm one of the first ones in the room, I quickly find my own name . . . and Taylor's. She's at a different table, but I make the switch speedy quick so she's now sitting beside me instead of my aunt Everly. Then I head to the bar at the end of the room. Of course there's champagne, so I grab two flutes and turn, searching for Taylor.

There she is, just entering the room. I make my way over to her and stop. "Champagne?" I hold out a glass to her.

Her lips quirk up at the corners as she reaches for the glass. "Why, thank you."

"You're most welcome." I gesture toward the table. "Apparently we're sitting beside each other for dinner."

She bursts out laughing. "Oh my God. Did you change the place cards?"

"How did you know that?"

"I helped set up the tables." She sips her wine, eyes dancing.

"Damn." I rub my chin, smiling ruefully. "Busted. But can you blame me for wanting to sit beside a beautiful woman instead of my aunt?"

She shakes her head. "Your aunt *is* a beautiful woman."

My aunt Everly is only a year older than me. It's weird, but my grandfather married for the second time later in life and had four more kids, Everly being one of them. She's also a bridesmaid, having become good friends with Lacey. "Well, yeah, she is. But she's my *aunt*. I can't flirt with her."

"You're going to flirt with *me*?"

"All night long." I meet her eyes. Hers darken, and heat slides down my spine.

"Well, calling me beautiful is a good start."

"It's the truth."

"I don't know." She tilts her head and studies me. "You seem a little cocky. You probably say that to all the girls."

I grin. "Only the beautiful ones."

Everyone is taking their seats for dinner, so I pull out Taylor's chair for her.

"Thank you."

I take my seat next to her. "We can get to know each other better over dinner."

Her eyes meet mine and she purses her lips.

"Why are you looking at me like that? I'm a nice guy." I lay a hand on my chest.

"That's not what I've heard."

"Oh no." I groan. "Théo's been talking about me."

"Well, yeah. But you also have a . . . reputation as a hockey player, Killer."

Killer. Great. "You like hockey?"

She nods.

"You've seen me play."

"I was at the game last year when you hit Novotny and got suspended."

I press my lips together, my jaw tightening. I look down at my place setting. "That shouldn't have happened." I lift my head and meet her eyes. "I don't play to hurt guys. Really."

She nods slowly. "But that wasn't the first time you got suspended."

I suck in a long breath. "True. Sometimes my emotions get the best of me. I'm working on it. Trying to do better."

It's true. This year I have to show the team I'm worth keeping on the roster. Last year didn't go so well. In a lot of ways.

The others are now sitting at our table—six people—so we make small talk. Lacey and Théo stop at the table to chitchat for a few minutes, and then servers start bringing out salads, so they take their own seats.

"How long have you known Lacey?" I ask as we dig into greens with blueberries, walnuts, and feta cheese.

"Not long. Just since she moved here."

"You must have become friends pretty fast."

"Yes. We met when she helped me catch my dog. And my dog liked her, so I knew she was okay."

"What kind of dog do you have?"

"Golden retriever. His name is Byron."

"Nice. So that's your test of whether someone is worth hanging out with? If your dog likes them?"

She nods, her lips quirked. "I've found it to be a reliable indicator. Dogs are smart."

"Yeah. I like dogs. We had a standard poodle growing up. He was so smart it was scary."

"And you know, sometimes you meet someone and things just . . . click." Our eyes meet and hold again and the air buzzes around us. Yeah, I know that feeling. "When I met Lacey, right away I felt like I could talk to her about anything. She's so . . . alive. Just fun to be with, yet she can be serious and she's smart, too."

I nod. I kind of feel like that about Taylor. This feels so easy . . . and yet so electrifying. "What do you do for a living?"

"I'm a speech language pathologist."

"Whoa."

She laughs. "Why? What's wrong with that?"

"I'm not even sure what a speech language pathologist does."

A server removes our plates and we sit back for a moment. I pick up the wineglass someone has thoughtfully filled with a golden wine.

"I help children who have speech delays or disorders, language delays, sometimes swallowing or feeding disorders," she says when the server has moved away. Her face softens. "I work mostly with kids. I love kids."

I'm . . . blown away, I guess. This is not what I expected. "Do you work at a hospital?"

"No. A private clinic. I haven't worked there long. I just graduated last year. You have to have a master's degree to practice."

Jesus. "Where did you go to college?"

"For my graduate degree, Seattle. University of

Washington. I got my undergrad degree here in California."

"Six years of university?"

"Yep."

"That's impressive." I could never do that.

"Thanks. I love it." She tilts her head. "You must love playing hockey."

"I do."

"What do you love about it?"

"Everything." I give her a lopsided smile. "I love the action, how fast it is, the skills you need. I love competing. I love winning."

"Don't we all."

I chuckle. "Yeah. Obviously, with my family, if you didn't love hockey you'd be a complete misfit."

Now our meals are served . . . charred lemon chicken piccata served over pasta. It looks delicious.

"There's nobody in your family who doesn't like hockey?" Taylor picks up her fork. "I mean, I know Everly doesn't *play* hockey, but she watches the game and works with the hockey team, sort of."

"Yeah." I nod and tip my wineglass to my lips. "The only ones who aren't really involved in hockey are Chelsea —my grandpa's wife—"

"Yes, I know who she is." She nods and cuts a piece of chicken.

"And my mom. But my mom was a hockey mom, driving Théo and me to practices and games at ungodly hours, lugging our equipment around, cheering us on at every game. So that counts, I guess."

"And Chelsea married into a hockey family."

"Right."

"I have to admit I didn't grow up watching hockey, but I got free tickets to a game once when I was about seventeen, and I loved it. It was so fast and fierce."

"Yeah." I like it that she enjoys hockey. "Do you play any sports?"

"I played volleyball in high school, and college."

"Hey, no kidding. That's awesome."

"I still like to get together with friends on the beach and play some ball."

Every nerve ending in my body goes on alert as I picture Taylor in a bikini, jumping up and down in the sand, setting and spiking the ball. "I'd love to do that."

"Well, sure. There are volleyball nets right near where I live. Which is right by Lacey and Théo. We should do that sometime."

Sparks crackle between us. I lean closer. "For sure. That would be fun."

"You know how to play volleyball?"

"Yeah." I shrug.

"You're probably good at it."

"Eh. Not as good as at hockey."

"Volleyball's not as rough as hockey."

"I play a physical game," I admit.

"Do you get in a lot of fights?"

"Not gonna lie, I've been in a few. Not so much anymore. But sometimes I piss people off. And sometimes they piss *me* off." I shrug. I've made some mistakes, but for some reason, I want her approval. When I meet her eyes I don't see judgment or disapproval, though. I see warmth and curiosity, as if she wants to understand. "I'm trying to do better."

"Aren't we all," she murmurs.

We share a long look of mutual interest that makes my chest fill with heat. "Okay, I know you like dogs and kids and volleyball. How about tattoos?"

She laughs. "Do I like them on other people? Or on myself?"

"Both."

"I have no tattoos. But I like them on other people. Do you have any?"

"Yeah. Just one, one my back." I pause, then lean closer to ask in a low voice, "What's your opinion on porn?"

She bursts out laughing again. "Wow, we're really getting to the good stuff."

"Just curious."

"Maybe we could talk about this later." She glances around at the others at the table.

"Absolutely." I don't hesitate, because I'm perfectly willing to talk to Taylor about porn later . . . preferably up in my hotel room, where I'm staying for the weekend nuptials.

For a while we join in other conversation at our table, until we're served a tiny slice of chocolate cake sitting in a pool of raspberry sauce.

"Raspberries are my favorite fruit," Taylor says.

With my fork, I lift the berries garnishing my plate and transfer them to hers.

She shoots me a startled glance.

I smile. "Enjoy."

"Thank you." She gives her head a small shake and pushes the tines of her fork into one berry.

With dinner finished, Théo and Lacey stand at one end of the room to say a few words, thanking all of us, and then presenting their wedding party—me, Taylor, Karine, Everly, Andy, and Leo—with our gifts: gold bracelets for the bridesmaids and for the guys, a wooden box with whisky stones and a shot glass, and a bottle of Crown Royal.

"This is awesome," I say to Théo. "Thanks, bro."

Some people are moving out to the hotel bar for another drink and since Taylor is one of them, I join them too. We're at a smaller table with a little more privacy. She orders a glass of sauvignon blanc and I go for a beer this time.

"I can't stay too late," she says. "Don't want to be posing for pictures tomorrow with big bags under my eyes."

I scoff. "You could never look bad." She really is one of those natural beauties, with high cheekbones, perfect skin, and full lips.

"And you're full of it." She smiles, though.

Damn, that smile. It makes me hard. "Now you can tell me what kind of porn you like to watch."

"Did I say I like to watch porn?"

I catch the teasing twinkle in her eye and grin. I pick up my drink.

"Okay, okay," she says. "Porn is fun sometimes. I'm kind of an 'everything in moderation' person. I don't like stuff that's demeaning to women, though. I like romantic porn. But I don't think it's good for anyone to watch too much of it. Real-life sex is better."

"Oh, hell yeah." I hold her gaze meaningfully. Heat slides through my veins, my dick thickening with arousal. "I bet real-life sex with you is amazing."

"That's . . ." Her eyelashes flutter, but she's looking at my mouth. "Inappropriate."

"I often am," I admit. "But I'm not taking it back."

I want to kiss her so damn bad. I've always had a little problem with impulse control, and it's all I can do to stop myself from leaning in even closer and kissing her. But there are others around us, friends and family, so I restrain myself, giving myself a mental pat on the back.

"Have you ever made a sex tape?" I ask.

Her eyes widen. "Uh . . . that's not really smart."

"Sadly, that's true. You have to trust the person you're with."

"Not only that! What about that actress who had her sex tapes stolen from the cloud? Hackers can get into anything."

"Right."

"And maybe you trust the person at the time, but then you discover he's a pill-popping addict with a gambling problem who hits on your friends, and you dump his ass, and next thing you know he's sending the video to all his buddies on Snapchat."

"Whoa." I frown. "You're not speaking from experience, I hope."

She winces. "Maybe."

Ugh. What kind of doucheholes has she been dating? "I would never do that."

"So you say."

"You don't trust me?"

"I don't trust anyone to make a sex tape with, but I'd trust you for . . . other things."

"Oh. I'm good at . . . *other things.*" Lightning-hot desire jolts straight to my groin.

Her eyes darken and her lips part as she leans forward. My breath sticks in my throat. "Too bad I'll never know."

"Ouch." I sit back, lips pursed.

She laughs lightly.

I shake my head. "Cut off at the knees by a gorgeous woman."

"Thank you. You're pretty gorgeous yourself." She pats my shoulder.

Her hand lingers on my shoulder as our eyes connect again. Excitement sparkles through my veins. "You're just busting my balls, Sunshine. You want to come up to my room with me."

Her breath hitches.

Leaning closer, I murmur near her ear, "No video, I promise. But I can guarantee you several orgasms."

"Th-that's a bold promise."

"Confident. Also I'm dying to taste you . . . and make you feel good . . ."

"Oh God." She gulps some wine.

I sit back and try to look casual, but when I meet her eyes, sexual urgency sizzles around us. I finish my beer. As I set it on the table, I lean in close to her ear. "I'm going up to my room. Four fourteen. I'd love for you to join me. Your call."

I say good night to the others there, who I'll see tomorrow for the wedding, and stroll out of the bar, across the lobby, and into the elevator.

My skin is prickling and my veins are buzzing as I enter my suite. I flick on a light, the door closing behind me, drop my gift from Théo onto the desk, and stroll over to the window. I have an ocean-view room, and I can see the lights of the Santa Monica Pier, the Ferris wheel glowing against the night sky.

I don't know if Taylor will come to my room or not. I'm going to be disappointed as hell if she doesn't, because there's some crazy chemistry between us. There's always tomorrow, though. A sexy bridesmaid makes a wedding a little more fun.

I kick off my shoes, sprawl onto the couch in the living room, and pick up the remote for the giant TV. Tomorrow, Théo and the other guys will join me here to get ready for the wedding and have some pictures taken. I've got drinks and snacks for the pre-game.

I flick through various channels and end up watching a sports news show even though hockey season hasn't started yet.

Soon.

After a while, I glumly turn off the TV. She's not coming.

I stand and as I move toward the bathroom, I hear a soft knock on the door.

My heart kicks against my ribs. I casually stroll to the door, though, and use the peephole.

Taylor.

I drop my forehead against the door, every nerve ending lighting up. Then I yank it open.

She eyes me, her mouth soft and uncertain, her eyes big and luminous. "Hi."

"Hi, Sunshine." I step aside so she can come in. "I thought you weren't coming."

She walks past me, carrying her purse and gift bag. "You promised me I would."

A surprised laugh erupts inside me. "So I did."

2

TAYLOR

Well, this is unexpected.

And . . . hot.

I've been dreading this wedding, knowing it's going to make me feel like a failure in the Department of Romantic Attachments all over again. I've been through bad dates, mad breakups, and sad disappointments.

But . . . wow. JP Wynn is such a sexy bad boy. And he wants me. Why shouldn't I have a one-night pre-wedding fling?

I saw the way every other woman there tonight looked at him. He's so brazenly masculine . . . big, hard body, dark hair and beard stubble, gorgeous blue eyes, and a cocky smirk that promises all the wicked things he'd like to do to me . . . some of which he actually said out loud, which is so . . . *bad.*

This is the Wynn brother I'm supposed to hate. He's a dick. He stole his own brother's girlfriend. What kind of jerk would do that? I know they're trying to get past it, but I formed my impression of him before I even met him—from that, and from his hockey play. I'm not supposed to like him. Only now . . . I'm ready to lose my panties over him.

I'm a little horrified by this.

And excited.

I told myself I should walk out of the hotel, get home early, and sleep alone the night before the wedding. I should *not* go to the hotel room of a man I barely know . . . but here I am.

I can't believe I'm doing this.

As I turn to face him, I register minimal details about the suite JP's staying in—doors onto a balcony that overlooks the ocean open to the fresh evening breeze, a thick rug on the dark wood floor, cream and blue décor, and a door to a bedroom with a huge bed covered in a white duvet.

"This suite is lovely," I say in a husky voice as I drop my purse and my bag on the coffee table.

A stupid thing to say. I should be making some kind of sexy, sophisticated remark.

He walks toward me, eyes on my face, stopping in front of me. He's tall. And I'm even wearing three-inch heels. "So are you."

He reaches for me and uses both hands to smooth my hair back, so gently, then he cups my face. His eyes smolder blue and his mouth is ridiculous . . . sharply carved, with a perfect full bottom lip.

"You keep looking at me like that," he says gruffly.

"Like what?"

"Like you want to kiss me."

"I . . . do."

"Fuck, so do I." With a groan, his thick eyelashes lower and his mouth touches mine.

It's a soft kiss, long and gentle and anticipatory. Sparks float through my veins. My belly flip-flops, heat pooling low inside me. Then he lifts his mouth, tilts my head with his big hands, and kisses me again, this time opening his mouth on mine.

I whimper and open to him as he licks inside my mouth. His tongue is strong and hot, sliding against mine, and heat sweeps through me like wildfire. I slide my hands around the back of his neck and press closer still, body to body, and he's aroused. So am I.

His kisses are delicious, his mouth firm and demanding, his tongue licking into my mouth so hot I think my bones are melting. I press myself harder against his erection and he groans. "Wow," he murmurs, kissing my cheek. "You are so fucking hot."

"So are you. You're a good kisser."

"Give me that mouth again."

His words have my belly squeezing with excitement and we kiss again, long, deep, wet, and scorching hot. Flames build inside me like a match thrown on dry kindling.

JP's hands move over me, sliding down to my ass to pull me up against him. I love how he squeezes me, then coasts his hands up my sides to brush against the sides of my breasts. I want his hands on my skin, everywhere. The ache between my legs is relentless. Insistent. I also want *my* hands on *him*, everywhere, feeling every hard muscle, especially that one that's so rigid behind his zipper.

"Let's get you out of this dress." His hands move over

me, seeking the zipper. "I need to see your sexy body. And get my hands on you."

"On the side." Breathless, I reach for the zipper myself, but he takes over, yanking it down and letting the dress fall off me. I undo my bra and toss it aside as he drags my panties down my legs.

I'm still in my suede heels and he pauses, his hands on my calves. My entire body quivers as his palms caress my legs. "Jesus, that's hot," he says hoarsely. Then he stands and yanks off his tie while I work on his shirt buttons. Together, we get him undressed too, and he picks me up and carries me to the bed, which has my belly fluttering again.

He disappears into the bathroom briefly, returning with a condom he rolls onto his stiff cock. I can only stare in desperate admiration as he walks toward me, his body so beautiful and perfect.

He comes down over me—wide shoulders, strong arms, knees on either side of me. His thick, strong thighs flex as he easily adjusts my position beneath him, shifting me on the bed with his hands on my hips, and I reach for his face to cup it as he kisses me. I bend my legs and reach down between us to find his cock, eager to have him inside me, filling this aching need.

"Wait, baby. Need to make sure you're ready." He pushes back up onto his knees and moves my hands aside. He strokes his fingers through my pussy, and yes, I'm ready. I'm wet and swollen and sensitive. "Oh yeah. That's fucking sweet."

My eyes fly open wide as he lifts his fingers to his mouth

and licks my taste off them. "Holy mother . . . I need you. Inside me. Please."

"Yeah. Want to fuck you so bad. Christ . . ."

He takes his shaft in his hand and rubs the head through my slick folds, over my clit. I jolt with sensation, holding my knees back, opening myself to him, watching him. He groans, then slowly finds my entrance, pushing inside deliberately, unhurriedly, watching my face with an intensity that mesmerizes me. Heat blasts through me as he penetrates me deeper, deeper still, my body closing around him. My mouth opens and my breathing picks up speed, my heart racing.

He moves faster. Faster . . . pumping into me, causing my body to shake with sensation. He grips one of my thighs and one of my hips, plunging deeper, harder. My breasts are bouncing, and he lifts his hands to cover both of them, squeezing, tweaking my nipples. Pleasure rolls through me, intensity building in my core and spiraling higher inside me.

I slide a hand down to my pussy to rub my clit.

"Want me to do that?" he asks in a low, gruff voice.

I roll my head on the bed in a negative, so needy I just want to come.

He nods, his gaze holding mine, his eyes dark and hungry. This only adds to the intensity, the feeling of connection between us.

My fingers work, finding the right spot, the right pressure, the power of his cock stroking over sensitive nerve endings inside me sending me flying up and up and up, filling me with dazzling sensation.

He lets out a shout and a long, harsh groan, going still against me. I feel him pulsating inside me, and I squeeze around him again and again. I'm dizzy and dazed, breathless and quivering.

He lowers himself to find my mouth with his, taking mine in a long, heated kiss, our bodies still joined so intimately.

He moves off me and collapses on the bed next to me. I'm panting, my body still quivering, my inner muscles pulsing. "Holy shit," I gasp. "I don't think I've ever come so hard."

"I don't want to be that guy and say 'I told you so' . . ."

I choke on a laugh. "I think you just were that guy. But I'll allow it, since I'm demolished."

JP reaches out a hand and flattens it on my belly. "I'm demolished too."

At the same moment, we roll to face each other. He studies me, stroking my hair, my shoulder, the top curve of one breast. Heat swells around us, thick and heavy. "That wasn't enough."

I slide my bottom lip between my teeth. "I know."

"Stay here with me tonight."

"That's crazy."

"I know. But why not?"

"I have to send a quick text."

He frowns as I slide out of bed to go find my purse. "A text to who?"

I pause at the bedroom door, looking over my shoulder. "Be right back."

Telling him I still live with my parents might be a mood killer. I'd rather do that when I'm back in bed, pressed up against him.

I send my mom a text to let her know I won't be home

tonight, then expel a sigh. I'm twenty-four years old. I lived on my own when I was in college. Moving back in with my parents has been rough. I've been independent, used to not answering to anyone, and it annoys me that I have to now, but I do it because I know my mom will worry if she wakes up in the morning and I'm not there.

I return to the bed and slip under the covers. JP is sitting up against the pillows, his eyebrows knitted, his mouth tight.

"Do you think I'm texting a boyfriend or something?" My lips lift with amusement at his black look.

"I have no idea." His jaw tics.

"It's my parents. I live with them."

"Oh." His face relaxes, and he lets out a short breath that almost sounds like relief. Then his forehead wrinkles again. "Uh . . . they're okay with you staying all night?"

"I don't ask their permission." I lay my hand on his chest and gently rub a circle. "I just tell them. Out of courtesy."

"Oh. Okay."

"I don't want to be living with them, but I just graduated. I have student loans, and homes are so expensive here . . . even renting a little studio apartment is more than I can afford right now."

He nods. "Yeah. I guess it's good you have that option. Pay off your loans, save some money."

"Right." He gets it. Whew.

He rolls me onto my back, moving over me. "Bottom line, you're mine all night. And I can't wait to taste that sweet pussy again. This time I want to feel you come on my mouth."

I melt into the bed. "Ohhh."

He parts my thighs with his rough hands, stroking the sensitive skin slowly up and down as he positions himself between them. His intent gaze on my pussy has my skin tingling everywhere.

He takes his time, massaging me, petting me, then finally bending his head to touch his mouth to me. My body is a mass of anticipation, quivery, needy for his touch. He licks leisurely along my outer lips, one side then the other, his hands reaching up to cup and squeeze my breasts. He takes his time exploring all around my pussy, sliding his tongue over my thighs, kissing my lower abdomen, then stroking over my flesh again. He kisses me, gently sucks me into his mouth and releases, his nose nudging me, then draws the flat of his tongue all over me again.

After long, excruciating, delicious moments, I'm writhing, heat pooling in my groin, my hips lifting off the bed. I set one foot on his shoulder.

"Beauty," he murmurs, lifting his head and using his fingers to probe deeper into my hidden parts. "So sweet and pretty."

A soft noise escapes my lips.

He pushes a finger deep inside me, then two fingers, crooking them, massaging my inner wall as he closes his lips over my clit. My body jolts like a live wire and I cry out.

He makes noises of enjoyment as he eats at me, pulling on my flesh, suckling and licking until I'm shaking, my abs clenching, my thighs trembling. Tension twists inside me, coiling and intensifying, drawing up and up, then bursting. I babble senselessly, fingers tugging at JP's thick hair, my hips elevating off the bed, pushing my pussy to his mouth as I come in endless, glorious waves of pleasure.

"Gorgeous." He gently licks me a few more times, slowly and almost reverently, then with another of those easy moves that demonstrate his strength, he flips me onto my belly. I gasp. I lift my head, but his warm hand presses on my middle back, then he lifts my hips. Shock reverberates through me as he once again presses his mouth to my pussy, this time from behind.

"Oh God."

"Making you come turns me on," he growls. "I'm so fucking hard now it hurts. Need to be inside that sweet, wet pussy."

"Yes." I close my eyes, my cheek pressed to the smooth sheet.

There's a pause as he gloves up, then his hands are on my butt cheeks, fondling me in a way that's both sweet and filthy. I know he's looking at me, seeing my most intimate secret places. My skin burns, my insides still tender and pulsing, aching for him to fuck me.

And he does, slowly easing into me. A long, low groan reaches my ears, thrilling me. I arch my back to take him deeper and he slides all the way in, thick and heavy, pressing his groin against my ass, holding my hips.

"Fuck, that's amazing," he rasps. "Your pussy all around me . . . I just want to fuck . . . and fuck . . . and fuck."

"Do it." My fingers curl into the sheets. "Fuck me. Fuck me hard. I like it hard."

I'll probably be embarrassed about that later, but right now, I don't care, I just want to feel him pounding into me. He moves carefully, as if holding back, and I push my ass back against him with each stroke. His hand rubs up and down my back, then tangles into my hair. The tug on my scalp is wickedly erotic and sweetly painful. Sensation skitters down my spine.

He pulls my hair as he thrusts, and I'm slamming against him, my body jolting. And there it is . . . another orgasm building. Really?

This time he does it for me, reaching around to find my clit, plucking it, then circling it with wet fingertips. I shudder and tense, another surge of sensation ripping through me just as he comes too, shouting out his pleasure.

He leans over me and fastens his mouth onto my shoulder in a love bite, his chest heaving against my back. I'm limp. Dazed. Ruined.

Wow.

3

———

JP

I catch Taylor's eye and smile.

I'm standing once again in front of the arch overlooking the beach at the Shore. Father Vincent from my mom's church is here, and Théo is next to me, all chill and happy now that his bride is standing next to him, looking beautiful in her wedding dress.

Taylor was the second bridesmaid to walk down the aisle, and she looked a little tense.

Jesus, I hope it's not because of me. Last night was amazing. Things better not be awkward today. But weddings are stressful; that's probably it.

She smiles back at me, her tense features relaxing.

Whew.

The bridesmaids' dresses are sexy—fitted and strapless, which shows off Taylor's great shoulders and toned arms. And her rack. She's carrying a bouquet of bright flowers. As I watch her, she glances out at the guests with another tight expression.

Jesus. I should be paying attention to the ceremony, not thinking about the bridesmaid's treasure chest. I'm such an ass.

For a while, I succeed at focusing on the wedding, but the next time I glance Taylor's way, she's watching me. *That way* . . . you know that way . . . remembering last night and all the dirty things we did to each other. I'm remembering how her cheeks flush pink when she comes. How sensitive her nipples are. How she . . . *Stop.* I'm getting a boner. Must stop thinking about naked Taylor coming on my face . . .

Maybe this wedding won't be so bad. I may be a pariah to everyone in my family, but at least someone here likes me. Weddings are a big party, and I like to party. I'm going to have fun tonight, family be damned.

Before the fun parts though, there are a few obligations to get through—photographs, dinner, the speech I have to make. We pose on the beach, eat the amazing meal, and then I get up to the microphone at the end of the head table and set my phone on the podium so I can see the notes I made on it.

"Good evening, everyone! I trust you're having a great night racking up the bar tab. Sorry about that, Mom and Dad."

A ripple of laughter flows through the ballroom.

"And I know we're all eager to get on with the evening, which means dancing and more trips to the bar." I hold up my wineglass. "So don't worry, my speech will be like a miniskirt: long enough to cover the essentials and short enough to hold your attention." I grin as people laugh again.

"For those who may not know me, I'm Jean Paul Wynn,

usually known as JP, and I'm Théo's brother. Being Théo's brother, I naturally have a lengthy list of blackmail-quality ammunition to talk about tonight. Don't get scared, though, Théo; what happened in Finland stays in Finland." I shoot him a grin and he shakes his head. The guests all laugh again.

"Technically, Lacey's already a member of our family, but she's a *beautiful* new member of our family. You look stunning tonight, Lacey." I pause. "So, too, do the bridesmaids. If any of you are interested, I can give you my number after this is over."

I flash a flirty smile their way, but my eyes are on only one bridesmaid as everyone chuckles.

I turn my attention back to the guests. "When Théo and I were young, we did everything together. We were attached at the hip even when we were fighting, which was often, as our mother can attest, especially on the ice. It wasn't a game unless we were trying to kick each other's asses. But done with love, of course." I smile. "Then when Théo went away to Moncton to play hockey, we were separated for the first time in our lives. And I was finally free."

More laughter follows this.

"We all know Théo is incredibly smart, but I don't know if any of you know the story about the time in university when Théo was writing a stats exam and he was completely hungover. Since it was a true/false test, he decided to flip a coin for the answers. At the end of the two-hour exam, he was still flipping his coin, flipping his coin, and the prof walked up and said, 'Look, clearly you didn't study for this test, if you're just flipping a coin; what's taking you so long?' And Théo replied, 'Shh, I'm checking my answers.'"

The crowd roars at that one, and Théo subtly flicks me his middle finger. The story's not true, of course, but it's so Théo.

"Seriously, Théo is a brilliant man who likes to thoroughly analyze all the data before making a decision. So now, let's toast to the best decision Théo's ever made—marrying Lacey. I wish you both a lifetime of love, happiness, and success." I hold up my glass in a toast, and everyone follows suit.

Théo rises from his seat to hug me as I move away from the podium. "I really am honored to be doing this, bro," I mutter to him, emotion rising in my chest.

He smacks my back.

Lacey too rises, and we embrace as well. "Welcome to the family, sis."

"Thank you."

I take my seat, again catching Taylor's eye. She's watching me, smiling, and I think she might be a little impressed with my speech. I lift my glass toward her and wink.

She toasts me back.

Let's get on with the dancing so I can put my hands on this girl again.

First I have to dance with Lacey's matron of honor, Karine, who's nice, and very pretty, but also very married. When that song ends, I try to make a move toward Taylor, but I'm waylaid by Everly.

"Come on, let's dance."

I don't have much choice, since she's standing right in front of me, so I take her hand and start moving to the music.

"Great speech."

"Thanks."

"I'm glad you and Théo have gotten past what you did to him."

One corner of my mouth lifts. "Thanks for reminding me I'm an asshole."

She shrugs lightly. "It's what I'm here for."

I laugh.

"Seriously." She eyes me. "We've never been super close, but since Théo moved here and I've gotten to know him better, and Lacey, I discovered I actually kind of like him even though he still thinks my mom is a gold digger."

I choke. "Uh . . . he said that?"

"Well, sort of. He said everybody thinks that, which I know."

I grimace. "Well, I'm not going to judge her. Being on the receiving end of that kind of judgment bullshit sucks, as I now know."

"True. Sorry everyone's being so jerkish to you."

"I deserve it." I sigh.

"They'll get past it. Eventually."

"Whatever." I try to pretend it doesn't matter. "I'm fine."

"Uh-huh."

My attention wanders over Everly's shoulder to where Taylor is dancing with Théo. I'll just keep an eye on her until this song's done.

"You've been staring at Taylor all day."

My eyes snap back to Everly's face. "What? No, I haven't."

"Yes, you have." She narrows her eyes at me. "She's a nice girl."

"What the hell does that mean?"

"Ha ha, I don't know. I just apologized for everyone else being dickish to you and now I am."

The song ends and we move apart. "Thanks for the dance. Catch you later."

I scrunch my face up in indecision. What the hell. I push my way through bodies toward Taylor. Standing in front of her, Everly's snarky comments and the pressure I've been feeling all day fall away. I feel lighter and calmer and . . . happy. I smile. "Dance?"

"Sure."

I take her hand and set my other hand on her back, pulling her closer than I did with Everly. "Having fun?"

"Yes." Her eyes glow. "Lacey and Théo are so happy, and I'm happy for them. There was a point when I didn't know if things were going to work out for them."

"I know. But thanks to me, Théo got his head out of his ass."

Her lips curve. "Thanks to you, huh?"

I grin. "Yep. That's what brothers are for."

"Okay."

"You seemed tense earlier. Were you nervous?"

A little notch appears between her eyebrows. "Nervous? No."

"That's good." I hesitate. "I was worried it was because of me. That you were regretting last night."

Her eyes soften. For a moment she doesn't reply. "Not because of you. Last night was amazing."

"It was, wasn't it." I twirl her and she laughs.

"I liked your speech." She tips her head. "Very funny. I didn't know hockey players could be so . . ."

My eyebrows shoot up. "Go ahead. Say it. You think hockey players are big, dumb jocks."

"No!" She shakes her head vigorously. "You were very comfortable up there in front of a crowd, that's all. You even have good comedic timing."

"Huh. Okay. Well, I don't mind making a fool of myself in public, it's true. Théo and I are different that way." I pause. "We're different in a lot of ways."

Story of my life. The older brother everyone worshiped . . . super smart, athletic, nice guy. Then there was me . . . Okay, I'm athletic too, but not a brainiac like Théo, and since I was always in trouble, some people didn't like me very much. Teachers. Coaches. Other parents. Sometimes I even wondered about my own parents.

"Yes, you are," she agrees. But she says it in a way that tells she likes the way we're different.

TAYLOR

The music changes, and now the DJ is moving the party along with a peppy Calvin Harris dance song. JP and I move apart but continue dancing together, laughing as we bust out some moves to impress each other.

He noticed I was tense.

It wasn't because of him.

It was because of Manny. Manny, the guy I'd been seeing who got traded to Nashville a couple of months ago and ghosted on me. Sure, we hadn't gone out that long, but I was falling for him, thinking I'd finally found a great guy, unlike my numerous dating disasters, and then he barely even said goodbye to me and took off to find a new place to live.

I haven't seen him since, until today when I walked down the aisle and saw him sitting with the other guests. Asshole.

I don't have a date for the wedding, but it appears neither does he. I'm determined to show him I'm over him. I don't care that he's here; I'm just celebrating my friends' marriage and having fun. And JP is here, dancing with me, flirting with me, and it's perfect for showing Manny I'm fine.

We dance another fast song; then, breathless, JP slides his arm around my waist. "Let's grab a drink and go outside to cool off."

"Sounds perfect."

We make our way across the dance floor, JP behind me with his hands on my waist like he doesn't want me to get away from him, both of us moving to the music as we walk. People are looking at us—okay, it's the women who are looking at us, no doubt wishing they were the one with JP Wynn's hands on their waist. I've seen the flirty smiles and breathy comments many of the female guests have bestowed upon him today. But he's with me.

He leads me to the bar, where I request a glass of wine and he gets a beer. Then he takes my hand and we walk out of the ballroom and onto the terrace. There are a few other people out here, and we head for a quiet corner and sit on a small wicker couch. The music from the ballroom is muted, the breeze off the Pacific Ocean soft and pleasantly cooling, the fronds of the potted palms around us swaying gently.

"Beautiful evening."

"It is. You're beautiful too."

I smile at him. "Thank you."

"These are very sexy bridesmaid dresses."

I glance down at my midnight-blue strapless dress. It's nice, especially considering the hideous bridesmaid dress I wore at my friend Ashleigh's wedding last year, but . . .

"Or maybe it's *you* that's sexy," he adds.

I shake my head at his compliments, but inside I'm buzzing and fluttering.

"You look good yourself in that tux." All three groomsmen are wearing dark tuxes over white shirts with midnight-blue pocket squares and a bright pink rose boutonniere. JP fills out the shoulders of the jacket spectacularly. "I'm a sucker for a handsome man in a suit."

"Oh yeah?" He leans closer. "Does the suit turn you on? Or is it me?"

"Oh my God. Your ego."

"It's me, isn't it." He brushes his lips over my cheek. "If you're turned on, maybe we need to take care of that."

"Maybe we do."

"You have my permission to put your hands down my pants anytime I turn you on."

He says this so earnestly, with a straight face, it takes a couple of seconds before I burst out laughing. "I don't think this is the place for that."

"You're right." He nuzzles my ear, and delicious shivers cascade down my spine and my inner thighs squeeze. "Especially when there's a perfectly good suite up on the fourth floor."

"We can't do that."

"Why not? Nobody's missing us right this moment."

"But . . ." His warm breath teases my hair and his hand on my knee gently squeezes. "But . . ."

"Come on. We have time for a turbo bang."

I choke on a laugh. "Oh my God." He's so bad. But he makes me laugh. My panties are wet already and I'm so, so tempted . . .

"Seriously. We'll be back down here before anyone notices we're gone."

I glance across the patio and see Manny standing, talking to a small group of people. He looks up and his gaze lands on me.

There's a moment of awareness as we make eye contact.

I turn back to JP, lean in to brush my lips over his cheek, and whisper, "Okay. Let's go."

"Perfect." He takes my hand and stands, bringing me with him. We leave our empty glasses on the small table and my heels click across the stone patio as we head back inside, hand in hand. I can feel Manny's eyes following us. Good.

We cross the lobby with its glowing table lamps, a fire flickering in the stone fireplace, toward the elevators. JP punches an up button, and soon we're walking down the carpeted hall to his room.

Inside the suite again, I trail my hand across the dark wood desk. "Looks like there was a party here earlier."

He grimaces at the bottles and glasses sitting on the dresser along with a tray of used dishes. "Well, there sort of was. The guys all got ready here this afternoon."

"We got ready in Lacey's suite. Théo and Lacey are staying there tonight."

"We've already tricked out their suite."

"What do you mean?" I turn to face him.

He walks me backward into the bedroom and pushes me to sit on the bed. "We got rose petals and, uh, arranged them on the bed."

"Oh, that's lovely!"

"Um . . . the petals spell out 'let me eat that pussy.'"

I fall back onto the bed, laughing. "You guys did not do that!"

He climbs on over me, grinning. "Oh yeah, we did. And we have more fun planned. Which is why we have to make this quick. Dammit."

He slides his hands up my thighs beneath my dress, pushing it higher, until his fingertips graze over my thong. Wasting no time, he has my underwear down my legs and off, and then his fingers slide between my thighs. "So wet," he murmurs. "Beautiful."

I bite my lip.

He turns his attention to the strapless bodice of the dress, tugging it down along with my bra to reveal my breasts. "Oh man. Your tits are fucking perfect." He presses his face between them. "I could stay here all night."

I slide my fingers into his hair. "We don't have all night."

"I know." He groans, turns his head, and licks one nipple. I twitch hard and then again even harder when he sucks my nipple into his mouth. Sensation flows down to my pussy, more liquid heat gathering there.

He cups my breasts, and sucks and nips at the tender tips until I'm writhing beneath him, my hips lifting against his erection. He lifts his head. "Can you grab that condom?" He nods at the bedside table.

I slap a hand out and close my fingers around it, my entire body aching and throbbing with need. I hand it to him, and he undoes his pants and pulls out his cock. With quick movements, he's gloved up and pushing my knees up and back, preparing to enter me.

"Can't wait to be inside you," he mutters. "You make me crazy."

"Oh God, me too." Here we are up in his room again, going at each other like animals in heat. "Do it. Fuck me."

"Oh yeah." He lets out a long groan as he penetrates me, filling me with exquisite pressure. "Oh fuck yeah."

We move together, my hands roaming over him. This is so dirty and decadent, fucking like this with our clothes still on, and I love it. I just need a bit more to come . . . just need to touch myself . . . I find my clit and circle wet fingertips over it as he drives into me again and again, so deep I can hardly breathe. Tension twists up inside me, higher, tighter, and it keeps building and building to the point of near pain before I come, shuddering hard, clenching around him, gripping his shoulders.

"Oh yeah, that's beautiful . . . I can feel you squeezing

me . . . damn . . ." He pumps faster, harder, then roars as he goes very still, pulsating inside me, his face buried in the side of my neck. *"Damn."*

I wrap my arms around him and tighten my thighs on his hips. My heart hammers so hard I can hear it in my ears, my breath coming in short pants. "Wow. Again."

4

TAYLOR

"I'D LIKE TO STAY HERE IN BED AND FUCK YOU ALL NIGHT long."

I smile lazily, my body wilted. "Me too."

"But I have to go back to the wedding—we have this, uh, thing planned."

"I guess I have to go back too."

"Let's go." He plants a kiss on my lips. "We'll be back here as soon as we can."

I have to smile. His eagerness to get me back into bed is a total turn-on. Not to mention his big, skilled hands, his strength, and his filthy mouth. God. Now I'm melting all over again.

He moves off me and adjusts his clothes—tucking his shirt in, zipping his fly. He runs his hands through his hair, and I tug my bra and the bodice of my dress back up over my breasts.

JP bends to pick up my panties and I reach out my

hand, expecting him to give them to me. But with a wicked smirk, he tucks them in his jacket pocket.

"Hey!"

He eases my dress down over my hips, down to my knees, and kisses me. "No one will know you're bare under there. No one but me."

"Oh God. JP . . ." But I kiss him back before zipping into the bathroom to clean up a bit, using his hairbrush to attempt to restore my hair. It's not going to look like it did earlier when the hairdresser did the loose, wavy updo. Actually, though, it doesn't look bad. I turn my head one way, then the other. The stylist used so much hairspray, it's still okay, just a little . . . looser. There are also some pink marks on my throat and shoulders that weren't there earlier. I didn't bring my clutch purse, so I don't have even a lipstick.

Luckily my dress doesn't look too bad.

JP of course looks amazing, but he grumbles as he adjusts his tie, frowning in the mirror next to me in the big bathroom. "Okay, let's do this."

He grabs the key card off the desk.

We walk into the ballroom to the sounds of "I Gotta Feeling" by Black Eyed Peas, people still rocking out on the dance floor. JP curls his hand around mine to stop me, leans in, and says, "I'll find you later."

"Okay."

I watch him disappear into the crowd, apparently on a mission. I take this chance to find my purse at the head table and make a beeline for the ladies' room to touch up my makeup as much as I can. But on my way out of the ballroom, I come face to face with Manny.

"Hi, Manny." I smile.

His gaze moves over me, taking in my messy hair, the whisker burns on my skin, my swollen lips. He doesn't know I'm commando under my dress . . . but I do. I'm acutely aware of how bare I am.

His face tightens. "Hi."

"So nice to see you again. Glad you could make it—I'm sure it means a lot to Lacey and Théo." I show some teeth. "Excuse me, I'm on my way to the ladies' room."

I dart around him, making my escape. In front of the big mirror, I inspect my appearance, seeing what Manny just saw. It's pretty obvious.

I don't even care.

Maybe I thought I wanted to show him I'm over him, but once JP started kissing me, the last thing I was thinking about was Manny. And that makes me realize . . . I *am* over him.

I pump a fist into the air just as two women walk in and give me puzzled looks. I smile back.

I return to the ballroom just in time to see JP up on the dais with the microphone in his hand.

"Hey, everybody! Some of Théo's friends have a special surprise for you tonight."

My eyes widen. I look around and see Jimmy, another groomsman, setting a chair at the edge of the dance floor, to which he then leads Lacey. Curious, smiling, I make my way to the head table to sit and watch what's going on.

The opening notes of "Beat It" by Michael Jackson fill the ballroom.

Everyone starts clapping and laughing as four men carry Théo in on a chair raised above their shoulders. They cross the dance floor and set him down next to Lacey. He's laughing too, apparently not expecting this.

The four men carrying him—his uncles Asher, Noah, and Harrison, and his cousin Jackson—move onto the dance floor, joined by JP and Leo, the third groomsman. All six of these guys are hockey players, dressed in suits over their muscular bodies.

As "Beat It" launches into its familiar, catchy rhythm, all six guys strike a Michael Jackson pose, then start dancing.

I can't take my eyes off JP, who's holding his crotch, thrusting his pelvis, and not even looking like an idiot doing it. I laugh along with everyone else as they dance. That song changes to Bruno Mars's "24K Magic." The men whip off their tux jackets and the women in the crowd all scream.

I can't stop laughing, watching JP mostly. He catches my eye briefly across the room and flashes a grin. This is so crazy. The guests are clapping along, many standing to watch the show.

The music now changes to "Gangnam Style" and the guys rotate their arms in the air and do the dance, bringing more gales of laughter. Finally, they end with "Time of My Life."

JP and Jimmy pull Théo out of his chair and then, along with Jackson and Harrison, lift him over their heads in the lift move from *Dirty Dancing*.

The room explodes with cheering and clapping as the show ends.

I'm laughing so hard my stomach hurts.

JP makes his way toward me, still without his suit jacket, his face flushed and eyes twinkling. Damn. This all just makes him even more attractive.

I could fall for this guy.

No, no, no. This is a fling. This is me letting go and forgetting about romance and happily-ever-after and just having fun for one night. Or two.

He holds out a hand to me, the DJ having resumed control of the music, playing "All of Me" by John Legend. We walk onto the dance floor to the piano chords and start to move to the music. Instead of taking my hand, he clasps my waist with both hands, and I drape my arms around his neck.

"That was hilarious," I say, smiling.

He grins. "It turned out pretty good. We practiced for weeks."

I shake my head, amused and touched by the effort he and the others went to for Théo. He can't be *that* bad of a bad boy . . . can he?

He bends his head close to mine and whispers, "I'm glad you enjoyed it."

And then he's gone. Stunned, I see him lying on the dance floor, Manny on top of him, having tackled him right out of my arms.

I let out a little screech.

Everyone else starts screaming, people scattering out of the way of the two men wrestling on the floor.

I watch in horror, shocked into inaction. "Oh my God! Manny, what are you doing?"

Théo charges up to them and grabs the back of Manny's suit jacket, trying to drag him off JP. "What the fuck, man?" he yells at Manny.

"You fucking asshole!" Manny shouts at JP.

Jackson and Théo's uncle Mark join in, trying to help

Théo get Manny off JP, but then two more guys rush up . . . Wyatt, who lives in the same building as Théo, and another man, and they grab Théo to get him to release Manny.

"Hey!" Lacey shouts, marching up in her wedding dress.

Attempting to defend Théo, JP throws a punch. More screams sound as Wyatt staggers back, holding his face. Then they're all shoving and wrestling with each other.

I throw a wild glance at Lacey, not sure what to do. Théo's mom, Aline, has her, holding Lacey back from charging into the fray. Then Théo's dad storms in and somehow breaks things up. The men are all shooting each other angry glares, shaking out bruised knuckles, and adjusting their clothes. JP touches his bleeding lip.

A hot gush of anger rises in me. I glare at Manny. "What the hell was that?" I demand.

He shakes his head, not meeting my eyes.

I turn to JP, unaccountably pissed at him too, with his bleeding lip, rumpled shirt, and mussed hair. My chest tightens and tears threaten. I'm not even sure what all the roiling emotions inside me are. I was terrified he was going to get hurt, and angry that Lacey's beautiful wedding was being ruined, and now I'm relieved and . . . and feeling guilty. This might have happened because of me. "Fucking cavemen," I mutter, covering my guilt with fury. "Good God." I stomp back to the head table to grab my purse.

My bridesmaid duties are done. Lacey's not throwing the bouquet, the cake has been cut and served, we've danced our duty dances.

I stalk across the ballroom to an exit, my legs unsteady from the rush of adrenaline, my cheeks burning.

"Hey, Taylor, wait."

I turn to see JP. I throw my hands in the air. "What the hell was that? You hockey players are all nuts! I'm out of here."

His mouth drops open as I whirl on a stiletto heel and march to the front of the hotel to wait for an Uber.

JP

I apologize a million times over to Lacey and Théo, even though I've done nothing wrong.

Nothing.

I met a fun, sexy woman, had a hotel quickie that I planned to turn into an all-nighter, danced with her a little, and . . . what the fuck? I get attacked on the dance floor!

How was I supposed to know that Manny and Taylor had been dating? I barely know the dude. Other than playing against him a few times, all I know is that Théo— the GM of the Condors, where Manny was playing— traded him away a couple of months ago.

I don't know what's going on between Manny and Taylor now, but I'm a little pissed that she was flirting with me and kissing me and, yeah, fucking me, if there's still something between her and Manny. Jesus.

This is bringing back some ugly memories, and not just for me, because everyone else has their panties in a twist now, thinking I was trying to steal some other dude's girlfriend.

Again.

Shit.

I want to chase after Taylor, but she's salty as fuck, and also if I do, Lacey will probably hurt me. Not to mention Mom, Dad, Grandpa, and even Everly, who's shooting me beady-eyed looks.

"I *told* you she's a nice girl," she hisses at me at one point.

As I suspected, she was warning me off Taylor.

It's not totally my fault. But even though I can be a dick, I'm not that much of an asshole that I'm going to try to get myself off the hook by telling the truth—that Taylor *very* willingly came up to my hotel room last night and stayed until this morning, and then again very willingly joined me up there for a flash fuck tonight. So as usual, I'm the whipping boy for whatever trouble goes down, and I keep my lips zipped.

If only I'd kept my fly zipped.

I sneak away from the wedding as soon as I can, taking a double shot of Crown Royal with me back to my room.

I toss the key card down and gaze glumly around the messy room, including the rumpled bed. Not how I expected this night to go. I fully expected Taylor and me to be back rolling around in that bed and messing it up even more.

I tip the glass to my lips and enjoy the warmth that fills my chest as I drink the whisky. The sting reminds me of my cut lip, so I head to the bathroom to survey the damage. It's stopped bleeding by now, but my lip's swollen. Hell, it's not the first fight I've ever been in, and not the worst I've ever looked after. I wash my face with cold water, scrubbing fiercely.

Back in the bedroom, I pile up the pillows on the bed and lounge against them, drinking the whisky and surfing through channels on the huge TV.

Nothing holds my interest.

I keep thinking about Taylor.

Why? I tip my head back. The last few months, since I broke up with Emma, I've been with a lot of women. I'm always clear that it's just sex. It's not that I don't want to get involved with anyone; I haven't met anyone I want to get involved with. Until tonight.

I finally meet someone who's hot as hell, also smart, sweet, and—I thought—genuine, and turns out she's dicking two guys around, just like Emma did.

I toss back more Crown Royal.

Training camp starts the Thursday after the wedding, which is good for taking my mind off the wedding disaster. I've been skating with some of the guys for a few weeks now, at informal get-togethers at the Golden Eagles' practice facility in the mornings. I also worked out hard all summer. The whole family lives here in California now, so I didn't have to travel back to Québec to see them like I have other years, but I went there anyway because I love Montréal. I still have a condo there, so I spent a couple of months working out with some other guys at a performance facility during the day, checking out the nightlife in the evenings.

Preseason games start the Tuesday after training camp. I've been away from hockey too long and I can't wait to play.

The top is down on my Jaguar convertible as I cruise along West Ocean Boulevard from my place to the arena in Long Beach. The wind flows through my hair, my sunglasses shielding my eyes from the bright early September sun.

This year I have something to prove to my team. And my fans.

On top of making some bad decisions in my personal life, I've made a few mistakes in my career as well. I've always been hotheaded, which last year resulted in a four-game suspension. Nobody was happy about that.

I also got a game misconduct penalty for yelling at a ref, and two years ago a one-game suspension for a hit. When I was playing in the minors, I got benched because I showed up late for a team meeting. I came to the NHL with a bit of a reputation already, fairly earned or not, and people are starting to wonder if I'm more of a liability to the team than an asset. I need to shut that down.

Not even my dad now owning the team and my uncle being the new coach will save me if I don't clean up my act. I know that. Blood may be thicker than water, but it's not thicker than hockey. Okay, that doesn't make sense, but when it comes to hockey, Uncle Mark and Dad are ruthless.

Which I think is partly why Dad bought the team . . . to show Grandpa he can't dick him around. Then he hired

Uncle Mark away from Grandpa's team. That message was unmistakable. They're out for blood.

The rivalry between the Condors and the Golden Eagles in California is legendary. The teams share a market. They both play a heavy, hard-hitting game. Every meet-up between them is billed as a "Beach Barn Battle." But only one team from the Western Conference goes on to the Stanley Cup final.

Years ago, the two teams met in the conference final. The series went seven brutal games and the Condors lost, while the Eagles went on to win the Stanley Cup. That left a lot of bruises and scars . . . and not just physical ones. Unfortunately, the Condors tanked the season after that, and pretty much every season since.

But now . . . the rivalry is personal too, Dad and Uncle Mark against Grandpa.

I pull into the parking lot, jump out of my car, and stride into the arena, preparing to die.

Today is the medical and fitness testing.

We'll be tortured with all kinds of cardiovascular, strength, and stretching exercises to see how physically prepared we are for the grueling hockey season. The regular season is eighty-two physically demanding games, not to mention practices and travel.

I get on the assault bike and start pedaling. I have to do one mile as fast as I can. Then I get a three-minute break. Repeat several times. Our time has to be less than six minutes, twenty seconds to pass this test. I climb off the bike sweating with a time of five minutes, fifty seconds.

"That's impressive," says Mick, our strength and conditioning coach.

"I did spin classes when I was in Montréal," I tell him. "Part of my workouts."

I don't tell him I can barely walk now, my legs like noodles.

But I immediately have to be tested to measure my power wattage output while fatigued. It's a crazy test that determines how much energy an athlete produces, measured in watts per kilogram of body weight.

Everyone's doing well at the tests, meaning nobody spent the summer golfing and drinking beer. Well, I did do that a few times, but I'm grateful for all the sweat and agony in the gym I endured to put up a good showing now as I do vertical jump tests, timed sprints, push-ups, and pull-ups.

Then we get on the ice for more testing, with different sprints and a sixteen-lap endurance test that nearly makes me puke. After that, we have "recovery time" in the training room with ice baths, massages, and brutal foam rollers. Because tomorrow we're going to work even harder.

I'm here for it.

I hang out in the locker room with the guys for a bit, catching up on news with those I haven't seen in a while, shooting the shit. It's great being with the team again. Last year when Dad bought the team, then hired Uncle Mark as coach, everyone was expecting a lot of changes. Over the summer Dad made a bunch of trades, and our draft picks are here trying to show their stuff and make the team, so we have a lot of new guys. This is going to change the makeup of the team this season, so there's some uncertainty for everyone.

When I get home, I crash for a two-hour nap. Not sure if that's a good idea, because I feel sore and a little grouchy when I wake up. I'm supposed to go over to Théo's place—he's going to grill some steaks for us since Lacey's working tonight—but I feel like texting him that I can't make it. But I have to go. I'm still trying to make things right between Théo and me, and backing out of this won't help.

Traffic is nuts on the 405, so I'm even crankier when I get to Théo's place. I've never been very patient. I'm working on it, but this traffic makes me crazy.

"Why are there so many fucking stupid drivers?" I ask Théo in his kitchen after he lets me in. "Why is traffic at a fucking standstill on a goddamn six-lane freeway? Why can't people just drive the speed limit?"

He eyes me with a raised eyebrow. "You sound a little stressed." He moves to the counter and starts shaking some kind of seasoning over two steaks. "Grab a beer."

"Uh . . . just one. Training camp." I rub the back of my neck. "Probably shouldn't have any."

"Here." He opens the fridge and hands me a beer. "Just one. What's got your jock in a twist? Just the traffic?"

"Nothing really. Well. Testing today was brutal."

"You passed everything?"

"Of course." I sound offended. "We all did. In fact, it was some of the best results they've ever seen. Everyone's in phenomenal shape."

Théo laughs, rubbing the seasoning into the meat. "Nice propaganda. Did Dad tell you to say that?"

"What? No." I frown. "Jesus. You think I'm here to gather intel about the Condors' camp?"

"Better not be."

For a moment I can't even speak. He can't seriously think that little of me. Can he? "Christ, Théo. We work for different teams, but we're not enemies." I hope. Jesus. The last thing I want is for the feud between our dad and uncle and grandpa to spill down into our generation. Of course, I didn't help that by screwing over Théo.

"I know, I know. I'm kidding. Sort of. Maybe we should agree not to talk hockey together."

"What else would we talk about?" I smile wryly, then tip the beer bottle to my lips.

"Politics. The economy. What the fuck happened at the wedding last weekend."

"Right. Look, I'm sorry. I had no idea he and Taylor were a thing." *She could have fucking told me.* "I was just dancing, minding my own business, when that lug nut jumped me."

Théo sighs. "I know. I don't know what got into him."

"Apparently he was jealous." Bitterness rises in my throat and I wash it down with another swig of beer.

"Yeah, apparently. Let's go out on the patio." Théo picks up the tray with the steaks, a couple of foil packets, and some barbecue tools.

I follow him outside and try to change the subject. "You've got a great place here, right on the beach."

"Yeah, I really like it. Lacey's obsessed with the ocean, so if we ever move, it's going to have to be beachfront."

I laugh.

"What's funny about that?"

"You. You're funny. You're completely whi—"

"Don't say it." He holds up a hand and gives me a stern look. "That's offensive to Lacey."

I snap my mouth shut. "You're right," I admit. "I didn't mean it that way. I love Lacey." His frown deepens.

"I mean, not *love* love. I like her a lot. Like . . . like a sister."

Things are still a little sensitive between us because of what happened with Emma.

He grins. "I know, I know." He lifts the lid of the barbecue, which has apparently been heating, and carefully lays the steaks on the grill.

"I actually like it that you're so in love with her you'll do whatever she wants," I continue, a little sheepish about trying to make a joke about it.

"She'll do anything to make me happy too," he says quietly, lowering the barbecue lid.

It's hard not to make a sarcastic "aw" comment. Clearly, I still have a bit of a chip on my shoulder when it comes to my big brother.

Okay, I'm a little jealous.

It's crazy, because Théo hasn't had an easy life. He got picked on for being a nerd when he was a kid. He worked his ass off at hockey because he thought that would shut people up. And it did. Then he took that puck in the face and lost a lot of his sight in one eye. He never played pro hockey again, after he'd worked so hard for it.

Luckily, he had his stats business that he built up into a mega success, and now he's managing an NHL team at only twenty-eight years old. If something happened to me and I got hurt, I'd end up living on the street, panhandling for change.

The idea scares the shit out of me, so I don't think about it. Even though I know I should have some kind of plan for my future. I'm only twenty-six. I have lots of years ahead of me. I *should* have, anyway. I still don't feel like I've "made it," like I've accomplished everything I want to do. But sometimes we don't get the choice.

"I'm glad shit's going right for you," I finally say. "You've been through a lot. I really admire how you've handled your life."

Théo nods. "Thanks."

"And I know I didn't help."

"I pretty much wanted to kill you." He takes a seat on one of the comfy chairs with a wry smile.

My guts twist. "I deserved it."

"It wasn't your fault that you had everything I ever wanted."

I stare at him. "I did?"

"Sure. You have the hockey career I worked my ass off for."

Ah, hell. My stomach plummets. "I'm sorry."

"Don't apologize. It's not your fault I got hurt." He pauses. "It was just . . . hard. And then you took my girl . . ."

"Shit." I rub my face. "That I've apologized for."

"I know. You said it was a mistake."

"I seem to make a lot of them." I'm thinking of Taylor now. Maybe it *was* a mistake, but damn, she was worth it, until I found out what was going on. "Like I want to have another beer right now."

Théo gives me a look.

"But I'm not going to. Not to brag, but I don't even need alcohol to make bad decisions."

Théo shouts out a laugh, shaking his head.

"How do you do it? Always make the right decisions?"

"I use careful analysis, logic, and reasoning."

"I need to learn that."

He snorts. "You know how to use logic and reasoning. But we're different people."

"True."

"Remember what you told me?"

My eyebrows pull down. "What?"

"About that Kenzimoto."

"What?"

"You know. Being horny makes you impulsive."

I start laughing. "Kenjataimu." The Japanese word for just that.

"Yeah, yeah. Maybe that's your problem. Not enough sex."

I consider that. "I do think some of my poorest decisions were made at a time I wasn't getting any." I rub my chin. Maybe that's exactly what happened when I slept with Taylor—I was so horny for her I was thinking with the stupid little head.

"You know what impressed me most?"

"Uh . . . what?"

"You never blamed Emma for what happened."

I give my head a shake at the abrupt switch from thinking about Taylor to Emma, an even bigger mistake. "Sure, I did."

"Well, okay, she did lie to you. But you took responsibility for what happened."

Huh. I guess I did, but to me it was pretty obvious I screwed up. "Well, thanks for that. In any case, I don't think I can blame all my problems on horny hormones. I have to have *some* kind of self-discipline."

"You should talk to Aunt Tori."

"I don't need a shrink."

"Come on, you know we all need help. It's not that there's anything wrong with you. She helps athletes perform better. That's all."

"Well, she's in Toronto, so I don't think that's going to work."

"The Eagles have a sports psychologist who works with them."

"I know. I've talked to him. We all have."

"Also, Jackson said at the wedding that his mom is considering moving here."

"No shit? Why?"

"She apparently has some big job offer. He didn't want to say who. And Riley's here."

"And Uncle Mark."

"They're divorced."

"Yeah, but . . . I always had this feeling they never really got over each other."

"Well, aren't you Mr. Perceptive."

I shrug. "I do pick up on things like that."

The scent of charbroiling meat drifts from the barbecue, teasing my hungry belly. Théo gets up and turns the steaks and checks the foil packets that I guess are veggies. "Medium rare, right?"

"Right."

"Almost done."

"I'm starving. I think I burned a million calories today."

"Here. Have some nuts." He pushes a bowl across the low table toward me. "Healthy fat."

I grab a handful to stave off my hunger.

Théo grills a great steak, I have to say . . . the spice rub he put on is excellent and the veggies are crisp, with a nice grilled taste. We've just started eating when the front door of the condo opens and Lacey's voice floats through to us, calling, "I'm home!"

The look on Théo's face is . . . I don't even know. He lights up like a thousand-watt lightbulb. "Out here, babe," he calls.

Lacey appears in the patio doors, smiling. "Hi, guys."

Then I see who's behind her.

Taylor.

6

TAYLOR

I stop behind Lacey, smiling, ready to greet Théo. I haven't seen either of them since the wedding. And my gaze lands on JP.

I freeze, my smile falling away.

Crap. What is *he* doing here?

Our eyes lock and his face tightens. Clearly, he's as thrilled to see me as I am to see him.

I grip Byron's leash, holding him back as he tries to dash out onto the patio, but he half drags me out and leaps toward Théo, one of his favorite people.

"Hey! Byron!" Théo greets him with ear rubs and back pats. "Hi, Taylor."

"I saw Taylor on the beach when I got home, so I invited her over," Lacey says.

"Hey, Théo." I lift my chin and turn to JP, my voice going icy. "Hello, JP. Last time I saw you, you were bleeding."

His jaw tightens. "Last time I saw you, it was your back

as you cut and run." His voice has an edge.

I shrug. "Testosterone-fueled brawls aren't my thing. I hope you've apologized to Lacey and Théo."

Lacey's jaw drops and she blinks, her gaze darting back and forth between me and JP. "Uh, he did," she mumbles.

Byron trots over to JP, who holds out a hand for him to sniff. "Hi, doggo." Byron sniffs and eagerly greets at JP, who then rubs his head gently. "You're a handsome boy."

Byron submits to the caresses, the canine traitor. I want to tell JP to keep his hands off my dog, but when JP stops rubbing him, Byron sets his paws on JP's knees to beg for more attention.

"Down, Byron." My voice is sharp as I tug the leash, displeased with Byron's affection for this jerk. "You guys are eating dinner, sorry—we'll take off."

"No, stay and keep me company!" Lacey says. "I've already eaten. How about you?"

"Yeah, I have."

"Let's have a glass of wine while they eat, then." She turns back into the house.

"Byron, sit." He obeys my command, his nose twitching at the scent of the meat on the guys' plates.

"Have a seat, Taylor." Théo waves to the patio furniture grouped near the glass dining table they're seated at.

"Thanks." I perch on the edge of a chair, wishing I could make a getaway. I don't want to hang around with JP.

Even though he looks so damn good . . . tanned and healthy, his dark hair thick and shiny, dressed in a pair of faded jeans and a T-shirt that hugs his shoulders and chest. I remember what his hair felt like when I slid my fingers into it, how that big, hard body felt against mine as he thrust into me . . .

Heat washes over me and I resist the urge to fan myself, instead reaching down to pat Byron, letting my hair fall forward to hide my burning cheeks.

I haven't told Lacey about what happened the night before her wedding. And the night *of* her wedding. Not the fight—obviously she knows about that—but why Manny went nutso and jumped JP while we were dancing.

Or maybe she already knows. Manny certainly figured out what happened.

My guilty conscience pokes at me again. When Manny and I made eye contact on the patio and then I left with JP, I *wanted* him to know what was happening. I wanted him to be jealous, to see what he was missing out on after dumping me without a word.

I feel like I was using JP for that, except . . . *ugh*. I kind of was. But really . . . I was so attracted to JP, I wasn't going to say no to sneaking away with him to his room even if Manny hadn't been there. After what happened the night before? Maybe my vagina was taking over for my good sense, but I wanted more of that. I definitely wasn't thinking about Manny when I was with JP. JP completely seduced me and pulled me under his magnetic spell. I was only thinking of him . . . and I've only been thinking of him ever since. Dammit.

Maybe JP told Théo all about it, and he told Lacey. Maybe JP told them I spent the night before the wedding in his hotel room, where we did dirty things to each other.

I was the reason for that whole shit show. I should have

resisted the temptation of JP and his sexy smile and hard body and bad-boy charm. And now, I don't even want to face him.

Awkwardness holds me in a tense grip as Lacey hands me a glass of wine. "Thanks." Even my voice is stiff. I'm on alert, jumpy, waiting for someone to say something.

Lacey sits too. "Look at poor Byron. He's dying for some steak." She relaxes into the chair cushions, clearly not feeling the same discomfort I am.

"Can he have some?" JP asks.

"Oh. Um." I'm tongue-tied and self-conscious. I swipe at my hair. "Not until you're all done. Otherwise he'll learn to beg at the table."

"He's very well trained," Lacey says approvingly. "I've almost got Théo convinced to get a dog. I'll need tips from you on how to train her."

My lips tick up into a smile, my unease lessening slightly. "Her?"

"I want a girl dog." She nods. "I don't know what kind yet."

"I haven't agreed to a dog," Théo says mildly.

Clearly, it's a done deal. Pretty sure Théo would do anything for Lacey.

I swallow a sigh. I'm only twenty-four. Too young to give up on love. But I'm definitely discouraged. What Lacey and Théo have is so beautiful. It makes me feel all warm and fuzzy inside, but it also makes me feel a pang of . . . yearning. And that has nothing to do with JP. Nothing.

I take a gulp of my wine. "I'd love to help train a puppy."

"Get a Great Dane," JP suggests.

I shoot him a wide-eyed, what-the-fuck look, but Lacey bursts out laughing.

"Maybe a bloodhound," he adds. "Those are cute."

"Those dogs are ugly!" Lacey keeps laughing.

Why is she laughing at his stupid comments? Annoyed, I drink more wine.

"Mastiff," he says. "Remember, Théo here needs a big dog to . . . compensate."

"Fuck you," Théo says. "Besides, isn't that what your Jag is for? Compensation?"

"The bigger the car, the smaller the penis," I comment.

JP narrows his eyes at me. "My Jag's not big."

I wave a hand. "A small penis car doesn't have to be big. It can be any fancy sports car–type vehicle. Usually driven fast, with loud music blaring."

"Hmm." Théo cocks his head, clearly trying not to laugh. "If the car fits . . ."

"Boys, boys." Lacey waves a hand.

JP gives me a pointed, fulminating look, and I know just what he's thinking—I'm very aware that he has no need to compensate.

"Get a Chihuahua," Théo says to Lacey.

Lacey claps her hands. "Yay! So you're saying we *can* get a dog."

"No! That's not what I . . ." Théo sighs. "Fine."

My eyes meet JP's in a mutual look of "we knew it." I have to fight back a smile and I tip my glass to my lips again to hide it. Shit. I don't like him. I don't want to share amused looks with him. Or any looks with him. Except the stabbing kind.

I don't know exactly why I feel so angry with him.

The guys are finished eating, so Théo stands and picks up his plate.

JP stands too. "Can I give Byron some steak now?"

I want to say no, but I love Byron, and he loves steak, and depriving him of a treat just seems mean, so . . . "Okay. A little."

I unclip Byron's leash and he happily dances after the men as they disappear into the kitchen.

"What's with you and JP?" Lacey immediately whispers urgently.

I give her a blank look. "What?"

"We haven't talked since the wedding. What was going on?"

My eyes flick toward the kitchen. "I don't want to talk about this right now."

"Oh my God." Her eyebrows fly up.

The men return, Théo with a beer in his hand, JP a bottle of water.

"On the wagon now?" I ask him. "Maybe that brawl was because of overindulging?"

He sits back down and casually leans back. "It wasn't a brawl."

"What would you call it? Saturday night?" I give myself a mental high-five for that one. "You're a hockey player. Just a normal thing for you."

A muscle tics in his jaw.

"Oh yeah, training camp started today!" Lacey exclaims.

"Yeah." JP holds up his bottle. "That's why I'm drinking water. And why I can barely walk."

My eyes widen.

"We did testing today," he explains to me, apparently seeing my confused look.

Damn. I don't want him to talk to me.

"And for the Condors, too," Lacey adds. "How did the first day go, Théo?"

"Can't talk about it." He nods at JP. "The enemy is here."

Lacey's mouth falls open. "What? You mean you guys can't even talk about hockey?"

"Better not to. In fact, he probably shouldn't even be here." Théo gives JP a smirk.

"You invited me!" JP shakes his head. "Asshole."

I find myself studying his mouth. His lip was bleeding the other night, but it looks okay now. In fact, it looks beautiful . . . sexy . . . He looks up at me, catching me. His eyes grow hot.

Shit.

I stare down at my wine.

"Okay, then, we can talk about something else," Lacey says. "How about politics?"

The guys groan, and I grin.

"Okay, then, let's talk about how Batman is not a true superhero," she says.

I laugh.

"Of course he isn't," JP says. "He's a fictional character. Therefore not a true superhero."

"Oh, come on!" My eyes bug out. "The very definition of *superhero* is that it's fictional."

"Says who?" JP meets my eyes, his chin jutting.

"Says me." I frown. I actually don't know why I said that.

"Taylor's right," Lacey says, consulting her phone. "Wikipedia says a superhero is fictional."

Now I lift my chin at JP with a satisfied smirk.

"Okay, then. He's not a superhero because he doesn't have superhuman abilities."

"What?" My eyebrows pull together. "Sure he does. He has superhuman strength. He just doesn't brag about it."

"That's not superhuman. He just works out a lot. Plus he has money to buy a lot of gadgets."

"There's no way working out a lot is going to give you the strength to punch someone across a room. I mean, I guess he can't fly, and he was never horribly mutilated or bitten by a spider or whatever, but clearly he has superhuman strength."

"No." JP shakes his head. "He just has training and money."

"Ugh." I can't believe I'm hearing this.

I catch Lacey and Théo exchanging glances at our heated debate, and I sag back into my chair. Why am I arguing about this with him? It's Batman, for cripe's sake. "Whatever," I mutter, and drink my wine.

"When's your first game?" Lacey asks JP brightly.

"No hockey talk, remember?"

She rolls her eyes. "I think that's pretty safe."

"Tuesday," he says. "Against Nashville."

My head jerks up. He's going to be playing the first game of the year against Manny? Uh-oh. I cast a wide-eyed glance at Lacey.

"Oh!" she exclaims. "Um . . ."

JP flashes an evil grin. "Yeah."

"JP . . ." Théo says warningly.

"What?"

"Remember those bad decisions we were talking about earlier . . .?"

"Yeah." He purses his lips. "I'm not going to do something stupid."

"Okay."

"I can't speak for *him*, though," JP adds bitterly. "Clearly, he's an asshole."

I catch my lower lip between my teeth. He doesn't know exactly why Manny was so jealous.

We make eye contact and a shiver works down my spine, both of us knowing we did a lot more than dance together.

Lacey wrinkles her nose. "We hung out all the time when I first moved here. I thought he was a good guy."

JP's jaw tightens.

As if sensing the tension snapping around us, Lacey changes the subject again. "Hey, today I saw one of the graffiti condoms."

We all stare at her blankly.

"Haven't you heard?" She gazes around at us. "There's a guy going around town finding dicks that people have painted on buildings and walls, and he spray-paints condoms on them."

"Uh . . ." I shake my head. "I hadn't heard about that."

"Oh, I did," JP says.

"I saw one today." Lacey grins. "It's hilarious."

"All those unprotected dicks do send a bad message," JP says with a chuckle. "Safe sex is important."

A vision of naked JP rolling a condom onto his impressive erection floats before my eyes. I whimper, quickly turning it into a cough. He shoots me a raised-eyebrows glance. My cheeks flame.

"Says the guy who thinks safe sex means not getting arrested," Théo says.

JP shoots him a narrow-eyed look. "Hey."

"You got caught in a storage room in the arena," Théo says. "And the backseat of a car. And—"

"Yeah. You believe in safe sex. You always took a condom when you went out." JP pauses. "Although it was always the same one."

Théo cracks up, as does Lacey.

"Also, I thought your definition of safe sex is a padded headboard."

Lacey wipes tears from her eyes. "Oh my God, JP."

My smile is stiff. "So funny."

Actually, he *is* funny. I just don't want to laugh at his jokes. Ugh.

He casts a slitty-eyed glance my way now, catching my sarcasm. And it's like flames ignite between us. Heat sears over my skin and spreads from my belly through my body. My pussy squeezes.

I toss back the rest of my wine and jump up. "I better get going."

At the same time JP stands and says, "I should go. Early morning tomorrow."

We eye each other. More static electricity builds around us.

"JP will walk you home," Lacey says.

"That's okay," I immediately respond. "I have Byron." I look down to where he's snoozing at my feet.

"It's dark," JP says roughly.

"I only live a few houses down the road."

"It's dark," he repeats and picks up Byron's leash.

Annoyance scrapes over my nerves. I grew up in this neighborhood, for cripe's sake. I grit my teeth and say to Lacey, "Thanks for the wine."

"No problem. Let's get together this weekend."

"Sure. You should come to yoga class Saturday morning." We all head to the door.

"Ugh." Lacey scrunches her nose. "The paddleboard yoga class?"

"Yeah." She keeps making excuses not to come.

"I'll end up in the water. Pass."

I laugh. "Oh, come on. It's fun! And even if you do fall in the water, so what?"

"I'll think about it," she says reluctantly.

I shake my head and wave goodbye as I step out into the fresh night air, scented with the ocean and the jasmine plant growing next to the door.

"She won't come," I tell JP.

"Yoga on paddleboards?"

"Yeah. It's cool."

"Okay, sure."

Clearly he's skeptical.

"You really don't have to walk me home," I tell him stiffly, setting out along the sidewalk of the narrow side street.

He follows. "I want to talk to you."

Great.

"What's with you and Manny?" he demands as he falls into step next to me. Byron trots along happily in front of us, making the left turn at Speedway that will take us home.

"Nothing."

"Bullshit. He fucking jumped me because we were dancing together. Apparently, you two were seeing each other."

"He's an idiot." I sigh. "He came to see me the day after the wedding and apologized."

"What the fuck? He apologized to you? *I'm* the one he should be apologizing to!"

He sounds so outraged I laugh. "He wasn't apologizing for the fight."

The air around us changes, vibrating with . . . something. "Fucker," he mutters.

I shrug. Let him be pissed. I'm pissed too. At both of them. And myself.

"This is my house. I mean, my parents'." I stop in front of the Craftsman home with the tall picket fence around it. "Thanks for walking me home even though I didn't need it." Byron is sniffing around the grass beside the gate. "Come on, Byron, let's go in. Good night, JP. Good luck with your season."

I leave him standing there as I open the gate and step into the yard, which is shadowed by palms and big fig trees.

"Wait."

I turn, firming my lips. "What?"

"I have something that belongs to you."

I frown, then it clicks and my eyes bug open.

He grins.

I start toward him. Does he have my panties in his pocket or something?

He shakes his head. "I don't have them with me. I'm keeping them. Just reminding you."

I freeze and glare at him. "Asshole." Then I spin around and slam the gate shut behind me.

7

———————

TAYLOR

Lacey doesn't come to yoga class, but she does agree to have lunch after it. She meets me at the marina and watches the last part of the class. Maybe she'll be convinced to try it.

I meet her on the beach, carrying my board. "I just have to put the board away and grab my stuff. Be right back."

Along with the others in the class, I trudge into the building housing Makara Yoga. It's cool today, so I'm wearing leggings and a long-sleeved tee. Lacey and I are just going to walk over to Bandit's, known for their fabulous shrimp, on the same marina basin as the yoga studio. It's a casual place, so it doesn't matter how I'm dressed. I slide my feet into my flip-flops and sling my purse over my shoulder.

"Did you hear about what happened in the game the other night?" Lacey asks as we walk there.

"What game?"

"The Golden Eagles versus Nashville."

JP mentioned it the other night. "What happened?"

"Manny and JP got into a bit of a shoving match."

"Oh Jesus. Really?"

"I didn't see it, but Théo told me about it. It looked like Manny was chirping at him."

"Damn. What is wrong with Manny?"

"Maybe he's still mad because JP got the better of him that night at the wedding."

"Men." I roll my eyes.

We're shown to a table for two outside, right next to the water, boats bobbing in the marina only a short distance away.

"So? Ready to join me next weekend for a class?" I ask Lacey when we're settled.

She smiles. "I have to work next Saturday."

"Phhht." But I grin. "You should just quit your job at Jolie." Lacey sells cosmetics at the big beauty supply store.

"I can't quit my job!"

"I think Théo can afford to support you."

"I don't want to be supported." She gives me an affronted look. Then she shrugs. "Actually, I *may* quit my job at Jolie if things keep going well with the movie gigs."

A few months back she got a job helping with the makeup on a Hollywood movie, and since then she's worked on two more.

"You like doing that, don't you?"

"I love it." She smiles. "It was really cool doing the makeup for Blake after the explosion . . . all the blood and dirt and gore."

I grimace. "Fun."

She laughs. "No, really!"

"I know, I know. So you and Blake Lively are best buds now, huh."

She chuckles again. "Right."

We order beers, and popcorn shrimp and spicy fries to share.

"Okay, what is going on with you and JP?" Lacey leans forward.

"Whatever do you mean?" Then I snort. "Okay, I made a big mistake."

Her eyes bug open wide. "What?"

"I slept with him. The night before the wedding."

"Oh." She blinks.

"And the night *of* the wedding. During the wedding."

"Whaaaat?"

"Yeah." I whoosh out an exhalation big enough to sail a boat across the nearby basin. "I don't know what got into me."

"Apparently, he did. More than once."

"Ha ha. Yeah. He was flirting with me and it was fun, and I was there alone and so was he . . . He *is* good-looking . . ."

She wrinkles her nose.

"Come on! He looks a lot like Théo. Only better."

"What?" Her spine straightens. "Take that back."

"It's in the eye of the beholder. You think Théo's better-looking because you're in love with him."

Her forehead creases and her mouth kicks up at one corner.

"Anyway, I figured, why shouldn't I have a fling with a hot guy?"

"Mm-hmm. But *at my wedding*?"

"We snuck up to his room." I nearly fan myself, remembering how hot it was. Damn.

"Your face is red. It was good, wasn't it?"

"It was amazing."

"Did Manny find out? Is that what happened?"

"He figured it out, yeah." I bite my lip and sit back as our waitress brings our beers. My stomach tightens, and then I confess, "I sort of wanted him to know."

Lacey slumps in her chair and closes her eyes. "Oh my God."

"I know, I know. It was stupid. I feel terrible about what happened."

"You slept with JP to get back at Manny?"

"No!" Now my eyes pop wide. "Manny wasn't even around at the rehearsal! That was all . . . JP." I lift my chin. "I'm not going to apologize or be ashamed of wanting to have sex with a good-looking guy who was into me."

"Ugh. You should know I'm not judging you for that. You have every right to sleep with whoever you want."

"Thank you."

"But it did, uh, cause a little problem."

"I know, and I'm so, so sorry." I lean forward, holding her gaze. "I feel responsible."

"I don't blame you. Is that why you took off?"

"Yes, but I was pissed, too. I mean, what right did Manny have to do that? He left without even ending things with me. I hadn't seen or talked to him in months. What a douche!"

"Did you talk to him?"

"At the wedding?"

"Yeah. Or, after."

"He came to see me the next day." I grimace. "He apologized. He said he didn't realize how much he missed me until he saw me leaving with JP."

"Idiot."

"I know, right?" I roll my eyes. "I told him to go back to Nashville and forget it. And forget me."

Lacey tilts her head and gives me a sad smile. "I know you really liked Manny."

"I really did." I pout.

"If only he'd figured shit out before he left, maybe things would have worked out."

"Who knows?" I hitch one shoulder.

Our food arrives, so we pause the conversation to arrange the baskets of shrimp and fries, then dig in.

"So that's why he was bugging JP in the game," Lacey says.

"Maybe. Idiot."

Lacey picks up a fry. "Back to you and JP . . ."

"Right. I don't want anything to do with him either."

"What did he do to deserve *that*?"

"They were fighting! On the dance floor! At your wedding!"

"He didn't start it."

"Well, I know, but . . . it was just stupid. Hockey players are stupid."

She lifts an eyebrow.

"Not Théo."

She nods.

"Also, he's an asshole. Look what he did to Théo, his own brother."

"You mean when he and Emma got together?"

"Right."

"But you knew that about him when you slept with him."

She's got me there. "Whatever. It was just a one-night thing."

"Okay. It might make things a little awkward if you two are going to snark at each other every time you're together."

"We're not going to be together."

She pushes her bottom lip out doubtfully.

"Even if we are, I can be friends with him." I shrug and munch on a shrimp.

"Mmm. Okay. If you say so."

"Why do you look like that?" I eye her.

"Like what? Like I don't believe you two can just be friends? Maybe it's because of the sexual tension that just about set the air on fire the other day when you were at our place. The looks you two kept giving each other. I knew something was going on."

I purse my lips. I muster up a weak denial. "There's no fire."

"I think you're protesting a little too much." She leans forward. "But I don't get why you're mad at him. Seems to me he did nothing wrong."

She's right. Why *did* that fight upset me so much?

I drop my gaze to the table. "I was scared," I admit. "I was afraid he was going to get hurt."

"Ah-ha."

"And I felt guilty. Because it was all my fault. I felt responsible for what happened. I did want Manny to know I was leaving with JP, but I never intended it to turn into a brawl!" I beg for forgiveness with my eyes and Lacey shakes her head, smiling.

"I don't want anything to do with guys who get into fistfights at weddings. So don't worry. If I ever see JP again, it'll be fine. And hey, I've been back on the dating app and there are a few guys who seem interesting."

JP

"Sorry about the wedding."

Grandpa shrugs. He's pruning a shrub with bright orange and yellow flowers in his backyard. He and Chelsea live in a big Spanish-style two-story house on a huge lot, not far from the arena in Santa Monica. Grandpa has developed a fondness for gardening and the backyard is spectacular, the shimmering turquoise pool surrounded by paving stones and a perfect green lawn, palm trees, shrubs, and flowers lining the perimeter. It's a bit of a trek from my place to his, but I made the drive this sunny Sunday, a day off for me and for him as well, I assumed.

"Not *my* wedding," he says. "Is that why you're here?"

"Yeah." I hate it that Grandpa thinks less of me. He was pissed about me dating Théo's ex-girlfriend, and I don't want him to be pissed about this too. "What is that plant?"

"Lantana."

"I like it."

He gives me a look laced with skepticism. "Really?"

I don't have a clue about plants. "Sure."

"Why'd Martinez start that fight?"

I sigh. "I didn't realize he and Taylor were going out."

Grandpa drops his shears and fixes me with a hard stare. "Jesus Christ, JP. You have to stop hitting on other men's girlfriends."

"I wasn't!" I hold up my hands, then drop them and bow my head. "I didn't know, I swear."

"She didn't tell you?"

"No." My words are bitter. *"Women."*

He lets out a gusty breath. "True. What really happened with Emma?"

I'm kind of surprised he remembers her name. "She told me she and Théo had broken up."

"You never mentioned that before."

"It didn't exactly come up in the conversation." We're both thinking of the family party Mom and Dad held to welcome Théo to California after he took the job managing Grandpa's team. Grandpa had given me shit for dating Théo's ex. "And it didn't matter. I shouldn't have gone out with her, even if they did break up. But I didn't steal her from him."

He scrunches up his face. "Are you sure?"

"What the fuck?" I gape at him. "Yeah, I'm sure."

"You and Théo were always close, but there's also a rivalry between you."

I stare at him. I don't like the thought that he knew that; that he knew I always felt like I couldn't live up to Théo. "Okay," I acknowledge quietly. "Maybe I did like the fact that Emma was interested in me." Ugh. I hate myself. "But I didn't go after her."

"And you didn't know that bridesmaid was dating Martinez?"

I frown. "No. I swear. She wasn't there with him the night before the wedding." *She came up to my hotel room and we banged all night.* "She wasn't wearing a ring. I'm not a complete moron."

Grandpa barks out a laugh and trims another branch. "No, you're not. You just don't always think through the consequences of what you do."

"I already got this lecture from Théo."

"Good."

"I just wanted you to know that . . . aw fuck, I hate even saying the words."

"What words?"

"It wasn't my fault."

He cocks his head. "You may not make the best decisions, but you always take responsibility for them."

I lift my chin. "Yeah."

He eyes me shrewdly. "Sometimes you take responsibility when it's really not your fault. I know you were trying to protect your teammate when you got in that fight last year."

I nod slowly. "I'm trying to do better, Grandpa. Really. I'm trying to make better decisions, on the ice and off. I screwed up with Théo and I'm not going to do that again. I really didn't know there was anything between Taylor and Martinez, and he started that fight out of the blue. I mean . . . I *had* to fight back." I grimace.

"Of course." He nods. "Also, you cleaned his clock."

I shouldn't like it, but damn, I do enjoy his approval.

"And I'm trying to do better on the ice, too. Control my emotions better."

"Passion is a good thing. But it can also be a curse."

I wait for him to say more, wanting his words of wisdom. Grandpa may be old and Théo worries about his decision-making lately, but he's learned a lot over the years.

"The same kind of drive that leads to success can also be destructive," he continues. "You can be so passionate about what you're doing, you end up wrapping your whole identity in it and losing sight of the real reason for why you're doing it in the first place." He pauses.

I frown and nod slowly. "Because I love the game."

"Yeah. We all love the game. But the best athletes in the world are at the top because they can control their emotions rather than their emotions controlling them."

"Thanks, Grandpa. I guess I have some stuff to think about."

His chuckle is dry. "You've already been thinking about them. How about lunch?"

"Okay." We head inside, where Chelsea's in the kitchen.

She looks different than when I usually see her, with her hair and makeup perfect, dressed in expensive clothes. Today she's wearing jeans, a tank top, and flip-flops, and her face looks even younger with no makeup. She smiles at me when Grandpa tells her I'm staying for lunch. "Great."

We eat out on the patio. Chelsea serves a salad with lots of healthy greens, chicken, and avocado, and pours us glasses of fresh juice that's orange in color but is actually orange, pineapple, and carrot juice.

"Tons of nutrients," she says, setting a glass in front of me.

"Good, I need that."

Grandpa and I talk about my summer in Montréal and the workouts I did to stay in shape. He shakes his head. "Times have changed," he mutters. "Training camp used to be when we got back in shape."

"Can't do that now," I say. "If you show up at training camp fat and lazy, you're gonna be in trouble."

"They shouldn't even call it training camp anymore. Did you know it was Conn Smythe who invented training camp?"

"No. No, I did not."

"That was back in the twenties, after he bought the Maple Leafs. Well, they weren't the Leafs; he changed the name to that. Made the players do a bunch of workouts and hikes and calisthenics. Guys complained, but they did it. Those guys didn't even take their skates home with them at the end of the season!" He chortles. "In my day it started changing; they started doing more scrimmages as a way to see who should make the team."

I've heard some of his stories before, but I still enjoy them. "Didn't you refuse to sign up one year?"

"Yeah." He grins and pokes his fork into a piece of avocado. "I thought I was worth more than they were offering. It was the day of the first game of the season when Joe Black, the Leafs' CEO, met me in the lobby of Maple Leaf Gardens before the game and said if anyone recognized me, he'd give me what I wanted. No one did." His grin goes crooked. "So I signed the contract, an hour before the game started."

I laugh. I love hearing these tales of how hockey used to

be, and Grandpa's full of them. "Was that before expansion?"

"Yeah. There were only six teams and not many spots for rookies. What the hell was I thinking?" He shakes his head.

"You were thinking you were a good player," Chelsea says. "And you proved it."

Grandpa snorts, but he and Chelsea exchange a look, and I'm struck by the affection between them.

A lot of my family thinks Chelsea married Grandpa for his money. But they've been married almost thirty years and have four kids together, so it has to be more than that. Grandpa's still pretty fit for an old guy . . . Ugh. I don't want to think about Grandpa's sex life.

After lunch, I drive back home, but as I'm passing Marina del Rey, I impulsively take the exit off the 405 that leads to Théo's place. I have no idea if he and Lacey are even home, but since I'm close, I decide to stop in.

Nobody answers the doorbell, but I hear voices on the beach, so I step onto the sand. Shading my eyes from the sun, I stare across the sand. Yeah, that's Théo over at one of the volleyball nets. And Lacey. And Taylor.

Damn.

Théo spots me and waves both arms in the air, then gestures for me to come over. I'm not dressed for beach volleyball, in jeans, loafers, and a long-sleeved T-shirt. I lower my sunglasses to my nose, kick off my shoes, and trudge through the soft sand toward them. The sun is bright but not hot, a cool autumn breeze blowing in off the ocean.

"Hey, man, what's up?" Théo calls as I get nearer.

"Not much. Just had lunch with Grandpa and Chelsea, and since I was passing by, I decided to stop in."

"Cool." Théo slings an arm around my shoulders. "I'd ask how Grandpa is, but I just saw him yesterday." He pauses. "And Chelsea. She spent most of the afternoon in Grandpa's office."

"Huh. That's weird." I like Chelsea, but the rest of the family doesn't trust her. "She do that often?"

"I've seen here there a few times." Théo shrugs. "Wanna play some volleyball?"

Taylor is on the other side of the net. She's not wearing a bikini, but even so she looks amazing in a pair of short shorts and a tank top, her legs long and bare. Her volleyball partner is a kid . . . a girl about eight or ten years old. "Looks like you have four players already."

"You can play with three," Théo says, meaning I can join Taylor and the girl.

"This is Ava," Taylor says, setting her hands on the girl's shoulders. "She lives next door to me."

"Hi, Ava."

"Ava, this is JP."

Ava smiles. "Hi."

"I'll just watch," I say, although I'd definitely rather play.

"I'm not very good," Ava says, wrinkling her nose. "You can play with Taylor."

Oh yeah . . . I'd love to play with Taylor.

"You're just learning," Taylor objects. "And you're doing great. You made a great save."

Ava's smile beams as she turns her gaze back on Taylor. Cute kid.

"I'll come over there," Lacey says, ducking under the net. "Boys against the girls."

"Okay, then." I join my brother and we high-five. "Like this is going to be fair," I mutter to him.

He grins and bends over, hands on his knees.

Taylor has the ball. She moves into position and tosses the ball a couple of times, eyeing us across the net. I smile.

She serves with a graceful arc of her arm and the ball comes toward me. I move with arms outstretched to bump it and it soars back over the net. Lacey gets it, bumping it into the air, and Taylor rushes the net, leaps up, and spikes the ball with vicious force straight into the sand at my feet.

I stare at it.

8

———

JP

I LOOK UP AT TAYLOR, TAKING IN THE GRIN SPLITTING HER face, then glance over at Théo. He shrugs.

The girls are all slapping hands.

"Lucky!" I call over to her.

She laughs. "Come on, Killer."

Lacey serves this time, and we do a few more back-and-forth rounds with similar results to the first one. Frustration mounts in me and when I finally get a chance to drive the ball down for a point, I hit it too hard and too far . . . and it's out.

More girl hand-slapping.

"Jesus," I say to Théo. He's having a hard time not laughing. "What happened to your competitive streak? Come on, man. You can't take it easy on them just because one of them's your wife."

"Take it easy on them?" His eyebrows fly up. "In case you haven't noticed, we haven't had a chance to take it easy."

I scowl.

I'm sweaty now, in my jeans and long-sleeved shirt. I reach for the hem of my tee and peel it up and over my head. I toss it aside and turn to face Taylor.

She's ogling my chest.

Well, if this gives us an advantage, I'm all for it. In it to win it.

I tighten my abs and straighten and bend my arms a few times to prepare, flexing my biceps.

Her gaze follows my movements, her lips parted.

Heh.

When Taylor misses the ball, I mentally congratulate myself. Maybe I should take my pants off, too.

But my self-laudatory moment is short-lived when she once again drills the ball. I dive for it and end up rolling in the sand.

"That's it!" Taylor shouts. "Game!"

"Shit." I spit out sand.

"You did great, Ava." Taylor gives the girl a hug.

"You're awesome." Ava stares at Taylor adoringly.

"Hi, girls!" A voice calls from across the sand. I see a woman approaching, carrying a toddler. "How's it going?"

Ava runs toward her. "Mom! We won against the boys! Taylor's fierce."

The woman grins. She's a little older than us, I'm guessing late thirties. She sets down the toddler, a cute blond boy, who immediately rushes to Taylor.

Taylor bends and scoops him up. "Carter, you handsome man, you."

He pats her face and babbles.

She props him on her hip as we all walk over to Ava and

her mom. "Elizabeth, I don't know if you know JP? JP is Théo's brother. JP, my next-door neighbor, Elizabeth."

I shake Elizabeth's hand with a smile.

"And this is Carter." Taylor bounces him.

"My man." I hold out my hand for a fist bump.

He frowns at me.

Taylor laughs and lifts one pudgy little hand to tap it against mine.

"Grandma's here now," Elizabeth tells Ava. "You have to come home."

"Okay." Ava bounces up and down, then hugs Taylor. "'Bye!" She waves at us all and takes off across the sand.

"Thanks for keeping her busy," Elizabeth says to Taylor.

"Hey, no problem. See you later. 'Bye, Ava!" She turns to the rest of us and cocks her head. "One more game?"

"I'm done," Lacey says. "I need a drink."

"Me too." Théo throws an arm around her shoulders. "Let's go have lemonade."

I eye Taylor. Well, I'm not going up against her myself. She'd probably nail me in the face with that ball. "Sounds good."

She shrugs and we all walk over the sand toward Théo's place, where Lacey serves us glasses of cold lemonade and sets out a bowl of snack mix.

"I need to work out more," Lacey says, sprawling out in a chair on the patio.

"I told you . . . come to yoga with me." Taylor grins at her friend.

"Yoga's not a workout," I scoff.

She gives me a chilly look, but her tone is mild and polite. "Sure it is."

"Phhht."

"Have you ever done yoga?"

"I stretch all the time."

"That's not the same."

Lacey's eyes are ping-ponging back and forth between us.

"Lots of hockey players are doing yoga," Théo says. "Some teams have hired their own yoga instructor. I've talked to Eddie about it. He says it's good for hockey players."

"Have you done it?" I ask him.

"No." He shrugs. "I'm not playing, remember? But I'd try it."

"You can *all* join me for paddleboard yoga," Taylor says with a grin. "But then again, maybe you should try it on dry land first. Not that there's anything wrong with falling in the water."

"It can't be that hard." I narrow my eyes at her.

"Saturday morning. Ten o'clock at the marina." She tosses her hair back. "I bet you can't do it without falling in."

A challenge. It's on. Yoga's not that hard and I have good balance. I play a demanding sport on blades that are a tenth of an inch thick. I mentally review our schedule, and we're home next weekend. "Might have a practice," I reply.

"Sure, sure."

My jaw tightens.

"Maybe the next Saturday," she adds, in a tone of voice that clearly indicates she thinks I'm making up excuses. Then she pulls out her phone and checks the time. "Oh hey, I better get going."

"Right, you've got a date tonight." Lacey stands, as does Taylor.

Date?

Is Martinez in town? I don't know the Preds' schedule. My back teeth grind even more.

"Nice seeing you again, JP." Taylor bares her teeth at me and flaps a hand in a casual wave as she walks out, followed by Lacey.

Théo gives me the eye. "You're a little salty. Did Grandpa piss you off about something?"

"No. I just don't like to lose."

"Jesus, it was just for fun." He scrunches his face up. "Or is it because it was girls? Or one girl?" He hoists an eyebrow.

I gulp some lemonade. "You're right. I'm too competitive."

He laughs. "You're a Wynn."

TAYLOR

Yes, I'm going on another damn date.

I believe in love—big, beautiful, crazy love that fills your heart and your soul, that radiates to everyone around you and makes the world go 'round. I want that. I'm not giving up on it.

Hockey players, on the other hand, I *am* giving up on. I

roll my eyes as I check out my reflection in the mirror in my bathroom.

It's Sunday and we're meeting at a sports bar, so I'm wearing jeans, a tank top with a big slouchy sweater over it, and ankle boots. I fluff my hair and turn to go.

Anthony's a guy I met on the dating app. He's cute and seems nice. He probably thinks the same about me. We'll see what we think when we meet in person. As long as the police don't show up to arrest him, I'm determined to do a second date (assuming *he* wants to) so I can't say I'm being too picky.

I grab my purse and my keys and jog downstairs.

Mom and Dad are in the family room with the TV on. They stop talking when I enter the room, which gives me a weird vibe. "I'm going out," I announce. "I don't think I'll be late."

"You're not home for dinner?" Mom asks.

"No. Sorry. I should have told you sooner." Too busy playing beach volleyball and drooling over JP Wynn's chest.

"Oh, that's okay. Who are you going out with?"

"A new guy. His name's Anthony."

Dad's face tightens. He hates that I date guys I meet online. But how else am I going to meet them? I work with mostly women, and now that I'm out of college it's not that easy. I could go hang out in bars, but would that be any better?

"I'm meeting him," I say to reassure him. "Don't worry."

He grimaces.

"Have fun," Mom says.

I jump in my car, an ancient Volvo my parents bought

me when I turned eighteen. Okay, it's not ancient, it's only six years old. It's not what I would choose, but since I can't exactly afford a new car, I can't be picky. It runs and it gets me from point A to point B, so that's all that matters.

Mom and Dad were probably talking about how to get rid of me. My older sister, Amy, lives with her family in San Diego. My parents had her when they were young and then six years later I came along . . . oops. They probably want to have another shot at a fun and child-free life.

After a short drive, I enter Jake's Tavern. It's a long, narrow space with wood floors, pressed tin ceilings, a dark wood bar along one side, and small tables on the other. I pause and search the patrons, looking for who I think is Anthony.

A man at a table against the wall lifts a hand. Yes, that's him—wavy, sandy-colored hair, a nice smile, decent shoulders. I smile and start toward him and he slides off his high chair to greet me.

"Taylor?"

"That's me."

He shakes my hand, holding it an extra moment and making eye contact, the corners of his eyes crinkling up attractively. "Nice to meet you in person."

"You too."

He helps me with my light jacket, which is very polite, hangs it on a nearby hook, and we take our seats.

"Have you been here before?" he asks.

"I have. They have great wings." Although chicken wings probably aren't a good thing to order on a first date —not exactly elegant.

A waitress approaches to take drink orders. I approve of

Anthony's choice of a craft Belgian wheat beer, and I request a house cocktail—lemonade with Maker's Mark bourbon. Two of my favorite things together.

We make conversation and look over the food menus. Anthony is a production assistant for a smallish film company. He has lots of entertaining stories, which he shares as we eat grilled chicken and avocado sandwiches, making me laugh. He's easy to talk to, interested in hearing about my job, and . . . there's no sparkly stuff happening. At all.

That doesn't matter. Probably I'm crazy to expect that after one date.

By the time we're done eating and have finished off a second drink each, the police haven't showed up to arrest him and he hasn't tried to recruit me to sell Amway or asked if I'm ovulating (these things all really happened to me on first dates), so really, we're off to a fine start!

On the sidewalk outside the Tavern, he offers to walk me to my car, another nice gesture. I'm only half a block away on the busy street, though, so we say good night.

"I'd like to see you again," he says.

I don't even hesitate. "Me too."

"Great. Let's chat next week."

He kisses my cheek, which is sweet.

So what if I don't want to climb him like a koala on a tree? I'm sure when I get to know him better, the attraction will develop. It doesn't always happen instantaneously. My friend Ashleigh ended up marrying a guy she was "just friends" with for years, so clearly it can happen. Anthony and I just need to be friends first.

I GET TO MY OFFICE EARLY MONDAY MORNING. I LIKE TO start my week by reviewing my calendar to see what appointments I have scheduled and what other things I have to get done, and prioritizing work.

I love my job. It's stressful and overwhelming at times, with all the paperwork and clients that are waiting to be seen, but it's also rewarding. It's all worth it when I have one of those moments when a child's face lights up in a breakthrough that I know is going to change his or her life. But dealing with kids with problems all the time can take its toll; dealing with parents too. Part of what I do is train parents to work with their children at home and it's frustrating when some parents begrudge their kids the time they need, or get annoyed because they feel like they're doing the work instead of me. I spend an hour with the kids once a week one-on-one, but they're the ones who spend every day with their kids.

My coworker, Catherine, arrives soon after me and we chat over coffee for a few minutes about our weekend. Our first appointment this morning is with a child who's new to the clinic, here for an assessment because of her language delay. We talk to three-year-old Laura's mom about her concerns, making notes, then do a play-based assessment. I get down on the floor to talk to Laura as we play with blocks and trucks, while Catherine observes and makes notes.

"That's it!" I tell Laura. "Now can you put the cow in the truck?"

She's making animal and truck noises as we play, and lots of gestures, but very few words.

I do a standardized assessment as well. Laura is dropping initial consonants, like *L*, *R*, and *Y*, and she's reluctant to imitate my sounds and words. This is quite typical. My clinical impression is that Laura has apraxia, which is actually a movement disorder. Her brain knows what she wants to say, but the muscles of her articulation structures—her lips, tongue, and soft palate—can't do it. It's very hard for her to put sounds and syllables together.

We explain this to Laura's mom, who's understandably distressed but also relieved to know the cause of her daughter's speech delay. My experience with children with apraxia is that they need to learn that when they make the effort to produce an understandable word, they'll be rewarded by being understood. I find that Laura can say *B* sounds, so I get out a ball and a stuffed bear that we play with. The idea is to associate a desired toy or activity with the word, which reinforces her effort.

We outline a treatment plan that will also include stimulating Laura's hard and soft palate, lips, and tongue using a toothbrush and tongue depressor to create oral awareness of the structures. I'll teach Laura's mom how to do this at home too.

"You're so good with the kids," Catherine says afterward.

"Thank you!"

"Building rapport is sometimes the hardest thing," she

adds. "Getting kids comfortable enough to participate—but you just bring that out in them."

I don't really think I do anything special; I just have fun with them. But it's nice to hear words of praise.

I'm typing up a report at my desk when my boss, Toni, stops by. "It's lunchtime, Taylor."

I smile. "I know."

"Shoo." She waves her hands. "Take a break! You know it's important."

I'm grateful for a boss who understands that. Burnout and compassion fatigue are real issues in this business. Toni tries to make sure we take breaks, and she makes our weekly team meetings fun as well as businesslike. She's been in the field for ten years and started this business five years ago, and I admire the depth of her knowledge as well as her management skills. I want to be her when I grow up.

I save my report and head out. Our office is in Torrance, and I drive to a nearby shopping mall to grab some food. I sit outside near the water fountains to eat, enjoying the autumn sun, and check my phone for Snapchat messages from Lacey or Ashleigh or Everly. We have a group set up on the app and send each other messages all the time.

Oh, hey, there's a text from Anthony.

He wants to go out on Thursday night. He has tickets to the Condors' preseason game that night.

Did I mention to him that I'm a hockey fan when we were out last night? Huh. *Used* to be a hockey fan, I should say.

What the hell, I still like hockey. So I text him back agreeing to go to the game with him.

Then I let my friends know about the date. This should end any thoughts Lacey might have about me and JP. She seemed to think there was still something between us. Well, she was right, there is—animosity.

Ha ha.

I sigh, thinking about the volleyball game yesterday. When JP took his shirt off, my bones turned to goo. His loose jeans slid so low on his hips I could see the waistband of his underwear, not to mention those incredible obliques, a couple of prominent veins, and a sexy trail of dark hair . . .

I wave a hand in front of my hot face.

I haven't seen Anthony's torso yet. It could be just as nice. I'll probably be melting and fanning myself over him, too. Probably.

I do enjoy remembering how my game had been so on point. I took a great deal of pleasure spiking the ball and making JP dive for it, futilely I might add. A smile tugs at my lips while satisfaction expands in my chest.

Take that, you cocky, smirky professional athlete.

But he was so cute when I introduced him to Carter, giving him a baby-sized fist bump.

Maybe he'll come to aqua yoga. It would be fun making him look foolish again.

Gah! Why am I thinking about JP? I should be daydreaming about seeing Anthony Thursday night.

I toss my trash into a receptacle and head back to my car, and as I drive back to work, I mentally review my wardrobe to plan what I'll wear on my upcoming second date.

"The Golden Eagles?" I tip my head back and stare at Anthony. "I didn't know that's who we're playing tonight."

"Yeah." His eyebrows pull together. "The Condors and the Eagles hate each other, so it should be good. Although it's just the preseason and not everyone is playing."

Okay, maybe that means JP isn't playing tonight. I'm not sure if I feel disappointed or relieved.

"Right." I force a smile. "Should be great."

He buys us beers and popcorn to share, and we find our seats, decent ones in the two-hundred level near center ice. We're there in time to see the end of the warm-up, and of course I check the handout we're given to see who's playing tonight. Yep, there's JP's name. Number thirteen.

Seriously? Number thirteen? That's like daring the devil.

I shake my head, smiling, and search him out on the ice. He's not wearing his helmet, so it's easy to recognize him.

My heart hops in my chest. I wipe a hand over my forehead. He looks extremely hot down there, all bulky in his equipment and even taller on skates. I let out a short sigh.

"You okay?" Anthony gives me a sideways glance, concern etched on his forehead.

"Yes! Fine. Did I tell you that one of my best friends is married to the Condors' GM?"

"No. Really?"

"Do I sound like a douche? I don't mean to sound like a

douche. We're neighbors. And Wyatt Bell . . ." I point to the end of the ice where the Condors are skating. "He's a neighbor too."

"That's so cool."

"I met Wyatt at the wedding, too. And of course JP Wynn, who plays for the Eagles. He's Théo's brother."

There. I said his name. Nice and casual.

"Wow. The Wynn family are like royalty."

"So I've heard."

The music is loud and catchy, and I watch the players shoot the puck at the net in fast, hard shots. JP pauses near the center line to talk to one of the Condors players. Neither of them crosses the line, but they prop their arms on their sticks for a moment while they chat. I check the Condors player's number and yeah, it's Harrison Wynn. It takes me a minute to figure out the relationship because that family's a little odd, but Harrison is my friend Everly's brother, which means he's Théo and JP's uncle. I seem to recall that he usually plays for the Condors' farm team in Pasadena, but I guess during training camp they all get a chance to play so the coaches can have a look at them.

What does it feel like for JP, playing against the team his grandfather owns, which his brother manages, and against another family member? It must be weird. On the other hand, he's a professional, so he probably just focuses on what he needs to.

JP laughs and the two men part, skating off in opposite directions.

The horn sounds to end the warm-up and JP does a weird thing—sprints from one side of the ice to the other, then back, as fast as he can, hopping off the ice as he arrives at the gate and disappearing down the tunnel.

"Glad you like hockey," Anthony says. "Could've been a dud date if you didn't."

I smile. "I love hockey. This is great." I munch on some popcorn. "Did you ever play?"

"Yeah, I did. Thanks to Bob Wynn and Wayne Gretzky, hockey started to get more popular here in the eighties and nineties. I was one of the kids who wanted to be like them. I was an okay player, but I sure wasn't ever going to make it my career."

"So you understand the game. You can explain things to me." I give him a wrinkled-nose smile. "I like the game, but I have to admit I don't know everything about it."

"Sure." He clearly likes this. Score a point for me for stroking his ego.

And he does answer my questions, when I don't understand an icing call, or when the Eagles get a penalty shot because one of the Condors interfered with JP on a breakaway.

"Why isn't it just a hooking penalty?" I ask.

"Because he had a breakaway and had a clear scoring chance."

I nod, tensing as JP prepares to take the penalty shot, pausing bent over to catch his breath. Then he strides forward, picking up the puck at center ice. My eyes go wide, watching as he skates in on Bergström, our goalie. He curves to his right, then crosses in front of the net with the puck. Bergström goes down in the splits, trying to block the net with his legs, but JP stops abruptly, spins around, and shoots the puck into the top of the net.

"Holy shit!" I jump up, clapping, smiling broadly. "He scored!"

Anthony tugs at the sleeve of my Condors sweatshirt. "Hey, uh . . . that was the other team."

I subside into my seat, my face going hot. People are looking at me like I'm an idiot. "Right," I mumble, picking up my beer from the drink holder and gulping some down. "It's just . . . I know him . . ."

Anthony chuckles, shaking his head. "Okay. But damn, they're up one–nothing, now."

The first period comes to an end.

"Still two more to go!" I say cheerfully, to make up for cheering for the wrong team. "Lots of time! And anyway, it's just an exhibition game."

"Let's go up and get another drink."

The Condors end up losing, three–two. JP has no idea that I'm there, but it's like he's showing off for me, scoring another goal and assisting on the third. I'm reluctantly impressed.

And he doesn't even get in a fight.

9

JP

"I'M NOT GOING TO THIS YOGA CLASS BY MYSELF." I FROWN at Everly. We're sitting on a patio having a Friday happy-hour drink.

"What do you mean? *I'm* going."

"I mean, I don't want to be the only guy there."

She laughs. "Why not? Seems like good odds to get lucky."

We've been talking about ways for me to manage my feelings so they don't control me and come out at the wrong time. Everly's not a psychologist, but she's smart, and I've confided in her my goal of controlling my emotions on the ice better this year to improve my game. For some reason, I feel like she gets it, and she surprisingly has some insight into it. From a couple of comments she makes, I have the impression she's had to learn some strategies herself. Not that she's angry . . . I don't think?

Apparently, Taylor convinced Everly to go to this yoga class on the water, and Everly's trying to drag me along, telling me yoga will be good stress relief and help me feel calmer. I'm not convinced of that, but what the hell, I'll give it a shot. Falling in the water is the worst that can happen, which isn't the end of the world.

I'm more worried about seeing Taylor again, to be honest. Because even though I'm pissed at her for not telling me she had a boyfriend when we slept together, and probably using me to make him jealous, which resulted in my split lip, I'm still mega attracted to her. But I can't go there.

That volleyball game last weekend just about killed me, watching her run around in those short shorts and tight T-shirt, her smile beaming brighter than the sun. Seeing that little girl gaze at her adoringly—which is kinda what I wanted to do, and that really pissed me off.

She slept with me while she was with another guy. *Not* going there again.

"Another thing you could try is knitting."

I stare blankly at Everly. "What?"

"Knitting. It's good stress relief."

"Ha ha. I am *not* going to knit."

She shrugs. "Think about it."

"Sure. Is, uh, Taylor going to be at the class?"

"Yeah, I think so."

"I'm surprised she's not in Nashville."

Everly's eyebrows pull together. "Why would she be in Nashville?"

"With Martinez." I shrug casually.

"They're not together," Everly says as if I'm a not-so-bright two-year-old.

Huh? "She's not seeing him anymore?"

"No." Everly frowns. "They broke up when he moved away."

"Then why the *fuck* did he jump me at the wedding?" I grip my glass so hard it nearly shatters.

"I can't answer that question." She shrugs. "I presume he got jealous seeing you with her and realized he made a mistake letting her go. I think that's basically what he told her the next day."

"She said he came and apologized. I thought it meant they got back together." Pressure builds inside me, the kind that makes me blow up. I take a deep breath.

"Nope. And good for her. He was an idiot to just leave like that. Doesn't say much for his ability to actually maintain a relationship."

"So . . . at the wedding . . . they weren't together."

"No." She squints at me. "You thought they were?"

"Yeah."

"You thought you were dancing with another man's girlfriend?"

"No!" I inhale slowly through my nose. "I had no idea they'd ever been together. I thought she was single." I pause, eyeing Everly. I guess Taylor didn't tell her about our sexcapades at the wedding. "We, uh, did more than dance." I shift in my chair. "Don't ask for any more details because I'm not talking."

Her eyes fly open wide now. "Holy shit." Her eyelashes flutter up and down rapidly. "Taylor never said anything."

"Which is why I'm not either."

She tips her head to one side. "You thought you slept with another man's girlfriend. Again."

"Yeah." I sigh heavily.

For a moment she says nothing, her lips pursed. Then, "You're actually a good guy, JP."

I rub a hand over my face. "Not really."

She slowly turns her head from side to side, smiling. "Whatever."

"She's not still seeing him."

Her lips lift at the corners in a near smirk. "Yes, that's what we've established. So are you coming to yoga class or not?"

I grin. "Oh, hell yeah." I experience a sensation of lightness in my chest, a little rush of adrenaline that has my hands tingling. *Taylor's not seeing Martinez.* This is the best news I've heard since we clinched a playoff spot last year.

"Oh, hey, I have an idea." Everly grabs her phone.

"What are you doing?"

"I'm texting Harrison. We'll get him to come too."

"Huh."

Harrison is her brother—my uncle, but he's the same age as me. We just played against each other the other night. I grin, remembering the bone-crushing check into the boards I gave him late in the first period.

"There." She drops her phone and smiles. "Now you won't be the only guy there. The idea of a bunch of women doing downward dog in bikinis convinced him."

"Bikinis?" I lift an eyebrow hopefully. "They do yoga in bikinis?" *Taylor in a bikini on a paddleboard . . .*

"No."

I laugh. "Damn. Whatever."

We arrange to meet at the harbor around nine thirty, before class starts at ten. Harrison's going to meet us there too.

Harrison has a twin brother, Asher, and another brother, Noah. Grandpa and Chelsea were popping out babies left and right twenty-some years ago, the same time my mom and dad were. My dad didn't like that. He thought it was fucked up that his father was having babies at the same time he was. He never liked Chelsea. He thought she married Grandpa for his money and only had kids so she could claim massive child support when she ditched him. Now their kids are adults and that hasn't happened, but to this day things are strained between Dad and Grandpa and Chelsea. Of course, the lawsuit Dad and Uncle Mark filed against Grandpa doesn't help any.

It's an overcast morning when I arrive at the marina. The sky is pale, the air damp and chilly against my skin. The ocean washes ashore in slow, easy laps, the water a smooth, silvery blue. This area is a popular spot for families with small kids, as it has a roped-off swimming and wading area where the water is nice and calm. We won't have to deal with big waves on our paddleboards. Piece of cake.

I'm alert and fidgety, drumming my fingers on my car in the parking lot, shifting from one foot to the other. I scan the area for any sign of Taylor. No luck.

Harrison pulls up, parks on the black asphalt in the lot, and jumps out of his SUV.

"Hey, man."

"Yo." We do a bro shake. "What the hell has Everly got us into?" he says.

"Eh. Not sure. But I have a feeling they expect us to make fools of ourselves." We meander toward the building that houses Makara Yoga.

"It's yoga. How hard can it be?"

"My thoughts exactly."

Everly and Taylor arrive a minute later. My eyes go straight to Taylor and connect with hers. I experience a little sizzle in my gut.

I smile and she slows her steps, her eyes widening.

She could be mine. My heart thumps and I can't stop smiling.

Taylor shakes her head and drags her gaze away from me.

Everly heads straight toward us, Taylor tagging along behind.

"You actually came!" Everly says to us with a big smile.

"Sure. You thought we'd bail?"

"I did wonder."

"Hi, Taylor," I say, keeping my voice even.

"Hi."

"Taylor, this is my brother Harrison. Harrison, Taylor Hart."

Harrison shakes her hand, his smile appreciative. "Nice to meet you."

I want to punch him.

"You too," she says. "I watched you play the other night."

"Oh yeah?"

"You were at the game?" I interject, frowning.

"Yeah." She smiles, nodding.

"Huh." I can't believe I didn't know she was there. "Guess you saw my penalty shot goal, then."

"I did." Her cheeks get a little pink. "Even though you play for the wrong team, it was pretty good." She hitches one shoulder.

"Pretty good! It was amazing."

"It kinda was," Harrison acknowledges, and I hold out a fist for him to bump.

"Thanks, man. Appreciate that."

"Hi, everybody!" a female voice calls out from near the front door of the building. "I'm Arya Ross. I'm the owner of Makara Yoga and your instructor today. I see we have a few newcomers to the class."

She smiles at me and Harrison, then Everly.

"Holy shit," Harrison mutters to me. "She's hot."

"She looks like every other chick you date."

"No, she doesn't."

"Whatever." Harrison definitely has a thing for blondes. I guess objectively Arya is good-looking—long gold hair in a bouncy ponytail, smooth tanned skin, and a big smile. Wearing a cropped bra top and leggings, her body is slim and toned.

I'd rather look at Taylor, though.

She's wearing a similar outfit, with an open zipped hoodie over it. I take in her taut abs, the only skin I can see right now, her flowered leggings hugging her perfect legs. She catches me staring and lifts an eyebrow.

I smile.

She turns away, but that just gives me an excellent view of her perfect ass in that stretchy fabric.

"Wonder if she'd like to join me for some downward

doggy-style later," Harrison says in a low voice, jerking his head toward our instructor.

I try not to laugh. "Douche."

He moves over to Arya and extends a hand. "Hi, I'm Harrison."

"Nice to meet you, Harrison."

"Looking forward to class. I'm looking forward to experiencing a higher consciousness."

She gives him an amused look. "Well, good. Let's get started."

We head out onto the water with our boards. The class is ninety minutes long, but the first part of it is spent making sure we know how to paddle our boards, so we paddle around a bit, which is easy; I've done this many times. Then Arya directs us into place and shows us how to lower the anchors we all have so we don't float away.

"Even if you've never done yoga, or never been on a paddleboard, you should be able to follow along," Arya says. "We're going to go through a Vinyasa yoga flow, which has been customized for the paddleboard."

"Vin what?" Harrison says next to me.

I shrug.

"I want to be closer to the instructor," he says to me in a loud whisper.

I roll my eyes but paddle along with him. This brings me closer to Taylor, so win-win.

We start off sitting cross-legged on the board, hands on our knees, focusing on our breathing. We're supposed to close our eyes, but I meet Harrison's and we both make faces.

Then I swallow a sigh. I really should at least give this an honest shot.

"Okay, open your eyes." Arya changes her pose. "Let's position ourselves on our boards, palms directly underneath our shoulders."

I watch Taylor instead of the instructor, taking in her smooth movements as she gets onto hands and knees. Of course this makes me think dirty thoughts about having her like that in front of me . . .

"Knees directly under your hips," Arya calls out. "And tuck your toes under."

I watch what Taylor does and emulate her as Arya talks us through arching our backs, then curving them the other way. When Taylor does it, it looks graceful and supple. I feel like I'm stiff and awkward, but I keep going.

"Feel your breath pulling your spine on the inhale," Arya says. "Okay, curl your tailbone down into our first child's pose."

"Curl your tailbone?" Harrison says skeptically.

I have to smile. He looks as uncomfortable as I feel.

"Walk your hands out in front of you," Arya directs us. "This is a really good way to ground your energy."

I choke on a laugh as I see Harrison, arms stretched out in front of him, banging his forehead repeatedly against the paddleboard.

We move into downward-facing dog. My hamstrings protest, and yet Arya tells us to walk our feet back even more. "Jesus," I mutter.

"I know," Harrison responds, his jaw clenched.

We're supposed to move our hands forward, asses up in

the air, and the board wobbles beneath me, making me pause.

"Bend your knees and stick those sit bones up nice and high."

"Sit bones," Harrison says with a laugh, this time loud enough for Arya to hear.

She gives him a quick, quelling glance.

At least it's him in trouble with the teacher, not me, unlike most of my school years.

"Press one heel down."

I grunt as this stretches the back of my thigh and calf, and bite back a curse.

"And switch it out." We do this a few more times. "Find one more breath . . . and steadiness . . . Inhale . . ."

Eventually we move into standing positions, which is more challenging in terms of balance. I watch Taylor again as we bend over, chin to chest, hands to the paddleboard. I'm tight and I know I look nothing like Taylor, who's literally folded in half, her head nearly touching her shins. Wow. Talk about flexible.

I glance over at Arya, who's the same.

The next move fucking kills my hamstrings again. I've always been tight there, so this is brutal.

Arya apparently notices Harrison and me struggling. "If it gets too intense, bend the knee," she says gently.

I wrinkle my nose, unwilling to give in.

We do a few more poses, and when we get to a high plank pose that we then lower into a push-up position, I'm good. I can do this.

"Exhale and bring your hands to heart center."

Harrison and I exchange another look as we press our palms together in front of our chests.

But then we're doing a one-legged pose with one foot on the opposite thigh. I'm wobbling, the board is wobbling, but I listen to Arya talk about pressing down into my left big toe, which oddly helps. It's satisfying to find that balance and center myself.

Splash!

The surprise almost makes me fall over, and I bark out a laugh at seeing Harrison in the water. "Way to go, man."

His smile is rueful as he shakes water out of his hair.

"It's fine," Arya says with a smile. "Climb back on and pick up again."

Dripping, Harrison gets back on the board and attempts the pose again.

I'm following along as we do another downward dog pose, but when we have our heads down between our hands and Arya tells us to walk our feet closer, my jaw drops. What the fuck?

I watch as everyone else does a handstand, their feet actually leaving the board. Should I even try?

If Taylor can do it, so can I. I tentatively lift one foot, and sway. My foot drops back down. I keep trying, but it is *not* going to work. I watch in awe as Taylor balances, not just on her forearms, but on a board floating on the goddamn ocean. This is my new life goal.

"If you're comfortable, lift your legs into a headstand position," Arya calls.

A few women do it, although Taylor stays as she is. Arya's legs slowly rise, and her body is straight, upside down, not even shaking. I glance at Harrison, who's staring at her, slack-jawed.

"This is too much," he says.

Arya's mouth twitches, but she doesn't move.

At last we're finished, ending the session stretched out on our boards, facing the sky. "Look up to the clouds," Arya says. "Feel your breath leaving your body."

"Feel the weight of the world on your chest, crushing you," Harrison says. "Life means nothing."

Arya lets out a little snort, obviously having heard him. "If you experience humor in yoga, that's also good."

This *is* nice and relaxing. I turn my head to look over at Taylor.

Our gazes collide like freeway pileup.

She's looking at me too. Instead of looking away, I hold her gaze. Heat builds around me, despite the cool ocean water surrounding us. Our gazes link for the stretched-out, quiet moment of peace and relaxation . . . and arousal. Dammit.

Arya ends the pose with a soft tone, and we begin paddling back to shore. I do feel . . . well, it's hard to describe. I feel both peaceful and energized.

As we get closer to the beach, my board is bumped hard, startling me out of my calm mood. I try to get my balance, but it's a lost cause and I crash into the water. Spluttering, I turn to glare at Harrison, who's sitting on his board with his paddle in his hands, laughing his ass off.

"That's for that hit the other night, asshole," he says.

"Fuck," I mutter, shaking my head. Good thing I actually like him.

The women around us are all hiding smiles behind their

hands and exchanging amused glances. Glad we're entertaining.

We're close enough that I can walk to shore, so I tug my board along after me and trudge onto the sand.

Taylor and Everly are already there, grinning.

"Well you *almost* made it through the class without falling in the water," Taylor says. "Guess I win the bet."

"What bet?" I frown.

"I bet you you couldn't make it through a class without falling in the water, remember?"

Oh right. "I *did* make it through class, though. If this asshole hadn't dumped me, I'd still be dry. Besides, we never agreed on what we were betting."

"You could buy us lunch," Everly says. "Too bad you guys aren't in any shape to join us."

"I have dry clothes in my car." I lift my chin. "But I'm not buying lunch, because technically I didn't lose the bet." That's total bullshit; of course I'm going to pay for lunch.

No way am I missing out on lunch with Taylor. I have to figure out a way to get her alone at some point . . .

Inside the yoga studio, we can see another class going on through a glass door. Harrison and I change in the locker room and meet Taylor and Everly outside the entrance. The sky is clearing, with patches of blue showing, the air warming a little.

"How about Bandit's?" Everly suggests, gesturing at the nearby restaurant.

"I was just there last weekend," Taylor says. "But that's fine—I love their shrimp."

"Wait, maybe we should invite Arya to join us," Harrison says.

I smack the back of his head. "I don't think you impressed her."

"She has another class anyway," Taylor says, fighting a smile.

We walk over, palm trees swaying around us, and enter the casual restaurant. We get a table for four and I make sure Taylor's sitting right across from me.

"She's single, right?" Harrison asks after we order.

"Who?" I frown. "Oh, Arya."

"I think she has a boyfriend," Taylor replies apologetically.

"Damn." Harrison pushes out his bottom lip and stirs his Coke with the straw. "Ah well."

"Why were you guys such idiots during the class?" Everly asks.

"Idiots?" I frown. "Not me. It was him." I point at Harrison.

He gives a guilty grimace, then changes the subject, looking at me. "What are you doing tonight?"

I'd made plans, but I can get out of them if I can just talk to Taylor and ask her out. "Not sure," I hedge. "Some of the guys are going to Sharky's to play pool and drink some brews."

"Oh yeah? Who?"

"Abs, Copper, and Dutch."

He nods.

Those guys are my best buds. They'll totally understand if I bail on them. I just want to get this lunch over so everyone else leaves and I can corner Taylor and . . .

"I have a date tonight," Everly says.

"Oh!" Taylor leans forward. "That's awesome. Who with?"

"Dan Diaz."

I frown. "Isn't he the mayor of Santa Monica?"

"Yes." Everly flicks her hair back.

Taylor's eyes pop wide open. "You're going out with the mayor?"

"Yes."

"Isn't he like sixty years old?" Harrison demands.

"He's not that old." Everly gives him a derisive look.

"Way older than you." He scowls.

"So?" She lifts one shoulder. "I like older men. They're more mature."

She grew up with a dad who was forty-something when she was born. Wonder if that has something to do with it. Ha. Look at me being an amateur psychologist. What the hell do I know.

"Wow," Taylor says. "I hope it goes well."

Our eyes meet and I can see she's uncertain about this too. We share a look of understanding. Warmth spreads through me at the feeling of connection.

Our server brings our food and we pause our conversation for a moment.

"How about you, Taylor?" Everly asks when the server has left. "What are your plans tonight?"

I perk up. I could even suggest something right now if it works out right . . .

"I'm going out for dinner." Her eyes flicker in my direction as she unrolls her cutlery from the paper napkin.

Everly flicks a glance my way, her mouth tightening. "Oh. Who with?"

"A guy I met online. Anthony."

I freeze. Anthony? What the fuck?

"You're seeing him again?" Everly leans forward.

"This'll be the third date." Her eyelashes flutter again. "We met for drinks one night, and he took me to the hockey game the other night."

Fuck! I curl my hands into fists beneath the table, staring at my food.

"Oh." Everly sucks her bottom lip into her mouth, sliding her eyes my way again. "Well. That's . . . good."

Tension flows off me in waves. I don't think Harrison is picking up on it, but clearly Everly and Taylor are. Taylor keeps shooting me jumpy glances.

Thank fuck I didn't ask her out. I close my eyes, imagining being shot down in front of everyone.

"So, uh, where are you going?" Everly asks.

"Delgado."

I snort. "You're kidding."

"What's wrong with that?" Taylor lifts her glass of ice water to her lips and meets my eyes.

"Hipster bar. They serve things like hand-pulled bison with homespun rice. Frightened tuna with distressed fennel."

Everly and Harrison crack up.

Taylor shakes her head, one corner of her mouth lifting. "Sounds interesting."

"Hopefully he's not as pretentious as the menu." I pick up my fried shrimp po' boy sandwich. It's messy as hell, dripping with coleslaw and tomatoes. Real food. Except I'm not so hungry anymore.

"He's not pretentious." Taylor's voice has an edge. "He's a nice guy."

"Nice. Okay." I let my disdain color my tone. "Sounds boring."

Heat washes through me and I feel sweat building under my arms and on my back. I want to throw my sandwich across the room, shove my chair back, and blast out of here.

I risk a glance at Taylor. Our eyes meet with a flash of heat and light and her cheeks turn rosy. Has she had sex with this fuckwacker? Because I know for a fact she wasn't bored with me in my hotel room.

Her cheeks now are scarlet. Good. She's remembering too.

Everly shoots me a warning glance, her head tilted, eyes wide.

I know, I'm being an asshole. Whatever.

10

—————

TAYLOR

Okay, maybe Anthony is a *little* pretentious. The restaurant menu was ridiculous, and I was inclined to snicker and make fun of it, but he was all into it.

He kissed me when he brought me home. It was okay. He's probably going to want the sex stuff soon, if we keep seeing each other. I've been thinking about sex a lot lately, but dammit, it's not Anthony in my fantasies.

It's Sunday and I'm in our sunny kitchen, toasting a bagel and sipping coffee before I take Byron for a nice, long walk on the beach.

Mom walks into the kitchen and stands beside the island. "Morning, sweetie."

"Morning, Mom." I look up at her, and instantly read her face. "What's wrong?"

Her lips are thin, her eyes strained. "Um, your father and I want to talk to you about something."

"Okay. Let me put cream cheese on this first." I smear

the bagel and, carrying my plate and coffee, I follow Mom into the family room.

They're probably going to kick me out.

I swallow a sigh. I know it has to happen sometime, and believe me, I *want* to live on my own and be independent. But I've looked at the kind of apartments I can afford and they're crappy. Nowhere near the beach. Some of them are studio apartments that don't even have a bedroom. Plus I'd have to leave Byron.

Well, hopefully they'll give me some time. Maybe this is just a heads-up.

We all sit, and I glumly wait for the bad news.

"We need to talk to you," Mom says again. "Because we have some . . . difficult news."

I nod and take a bite of bagel and cream cheese.

"Your dad and I are separating."

I choke. My eyes water. I cough. *"What?"*

Mom's eyes flicker to Dad, then back to me. She twists her hands together on her lap. "We've decided to separate. It's a mutual decision. We want you to know it has nothing to do with you."

My mind is spinning. I can't make sense of this. "You've been married for over thirty years!"

"I know. It hasn't been easy coming to this decision. But it's for the best."

"But . . . why?" I stare at her, then Dad, who can't even meet my eyes. He looks like he's going to cry.

"We've agreed that we won't discuss the details with you and Amy."

"Amy! Does she know about this?"

"We're going to Skype with her right away."

"Oh my God." Shaking my head, I set my plate down on the coffee table. I can't eat it now. My throat is clogged up. This can't be happening. This really can't be happening.

I look back and forth between them, seeing the anguish on both their faces. "What about some counseling?"

"We've been for counseling," Dad says in a choked voice.

"It did help us come to terms with things," Mom adds, her voice also thick. "And to decide how and when to tell you and your sister."

"You can't do this." I look between them again. "You can't lose everything you've shared all these years."

"We don't lose that," she says gently. "We'll always have that. We'll always have our two beautiful daughters and all the memories."

"But . . ." I don't even know what to say. It's horrendous. Unspeakable. After thirty-two years of marriage, you'd think they'd made it through everything. I can't comprehend this. At all. "It's because of me. Isn't it? If I move out, will that help? I mean, I can't really afford it, but if it will save your marriage, I'll do it."

Mom's eyes get wet. "No, sweetie. That's not it. It's not because of you."

My heart throbs painfully, not entirely convinced. I don't want this to happen. I'll do anything to keep this from happening. "But your future . . . retirement . . . what are you going to do?"

"Well." Mom bites her lip. "That's another thing we need to talk about. I'm going to move out. We need to sell the house."

"Sell the house?" My voice rises.

"Yes." She shifts in her chair. "Neither of us can afford to buy the other out."

"But . . . we love this house."

"Yes," she says sadly. "We do. That makes it even harder. But again . . . we'll always have the memories of living here, of you two girls growing up here."

My chest hurts so much I press a hand there. My eyes burn. "Where are you going?" I look at Mom.

"I'm going to stay with Shirley."

I nod slowly. Her best friend. "Okay." I suck on my bottom lip, then look at Dad. "I can stay here for a while?"

"Of course!" His eyes are red. "I've already found an apartment. The house is going on the market tomorrow and it should sell quickly. You can stay with me here or at my apartment if it takes you a while to find a place of your own."

Tomorrow. Holy shit. I swallow. "O-okay." I stand. "I need to leave."

"Taylor . . ."

"I'm okay." Almost blind with tears, I manage to find Byron's leash. "Byron! C'mere, boy! Let's go for our walk."

Seeing his leash, he prances up to me all happy from where he was lying on the carpet.

"Good boy," I choke out. "You're a good boy." Then I pause in clipping the leash to his collar. I straighten. "What about Byron?"

My parents give me pained looks and exchange a glance. "We're not sure," Mom finally says.

Now my heart cracks; it actually feels like it's splitting into pieces with agonizing pain. I suck in a shaky breath. "We can't . . . give him up."

Mom sinks her teeth into her bottom lip. "I know you love him. But I can't take him to Shirley's."

"And the apartment I found doesn't allow pets," Dad adds. "But eventually I hope to buy a smaller house . . ."

That doesn't help right now. My chest constricts. I won't be able to afford the kind of place that allows pets. And the apartments I've looked at online are way too small for him. I nod and turn away, tears sliding down my cheeks as I head outside with Byron.

The breeze off the ocean cools the moisture on my hot cheeks and I turn my face into it, eyes closed. Then I let Byron pull me along briskly, my feet sinking into the soft sand.

I walk mindlessly, for how long I don't even know, staring out at the ocean, trying to process what is happening and what is going to happen. Mom and Dad seem like the perfect, happily married couple. It makes no sense. They don't have fights. I don't think either of them has cheated on the other. Of course, nobody really knows what happens in a marriage except the two people involved. Maybe I've just been blind.

I was away at college for two years, but I've been back for a while now. Surely I would have seen the signs if things were wrong. Am I that self-absorbed that I missed it all?

We meet another dog that Byron stops to greet, which means sniffing each other's butts. I force a smile for the woman with the other dog and we make small talk for a few minutes, then continue on.

How can I live without Byron? He's my best buddy. We've had him for eight years, since I was sixteen. I was the one who trained him to do his tricks, took him for walks on the beach. He sleeps in my bedroom. I mean, Mom and Dad love him too, but Byron and I have a special bond.

I guess I'm going to have to figure it out.

When I'm near home, I turn and walk toward Lacey and Théo's place. She's my closest friend right now, literally in terms of physical proximity, but also we've gotten close in the months she's lived here. I need someone to talk to.

Luckily, she's home, although I feel bad because I think I interrupted her and Théo having some afternoon fun.

"No, no, we were just napping," she says, ruffling her hair.

"Uh-huh. That's what my parents used to say when they went into the bedroom on Sunday afternoons." And I burst into tears.

Horrified, Lacey wraps her arms around me. "What the . . . what's wrong, Tay?"

Sobbing, I managed to choke out the words about what just happened. She leads me into the living room and sits me down on the couch. Byron pads after us, does a quick sniff around the room, then lies down on the rug, panting a bit from our long walk.

I tell Lacey what I know, how I feel, the questions I have. She listens, rubbing my back, being the best friend you could ever have, sympathy pouring off her.

Théo wanders in, sees me crying, and quickly starts to leave, which is fine, because I'm an embarrassed disaster. A pile of used tissues sits on the table in front of us, some of them smudged with my black mascara. I can only imagine what a horror I look like.

"Théo!" Lacey calls. "Could you get Byron some water?"

"Thank you," I mumble, ashamed of not realizing he was thirsty.

Of course that's when JP has to show up.

Fuck my life.

I bend my head, letting my hair fall forward as he greets us, trying to hide my face.

"Uh . . . everything okay?" he asks. He absently reaches down to rub Byron's head when my dog joyfully prances up to him.

"Taylor just got some bad news," Lacey says.

"Oh." I sense his hesitation. "You okay, Taylor?"

Like he cares. He was such a jerk yesterday when we were all having lunch after the yoga class, being snarky about Anthony. "Fine," I snap. "I just need to use the bathroom." I jump up and try to escape before he sees my face.

I splash cold water on my swollen eyes and red cheeks, then stare at myself in the mirror. Yep, I look dreadful. I close my eyes on a wave of self-pity.

But this isn't about me. Mom and Dad are hurting too. And I'm sure Amy's devastated. I'll have to call her tonight. And Byron . . . poor Byron has no idea what's going on. An ache pulses behind my breastbone and I press the heel of my palm there.

I blow out a breath and return to the living room.

"I told them what happened," Lacey says. "I hope that's okay."

I nod. That's actually way easier than telling them myself. "Thanks."

"Sorry, Taylor," Théo says.

I nod.

"It sucks," JP adds gruffly. "Sorry you're going through this."

I meet his eyes, trying not to, but unable to resist. And I see warmth and compassion there, and that nearly undoes me all over again. Tears well up in my eyes and I have to fight them back, dashing at them with my knuckles. "Do you have any tequila?"

"You know we do." Lacey jumps up and returns with the bottle and some small glasses. "And it's not stupid to worry about Byron. You love him."

"I do." I pout a little, petting Byron's silky back as I watch her pour the golden liquid. "So much." I swipe at one more lone tear.

JP clears his throat, then picks up a glass of tequila and downs it.

I lift my own glass, stare glumly at it, then take a sip. "Thanks for this. And thanks for listening and letting me cry all over you."

"Of course." Lacey smiles. "You listened to me when I was crying over Théo."

"You were crying over me?" Théo lifts an eyebrow.

"Of course I was."

"He was crying over you too," JP says to Lacey.

Théo flashes him a middle finger. "I was not." He pauses. "Okay, I got a little choked up."

I smile at this interplay. I love these people.

I mean, not JP. Not *love* love.

But they're making me feel a bit better.

JP

This sucks camel dick.

I fucking hate seeing Taylor so upset. A lump of cold granite lodges in my gut and all I want to do is pull her into my arms and comfort her. Dry her tears and tell her it's all going to be okay.

But I can't do that.

Just when I discover she really wasn't with Martinez and I'm free to . . . what? "Go after her" sounds kind of dickish. "Court her" sounds ridiculously old-fashioned. Whatever you call it, I'm attracted to her and I like her and I want to see more of her. But she's seeing someone else, that fuckstick Anthony. I've already screwed up once by, uh, screwing her when another dude thought she was his. And I did that big time with my own brother. No way can I even think about going there again.

Fuck my life.

The hockey season hasn't started yet; it's almost two more weeks until the start of regular season. I haven't even had a chance to show the team that I can stay out of trouble and be an asset, other than in a couple of preseason games. And damned if I'm going to give in to some kind of weird temptation when it comes to women and just prove I'm a total asshole. It's too soon to fail. No . . . I'm not going to fail.

It's killing me, though, seeing the droop of her lips,

mascara smudges beneath her puffy eyes, her cheeks blotchy. She should look terrible, but she's never been more appealing.

"You want to stay here for dinner?" Lacey invites Taylor. I've already been invited. "We're going to make fajitas."

"Sure." She nods listlessly. "I don't want to go home yet. God." She closes her eyes and tips her head back. "This is going to be so awkward."

"When is your mom moving out?"

"I don't know." She scrunches up her face. "I assume right away, since they told me and Amy today."

"You'll still see her."

"I know."

"You two are pretty close."

Taylor nods. "I'll have to start looking for a place too. The house is going on the market tomorrow."

"We should buy it," Lacey says to Théo.

"What?" His eyebrows fly up.

"You're just renting this place. It would be nice to have our own place, and we love it here."

"Uh . . . that's a bit sudden," Théo says, being his usual careful, controlled self. He would definitely not make an impulse buy of something like a house. He'd research the market, check out interest rates at different financial institutions, and make a list of everything they needed and wanted in a house before even looking. "I was planning to look at buying somewhere after my first year here, when we have a better idea if I'll be staying."

"Oh." Lacey makes a face. "Okay."

"I think I'll look in Torrance," I say. "Near work."

Torrance isn't far from where I live.

"That's a good idea." Lacey pushes out her bottom lip. "But I'll miss having you so close."

"Our friendship is probably over," Taylor says sadly.

Lacey chokes and my eyes shoot open wide at this dramatic statement.

"I'm kidding," Taylor adds. "Sort of." She lifts unhappy eyes to look at Lacey. "But I did think of that. What if you don't want to bother with me when I live farther away?"

"Don't be silly." Lacey laughs and hugs Taylor. "Of course we'll see each other. And we'll send Snaps all the time, just like we do now."

"Okay."

My heart aches a little at Taylor's fears. She'll be losing a lot—her home, her family, and she's worried about losing her new friends.

We all help Lacey and Théo in the kitchen, making the marinade for chicken and beef, slicing up onions and peppers. It's comfortable and yet it's not, because just being near Taylor is a challenge to my resolve. My body vibrates and my mind hums with wanting her.

My mind twists and turns with the effort to resist. It's killing me.

I have to fucking get over this.

"You know what's stupid?" Taylor says. "I'm m-most broken-hearted about Byron."

I frown. "What about Byron?"

"Neither of my parents can take him, and I'm sure any place I can find won't allow p-pets." Her voice catches and tears glint on her eyelashes. "My dad wants to buy another house eventually, but I don't know what we're going to do with him right now."

My heart contracts and my gut tightens. Fuck. She loves that dog. She's losing everything.

"I'll take him."

For a couple of seconds, I don't know where the words came from. Oh . . . me. They came from me.

She gapes at me. "What?"

"I'll take him. I love dogs. He likes me. I don't live right on the beach, but close."

"Can you . . . have dogs where you live?"

"Oh yeah. You can visit him. In fact, you'll *have* to when I travel."

She gives her head a shake. "That's crazy. You don't have to do that."

"Well, the offer is there."

"If you're going to live in Torrance, that would be closer than us," Lacey says. "We'd take him too, but JP's place would be easier for you to get to."

"You want to get your own dog," Taylor says to her with a sad smile. "I know. But thank you."

"Just let me know," I say, not sure why I'm doing this except I can't stand to see her so broken-hearted. And I really like Byron. "Seriously."

She catches her lower lip between her teeth, looks up at me through wet eyelashes, and slowly nods.

Saturday is the Fan Fun Fest the Eagles hold every year during training camp. It's held outside the ExCorp Center in Long Beach, where the Golden Eagles play. There are a bunch of stations where kids can do fun things like shoot pucks at targets, and we have places to sit and meet and greet the fans and sign autographs. We're all expected to be there for a while.

It's a kick meeting fans, especially the kids, who are all big-eyed with hero worship. Lots of parents are too. I find it funny, because it's such a different atmosphere than what I grew up with. Yeah, Montréal fans are unique in the intensity of their relationship with their hockey team. Hockey is more than just a game. But they're hard-core *serious* about it. Hockey players aren't rock stars, like they are here in California; they're *gods*. Or pariahs, depending on how they play. Or how they treat the fans. Ha.

Anyway, it's a nice day, the sun is shining, people are smiling and happy, and I'm signing sticks and hats and jerseys and random stuff.

Even my dad and Uncle Mark are here, on the periphery, probably making brief appearances. I pause in chatting with fans to glance over at Uncle Mark, surrounded by a group of puck bunnies.

One corner of my mouth lifts and I shake my head. Jesus. He's forty-five years old and there are twenty-year-old women fawning all over him.

He seems to be enjoying himself.

He's been single for a long time, although I know he's had relationships. I don't even know if he's seeing anyone right now; he kind of keeps his personal life . . . personal. Understandable. When he first came to California from

Hershey, he went out with a pretty well-known TV actress and the media was all over that. He (and Dad) don't like anything that takes away from the hockey, which we've all learned after a couple of stories hit the news about players and their, uh, social lives. Dad and Uncle Mark both have a way of looking at you that can make your nuts shrivel. You don't want to go there.

The woman in front of me follows my gaze. "Your coach is hot."

I don't even know what to say to that. I force a smile. "If you say so."

"It must run in the family," she adds.

"Uh. Thanks."

Normally, I'm all into girls flirting with me. But it's hard to work up enthusiasm when I keep thinking about Taylor. Also, it's creepy that this woman finds me *and* my uncle attractive. So instead of flirting back, I quickly sign her jersey and move on to whoever's next in line.

Three women. All beautiful, with long, wavy hair, shiny lips, and big smiles. "Hi, JP," one of them says.

"Hello, ladies." I smile back at them.

Maybe they should rename this the Flirt Fest.

A FEW DAYS LATER, I'M IN UNCLE MARK'S OFFICE AT THE ExCorp Center—or should I say the coach's office—for a meeting that every player is having. They've got the roster down as of today, and I made the team. I wasn't really doubting it. I know my hockey skills are good.

But I'm getting the expected lecture about my behavior.

"And don't think that your last name is going to get you any preferential treatment," Uncle Mark says.

I sit up straighter. "I've never thought that."

He narrows his eyes at me. "Are you sure?"

I frown. "Yeah, I'm sure."

"You don't think you can get away with stupid shit because there won't be any consequences because of your name?"

"No!" My jaw drops. "Hell, no. There *are* consequences. The Department of Player Safety doesn't give a shit what my name is."

I think. They wouldn't go easy on me because of who my family is, would they?

I've never thought that. I've never *wanted* that. That Uncle Mark would think it about me burns.

"No," he agrees. "Likely not. But that's supplemental discipline. You also gotta face the consequences from the refs . . . the fans . . . your own teammates."

"I know that." I clench my teeth. "Believe me. I'm trying to do better this year. Control my emotions."

"And not taking stupid penalties. You gotta keep your feet moving. Too many of those stick infractions were because you were behind the play."

Ugh. He's right. I know it. I nod slowly. "Yeah."

"We'll work on that."

"You talk to everyone else like this?"

He grins. "Yeah. You think you're special or something?"

One corner of my mouth lifts. "Nope."

"Everyone has a part of their game they need to work on," he says.

"Yeah. I want to work hard."

"Good. I want everyone to be the best player they can be."

"Yeah."

"And I know you can be the best," he adds. "Both as your uncle . . . and as your coach."

My chest expands and I lift my chin. "Thanks, Uncle Mark. Er. Coach."

His faith in me, despite his warning, means a lot. I'd be lying if I said making my dad and my uncle proud wasn't important to me. It is. Also Grandpa Wynn. Even though I play for the "wrong" team, I want him to be proud of me too.

Most of all . . .? I want to be proud of myself.

11

JP

I'M ON MY WAY TO YOGA CLASS.

Things have been busy with a bunch of road trips—San Jose, Phoenix, Dallas, Vancouver, with home games in between. I wanted to go to another class, but with games every Saturday for the last three weeks, I haven't been able to. I hate to admit it, but I liked the way I felt after the class and without Harrison there showing off for the instructor, maybe I'll be able to focus even more.

Although Taylor in tight leggings and a bra top is hella distracting.

I sigh. She's *not* the reason I want to go to another yoga class. Seriously. I don't even know if she'll be there. The last time I saw her, she was broken up about her parents' marriage ending, crying her eyes out. I've had a hard time not thinking about that over the last month, wanting to get hold of her somehow to see if she's okay. I considered texting or calling Lacey to ask but knew how she'd take that.

I saw Everly once and managed to casually ascertain that she was "okay," but that was it.

This is all about improving my game. So far this season I'm playing okay, but I know I can do better. It always takes a few games to get back into the swing of things—working out in a gym, even training camp and exhibition games can't totally prepare you for the reality of a regular-season game. It's hard.

We've lost a few games, and I've taken a few penalties. One of them, I'd take again—I likely saved us from a goal against us, and we managed to kill the penalty. I deserved a couple of them, they were dumb, but another was a fucking horrible call that just about made me lose my mind. Hence the yoga class.

I need to find my Zen. Or whatever.

This is the second year having my uncle as my coach and it's stressful. I mean, he's a good coach, but . . . he's my uncle. I don't want any special treatment, and I especially don't want my teammates to think I'm getting any special treatment. I also don't want them to be awkward around me when they're pissed at Uncle Mark, which happens even though he's a good coach. He's tough and honest, but fair. And damn smart. I think every guy on the team feels like I do . . . we listen to him and do our best to give him what he asks of us. And I want to show him my best, not me breaking my stick and shouting obscenities at the ref. (I didn't do that, but I wanted to.)

I park in the lot. Unlike last time I was here, it's a beautiful sunny day, the sky a clear, cloudless blue, the ocean a deeper shade of cobalt. I stroll inside Makara Yoga, trying to feel chill, not hyper-alert on the lookout for Taylor.

She's not here, and I'm not sure if I'm disappointed or relieved.

"Hi again," Arya says to me with a friendly smile, clearly remembering me. "It took you a while to come back."

"I've been away the last three weekends." I have no idea if she knows who I am, but I tend to assume people don't know me.

"Your friend's not with you?"

"Not this time." I grin. "And he's not my friend."

She blinks.

"Actually, he's my uncle."

She gives her head a confused shake. "Okay."

"Yeah, we're the same age. Weird family."

"Hey, you're not the only one!" She turns her attention to the rest of the group, and we start grabbing boards to carry outside.

Just as Taylor rushes in. "Sorry I'm late!" she says breathlessly to Arya.

"We're just starting. Grab a board!"

It's been a month since I saw Taylor. My breath sticks in my chest as I watch her. Her hair's up in a messy knot on top of her head, and yeah, she's wearing form-fitting pants again and a different bra top, this one lime green and black. She hasn't noticed me yet. But, as if she feels my gaze on her, she turns and we lock eyes.

My blood fizzes in my veins. I manage a smile. "Hey."

"Hi, JP." She tilts her head. "What are you doing here?"

"Uh . . . yoga?"

"Smart-ass."

I grin. I'm still fizzing, my chest filling with it. "Yeah. I wanted to take another class. This time I won't have that clown Harrison distracting me."

She laughs. "Yeah, he didn't really seem into it."

We follow the group outside and across the sand to the water. I'm going to focus on the yoga. Not on Taylor.

Apparently *I'm* the distraction, though, for others in the class, as women are whispering and eyeing me. I'm not the only male here; there are two other guys today, but I guess the women recognize me. I smile politely, then ignore them to follow Arya's instructions.

Ignoring Taylor is easier said than done, but I use the focus I've learned from years of playing hockey to block out the things that take away my concentration.

"A main concept of yoga is being nonjudgmental," Arya says when we're out on the water. "Meaning both toward others and toward ourselves. A lot of our stress comes from being hard on ourselves."

This strikes me as true.

"Our minds and bodies are one and connected," she continues.

Okay, here comes the woo-woo stuff.

"Stress in one affects the other," she adds.

Okay, this I know is true. The mind *is* powerful.

Determined to actually get something out of this, I focus on the various poses, starting with child's pose and flowing through a series of movements including downward dog.

"On the paddleboard you have to be more mindful of your balance," Arya says in a gentle tone. "Where your hands and feet are."

It's true, and that makes the focus even more important.

One look at Taylor while doing Warrior 2 makes me wobble dangerously. I grit my teeth and resume my pose, trying to find that balance again and relax.

I leave the class feeling good. Nice and calm and relaxed. That'll probably last until I get on the freeway.

Nonjudgmental toward myself and others. I won't curse the stupid drivers on the freeway. Wait, that was judgmental. I mean, I won't curse the drivers on the freeway.

"I'm surprised to see you here," Taylor says after we've taken our boards back. "I didn't think you were really into this."

"That was Harrison." I throw him under the bus. "I felt good after, and I'm working on being more Zen."

Her lips twitch. "Ah. That's good. Did it work?"

"Yeah. I think so."

"You're ready for the party tonight, then."

"Ah . . . yeah." I eye her. "Lacey told you about it?"

"I'm invited."

It's Théo's birthday party tonight. His birthday was last week, but Lacey planned the party for tonight, a Saturday night both the Condors and the Eagles are off. We've had three Saturday games in a row, now a few weeks into the season. "I hope Lacey knows what she's getting herself into. The Wynn family parties are usually a bit . . . uh . . . well, you know what happened at the wedding."

She rolls her eyes. "Oh yeah."

"I'm sure it'll be fine." *I'll* be on my best behavior. I can't speak for everyone else. "How are you doing?" I ask, holding her gaze.

"I'm fine." One corner of her mouth lifts, as we both remember how upset she was last time we saw each other.

"I found a new place. I'm moving in next week, which is good because our house sold right away, and the new owners take possession November first."

"Wow. Well, that worked out. What about Byron?"

Her eyes shadow and her eyebrows slope down. "Looks like—" Her voice catches and she stops.

"I told you I'll take him." My voice is low and intense. I'm pissed because she hasn't contacted me about this when she's clearly upset about it. "Why didn't you let me know?"

"I, uh . . ."

"Where's your new place?" I ask. "Is it an apartment?"

"Yes." She bites her lip. "On Frampton Avenue."

"I'm not sure where that is."

She describes the location.

"That's not far from my place at all." I shake my head. "Come on, Taylor, this is a no-brainer."

Our eyes meet in a sizzling, penetrating connection. She's being stubborn about this because it's me. It pisses me off. And makes my chest feel heavy.

She nods. "Okay."

"How about we get lunch and we can talk about it?"

"Oh. Um, I'd better get home. Anthony and I are going to a movie premiere tonight."

Anthony. Fuck. "Ooh, all Hollywood." I try for a light tone, but it comes out with an edge.

Taylor's lips tighten.

"I thought you were coming to the party."

"We're going to stop by for a bit. So, I'll, uh, see you there."

"Right. Okay." I nod and watch as she hustles over to her car in the parking lot.

I blow out a gusty breath. Anthony's going to be there. Okay, I said I was going to be on my best behavior. I may have an urge to punch the dickwad in the mouth, but I've just found my Zen . . . I'll think happy thoughts, or imagine I'm floating on a paddleboard on the water . . . or something. It'll be fine.

LATER, WHEN I GET TO THE PARTY, I HAVE TO PARK ABOUT ten blocks from Théo's place. It's hard enough to park near there with those tiny little side streets, and tonight, Pacific Avenue is lined with cars. I recognize some of them. Apparently, I'm late.

I hear noise coming from the house as I approach the door. People are outside on the terrace talking, there's music playing, and a loud burst of laughter greets me as I open the door and step in. I rang the bell, but I don't know if anyone heard it.

Lacey appears with a glass of wine in hand and a big smile. "Hi!"

"Hi, Lace." We do a brief embrace. "How's it going?"

"Ooookay." She grimaces. "So far so good."

I grin. "Good to hear. I'll see if I can stir things up."

She gives me an alarmed look.

"Kidding." I hold up my hands. "I'm on my best behavior tonight."

"Whew. Come on in. What can I get you to drink?"

The party is clearly casual, people in the kitchen, dining room, living room, and, like I said, spilling outside. There are more than just family members here; I recognize some of the Condors organization—Dave Martin, their coach; their new assistant GM, Scott Jermey; and a few players including Wyatt Bell, who lives in the same complex as Théo. I haven't seen him since the wedding. He gives me a slitty-eyed scowl.

Right; I punched him in the face when he was trying to get Manny off me. I apologized to him that night, but he obviously hasn't forgotten.

Then I see Taylor.

As I take the beer Lacey hands me, my eyes lock with Taylor's across the open space. She's talking to Everly in the living room. There's a guy sitting beside her I don't know.

Craptastic. That must be Anthony.

My insides twist up into knots. I can't exactly cut and run. I greet Théo with a hug and backslap. I chat with him and Harrison and Wyatt for a few minutes, then make my way around to greet other family members—Mom and Dad are here, Uncle Mark, Grandpa and Chelsea. Eventually I wind up near Everly and Taylor.

Everly bumps me with her shoulder. "Hey. How's it going, bad boy of hockey?"

The nickname bugs me. "I'm not a bad boy anymore."

She lifts an eyebrow. "Since when?"

I don't want to talk about this, especially in front of Taylor and her boyfriend. Gritting my teeth, I smile and extend a hand to him as Taylor introduces us.

"So cool to meet you," Anthony says. "I'm a big hockey fan." He looks around. "This is wild, being here."

I look at Taylor. "We need to talk. About Byron."

"What about Byron?" Everly asks.

I tell her about the plan.

"That's a great idea!" she says. "Taylor, your new place isn't far from JP's. This'll work perfectly."

Taylor nods, her lips pressed together.

"Maybe Byron should come for a visit before he actually moves in," I say. "I assume he's housebroken."

"Yes." She gives a little eye roll. "He's very well trained."

"Okay, then."

"I'll pay for his food. And vet bills, of course."

"Whatever." It's not like I can't afford a few cans of dog food.

"Okay." She beams. "This is really so much better than . . . than having to find a new home for him with people I don't know."

"Yeah."

"You're a hero." Everly nudges me. She's teasing, but I can see she's happy too. She looks up. "Oh. I'd better go help Lacey with the food."

She departs, and a blanket of awkwardness drops over Taylor, Anthony, and me. Well, *I* feel it, anyway. I want him gone. But it's me who has to clear out.

I grin, trying to lighten the mood. "You'll have to switch to being an Eagles fan now, since you're practically in Long Beach."

She rolls her eyes. "Never."

I laugh. "Nice meeting you," I say to Anthony. I turn to Taylor. "We'll talk more about Byron, okay?"

"Okay. Thank you."

I meet her eyes, hold her gaze for a couple of heartbeats, then nod and move away.

I walk outside, where I see Grandpa and Chelsea sitting. There are other people out here . . . Rosa and Marshall, neighbors of Théo's, talking to Wyatt. But no other family members. Grandpa and Chelsea are by themselves.

I get it, but it annoys me, too.

I pull up an empty chair. "Hey there."

"Hi!" Chelsea says with a smile. I lean over to kiss her cheek.

"Hello, kid," Grandpa says. "Haven't seen you in a while. You bring a young lady with you tonight?"

"No. Didn't go well the last time I brought a date to a family function."

"That's because you were screwing over your brother."

Ouch. "Yeah, yeah. Anyway, I haven't been seeing anyone lately."

"Unusual for you. From what I hear."

Actually, it is. I just haven't been interested lately. There were women at the Fan Fun Fest who were clearly interested. I've gone out with the guys a few times, and there are always women who want to hang out with hockey players. I've flirted a little, danced a couple of times, and bought a few drinks, but I haven't done anything more than that. "Saving my energy for hockey," I tell him.

"Ha! That's a good one. My coach used to tell us not to have sex before a game."

"Jesus." I rub my forehead. "Thank Christ Uncle Mark doesn't tell us that. I think they've debunked that old myth."

"We always believed it," Grandpa says sadly. "Of course, most of us just ignored it."

Chelsea laughs.

"It's time for dinner!" Lacey calls from the door onto the patio. "Just buffet style, so we're all helping ourselves."

I follow Grandpa and Chelsea into the house. Chelsea sticks close by Grandpa while they fill plates. My family may be pissed at Grandpa for allegedly stealing money, Grandpa may be mad at his sons for suing him, and they all may hate Chelsea because they think she's a gold-digging opportunist, but everyone is respectfully letting Grandpa go first at the buffet.

Lacey hovers around, apologizing for using paper plates and napkins, making sure they have everything they need, then others move in. I head into the kitchen for another beer first.

The kitchen is still crowded with people, including Théo and Harrison. Without asking, Théo opens the fridge door and hands me a beer. I grin.

"You gotta make sure people talk to Grandpa," I say to him in a low voice.

He sighs. "I know."

"This family feud is bullshit," Harrison mutters. "We need to do something about it. Can't you get your dad to withdraw the lawsuit?"

I grimace and glance at Théo. "I don't know. They seem pretty convinced that Grandpa stole money from them."

"Why would he do that?" Harrison shakes his head.

Théo's lips pinch together, but he says nothing.

"I don't know." I don't want to get into it with Harrison, because I like him and we get along. "Maybe all of us should get together sometime and talk about what we could do."

"What do you mean 'all of us'?"

"Like . . . this generation. You, Noah, Asher, Everly . . . us . . . Riley. I doubt if we can get Jackson here, but maybe."

Harrison purses his lips and nods. "I'll talk to Everly about it. She's like the boss of everyone."

I laugh. "True."

Taylor and Anthony appear.

"We're on our way out." Anthony extends a hand to shake mine. "Good to meet you, man."

"Yeah." I resist the urge to curl my lip.

He says goodbye to the others, then tells Taylor, "I'll get the car, babe. Pick you up in a couple of minutes."

"Okay, thanks." She smiles at him as he leaves.

"You had to park in the next county too?" I joke.

She laughs. "Just about."

"Give me your cellphone number. And we'll get things sorted out with Byron." She tells me her number, I enter it in my phone, and I immediately send her a text so she has mine.

"I still can't . . ." She hesitates.

"It's fine, Taylor." Jesus. She sinks her teeth into that plump bottom lip and it's all I can do not to swoop down and kiss it. I know how that lip feels . . . against mine. How she tastes . . . My entire body heats and tingles remembering. I have to curl my hand into a fist to resist reaching out to touch her. I want to stroke a hand down her silky hair and over her velvety skin. I want to assure her that Byron is going to be fine, even though he'll be living with someone else.

She gives a small nod and looks up at me through her

eyelashes. Electricity arcs between us and I feel a tug of desire in my groin. Oh for Chrissake.

Maybe this isn't a good idea. I'm going to be tormented every time I see her. I'm being a dumbass, suggesting this. I know it's for selfish reasons—I want to see her. But I fucking can't.

Harrison and Théo are watching us.

"I'll walk you to the door," I murmur, setting a hand on the small of her back.

Her eyes flicker.

A minute. Just a minute alone with her. In the foyer, we pause. I gaze at her face, my eyes moving over her flushed cheeks and glittering eyes, lingering on her mouth. Heat crackles around us and I feel a tug of desire in my groin.

"Stop looking at me like that," she whispers.

"Like what? Like I want to push you up against that wall and kiss the breath out of you?" I edge infinitesimally closer, barely at all, and she takes a step back, her breath hitching.

"Yes. Like that."

"Then stop looking like you *want* me to."

"I . . ." She swallows. "Don't do this, JP."

I sigh. "I'm not doing anything. I'm not going to hit on another guy's girl. *Again.*" I bite out the word, remembering how pissed I'd been when Manny jumped me at the wedding because he was jealous.

"Okay, good." She nibbles her bottom lip. "We can still be friends . . . right?"

I stare at her incredulously. "Friends?"

"Sure. Because of Théo and Lacey." A tentative smile touches her lips. "And Byron."

My forehead tightens. "Uh . . ."

"If you're going to look after my dog, we should at least be friends."

"Friends," I say again.

She smiles tentatively.

My heart is withering and shrinking in my chest.

This isn't a shocker. She's with someone else now. Why would I think we could be anything more than friends? I draw in a long breath through my nose and straighten my slumping shoulders. "Sure. Of course. Friends. Have fun at your Hollywood premiere." I stretch my mouth into a smile before turning away from her.

Lacey's in the kitchen and shoots me a nervous glance when I stalk in. I grab the beer I left on the counter and march through the living room to the doors to the patio. Everyone's inside now, eating. I lean on the low wall and gaze out at the dark ocean as I tip the beer to my lips and chug down half of it.

Everything inside me is buzzing. I'm wired and edgy. I try to calm myself down, using some of the things I've learned about preparing for a game when the adrenaline is running high. Except I don't really want to calm down. I want to punch something.

I draw in a long breath, let it out slowly, and raise the beer again.

"You okay, man?" Théo's voice comes from behind me. He slaps a hand on my shoulder as he joins me.

"Yeah."

"Something's got your shorts in a twist."

"I don't like this shit about making good decisions. It's too hard."

Théo cracks out a fast laugh. "Not for me."

"I'm not you." The words come out on a growl.

Théo tips his head. "I know, man. And thank God, right? Sometimes going with your gut is the right thing to do."

"I can't believe you just said that."

"Well, in fairness to myself . . . intuition has been shown to be information acquired through associated learning and stored in long-term memory, which is accessed unconsciously to form the basis of a judgment or decision."

"What?"

"You learn things throughout your life." He shrugs. "You hold that knowledge in your subconscious and use it unconsciously to make decisions. It's not just letting emotion guide your decisions; there's some factual basis for it."

"Huh. So you're saying I should go after Taylor?"

He chokes. "Uh . . . that's what this is about?"

I drop my head forward. "Yeah."

"She's seeing that dude . . ."

"I know, I know." My voice comes out like a snarl. "First I thought she was still with Martinez. Then I found out she wasn't. Before I could move, I found out she's dating Anthony Hipster."

He chokes on a laugh. "Um, yeah. Well, shit. I didn't know . . ."

"Seriously?" I lift my head to peer at him. "Lacey didn't tell you about the wedding?"

"Okay, yeah, she did."

"Asshole." I punch his shoulder.

He laughs. "Guess it wasn't that good with you. She found someone else pretty quick."

"Sure, kick me when I'm down." I exhale sharply. "I can't stop thinking about her. And she wants us to be just friends."

"Ouch." He winces.

"Yeah."

"Well, I'd say it's pretty clear. You gotta forget about her."

"*That's* your advice?" I scowl.

"You know it's the right thing."

I nod reluctantly. I'm trying to do the right things. But it's fucking killing me.

12

TAYLOR

JP texts me on Sunday morning about bringing Byron over so he can see his new place and get acquainted with it. A great idea.

No. It's a bad idea. The worst idea. This is like jumping into a bonfire with gasoline-soaked clothes on.

I feel like I'm about to give a speech to a thousand people, naked, as I drive to his place, my hands sweaty on the steering wheel, my belly a mass of jumping nerves. Byron is happily oblivious in the backseat, his face up to the window I've cracked open, panting eagerly.

I love him.

Byron, I mean. I love Byron.

I'm doing this for him. I know he's only a dog, but there's no such thing as "only a dog" when the dog's been in your family for years and he's such a sweet guy and . . . well, I love him.

I sigh. I can do this.

JP and I are friends. That's what I suggested to him the

other night. We're both always so . . . tense . . . around each other. We need to get past that and just be friends.

Sure.

He'd looked at me as if I'd just told him I was going to become a sex worker when I suggested that. And I'm not sure if it's because he hates me or because he wants to bone me. Maybe both.

I sigh. That's pretty much how I feel about him.

No. That's a lie. I don't hate him. But I do want to bone him.

Shit! I'm dating someone else! I can't be thinking things like that about JP.

Standing in the foyer at Lacey's place the other night, heat crackling between us, melting my panties, tightening my nipples . . . I forgot all about Anthony.

What is *wrong* with me?

I've mapped out my route on Google Maps and my phone tells me to take the next exit off the 405. It's another five minutes or so until we turn again to find JP's street and then his condo complex. It's a high-rise building, right near the ocean, and my heart drops as I study it.

This isn't a place for a dog.

I fight back tears. "Look!" I say to Byron as I open the back door and reach for his leash. "This is where you're going to live!" My eyes sting and I squeeze them shut briefly. "It's a really nice place!"

Leading Byron inside, I take in the elegant lobby—all glass walls, marble tile, and carpet, with furniture groupings and potted plants.

"There's a freakin' doorman," I mutter to Byron, clutching his leash.

The doorman lets us go up to the twenty-fifth floor with a friendly smile. JP greets us at his door.

Oh God, he looks so good, my knees actually go weak. Stubble dusts his square jaw, his thick hair is messy, and he's wearing loose athletic shorts and a Golden Eagles T-shirt that hugs his biceps and chest. I could just stare at him all day.

Damn him, I don't know why I'm so attracted to him. Sure, he's good-looking and built, but . . . there's something else. The way he looks at me . . . I tried to tell him we could just be friends, but inside I was a melting pool of lust. The urge to press myself up against him was so powerful I had to tense every muscle in my body. My mouth longed to feel his against mine. I wanted to taste him. Breathe in the scent of him. Put my hands on him everywhere.

God.

It's happening all over again.

Friends.

I gird my loins and smile. "Hi."

"Hi." His smile is easy, friendly. Just what I want. "Hey, Byron." He takes the leash and Byron happily trots into the condo, his toenails clicking on the dark wood floor.

The door closes quietly behind me as I follow them.

Looking around, I sigh. "This isn't going to work."

The place is amazing . . . Light pours in through floor-to-ceiling windows with an ocean view. A massive sectional upholstered in tan distressed leather takes up one corner of the room, a glass coffee table centered in front of it on a patterned rug.

"What? Why?" JP straightens from unclipping Byron's leash and faces me.

"Look at this place." I shoot out a hand. "It's . . . Byron will scratch your beautiful floors and jump all over your furniture."

JP shakes his head, a smile tugging at his lips. "Your house had hardwood floors and they were fine. And leather is the best thing. If he gets it dirty, I'll just wipe it off."

My chest is tight. "It's twenty-five floors down, every time you have to take him out."

"Yeah, that's okay. I mean, it's not ideal, but I don't mind. I go out for coffee across the street every morning anyway."

"What about . . . I'm sure you must, uh, have an active social life. There'll be times you'll have to come home to let him out."

He shrugs. "I'll figure it out. We'll keep in touch, and like I said, there'll be times you'll need to come by. If we're both busy, I'll hire a dog walker."

My mouth falls open. "A dog walker! That's—"

"Lots of people do it. Lots in this building."

"There are other dogs?"

"Hell yeah."

I suck on my bottom lip, hands clasped together. What other choice do I have? My apartment is strictly no pets and so is Dad's. I couldn't find anyone else who could take him, much as I tried.

Byron is nosing around the room, checking things out. Without me asking, JP strolls into the kitchen, which is separated from the living/dining area by a big granite counter, grabs a bowl from a cupboard, fills it with water, and sets it on the floor. Byron happily slurps, then continues his exploration.

"I brought a few things." I set down the reusable shopping bag on the coffee table. "A few toys and chews."

"Good." He dumps them on the rug.

I laugh. "He doesn't need all of them at once."

"I know, but maybe they'll make him feel at home."

"I hope he feels like it's home." I'm being such a baby about this, but he's my *dog.* "You have to keep an eye on him. He sometimes likes to eat weird things. A loaf of bread off the counter. A twenty-dollar bill. One time he ate a bottle of glitter." I pause. "His poop sparkled for three days."

JP bursts out laughing. "Noted. How about we take him for a walk? You can see the neighborhood."

"Okay, sure."

I grab the leash and some poop bags and we leave the condo.

After locking the door, JP hands me the key. "Here."

I look up at him.

"For you. So you can get in when I'm not here."

"Right." I blink and shove the key in the pocket of my jeans. Of course I have to be able to get in. It just seems . . . personal.

Weirdly, despite my nerves on the way over here, there's no awkwardness between us. He seemed taken aback when I suggested we just be friends, but today he's casual and relaxed, and . . . well, friendly.

Down on the main floor, we leave the lobby by a rear exit and follow a well-groomed path through palm and fig trees toward the ocean. We have to cross under a busy street to a grassy area, where Byron decides to do some business.

I glance at JP as I pick up the poop in a bag. "You prepared for this?"

"Sure." He appears unconcerned.

I get rid of it in a nearby trash receptacle and we continue on until we're at the beach—volleyball courts. I smile.

"You'd think you'd be better at volleyball, living so close to beach courts."

"Ha. That was quite the show you put on that day."

I rein in my smile. "I wasn't showing off."

"No?" He slants me an amused look. "I think you were."

"Phhht." I totally was.

"We could have a little one-on-one action here sometime."

I stare at him.

"Volleyball."

"Right!"

He laughs. "You have a dirty mind, Sunshine."

My cheeks flame. "Why do you call me that?"

He hesitates, then says lightly, "Because of your smile. It's like sunshine."

My heart skips a beat as tension shimmers between us. Then I kick off my flip-flops and bend to pick them up. Carrying them in one hand, I start across the soft sand. JP follows Byron and me toward a grouping of tall, slender palm trees, their fronds glistening in the sun. The breeze is cool on my hot face, despite the bright sun.

"See, Byron's right at home here," he points out.

"He is. See, Byron? It's the same beach as at home, just farther down the coast."

"I like how you talk to him."

"Are you making fun of me for talking to a dog?"

"No! I said I like it. It's cute."

"You'd better talk to him, too," I say fiercely. "Or he'll feel . . . rejected. You have to play with him and give him hugs."

"I will." He presses a hand to his heart. "Promise."

I study him from the corner of my eye as we walk. He seems more relaxed today. Too bad I'm not, remembering the sparks and heat surrounding us the other night. I'm tingling all over again just being this near to him.

My hair is whipping around in the wind, so I pause. "Can you take him?" I hand JP the leash. Then I pull a hair tie from my pocket and scoop my hair up into a ponytail. JP watches me, his eyes darkening.

Heat darts in my lower belly.

Friends.

He clears his throat and we resume walking. "So are you all packed to move?"

"Getting there. I move in Wednesday."

"How are you handling it?"

I'm surprised at this question. I guess I don't expect him to ask a question like that, knowing he's probably going to get an earful about how sad I am and how heartrending it is to leave the house I grew up in most of my life. Most men would rather avoid that. So I lie. "I'm okay."

"Sure." He nudges me with his big shoulder. "You're going to be fine. This will be a good move for you. How about your parents? How are they doing?"

"Well, my mom is gone. But we had lunch the other day, and text all the time. She seems . . . fine." I shake my head.

"My dad I'm not so sure about. I saw him the other day, wandering around the house looking at things, and he seemed so . . . lost."

"You don't know what happened with them?"

"No. They're pretty firm that they won't discuss it with me and Amy. My sister. She's coming up from San Diego today to see if there's anything at the house she wants." I chuckle. "I think there are boxes of her Sweet Valley High books there." I pause. "I guess it doesn't really matter what happened, if this is the best thing for them."

"Relationships can be complicated."

I narrow my eyes at him. "Speaking from experience?"

"Well . . . to be honest, I've never had a really serious relationship. As an adult."

"No?" I shrug. "Me either."

"Until now. Things seem pretty serious with Anthony." His tone turns rough.

I don't know what to say. I keep trying with Anthony because he's a nice guy and I do enjoy going out with him. We still haven't had sex. I'm just not feeling it. He's made a few moves and asked me to stay over at his place, but he hasn't pushed too hard, which makes me feel both relieved and kind of miffed. Which is somewhat perverse of me, but there you have it. I may not want him, but I want to be wanted.

I know JP wants me. Or should I say, *wanted* me. I put an end to that with my "let's be friends" speech.

"We haven't been seeing each other that long," I finally say. "But you're right. Relationships can be complicated."

We let Byron off the leash. JP picks up a stick and

throws it for him. Byron flies over the sand to retrieve it and return it. This continues as we walk.

"Can he swim?" JP asks.

"Of course. He's a retriever."

The next toss has the stick sailing into the ocean, and Byron doesn't hesitate to splash in and swim for it.

"You're really a sucker for punishment. He's going to be wet and sandy now."

"I'll introduce him to my big bathtub. And my cleaning service comes tomorrow." He pauses. "Why does it seem you're trying to discourage me from taking him?"

I twist my mouth up. "I'm not. I just . . . want you to know what you're getting yourself into."

"I'm aware." His words are loaded, and I just *know* he's thinking about us . . . about me coming to his place all the time. "I'll give you my schedule and we can plan out what days you'll need to come by."

I nod.

"But you can come anytime," he says. "I know you're going to miss him."

"I am. But I won't just drop in. I'd, uh, hate to interrupt you in anything." Blergh.

"I guess that's fair."

Byron has had enough and flops down on the sand.

"Buddy." I plant my butt in the sand next to him. "Are you exhausted?" I rub his head.

JP starts to sit beside me, then appears to change his mind. He moves around Byron and drops down to sit on the beach with Byron between us.

I stare out at the ocean, white sailboats sliding along the horizon, the sun creating a shifting pattern of silver on the blue water. People walk along the hard-packed sand and a few surfers are sitting on their boards, waiting for waves. The breeze lifts loose strands of my hair.

I stroke Byron's back. "How long have you lived here?" I ask JP.

"Here, in Long Beach? Or my condo?"

"Both."

"I've been in Long Beach six years. I got drafted by the Eagles eight years ago, but I played a couple of seasons in San Diego, and when I first got called up, I rented a place for a while. Bought the condo four years ago."

I nod. "It's really nice."

"It's okay. It's close to the arena."

"You grew up in Canada, right?" I already know this from my Google search. Don't judge me. You'd do the same.

"Yeah. Québec. My dad bought an AHL team in Drummondville when I was about four or five, so I grew up there, surrounded by hockey. Ended up playing in Gatineau when I was a teenager. I lived there for three years."

"What's it like being part of such a famous hockey family?"

"Eh. They're my family. The fame is weird, but I get it. Bob Wynn is the King of Hockey. To me, he's Grandpa. Which actually makes it worse."

"Worse?"

"I mean, grandparents are always proud of their grandchildren, right? But when you play the same sport your grandfather did and he's 'the king,' it's a little intimidating. It's a lot to live up to."

"You think he's not proud of you?" I take in the tightness of his jaw as he stares out at the ocean.

"Well." He bends his head. "I haven't given him a lot to be proud of lately."

"What? Why? Oh, you mean the suspensions."

"Yeah. And there've been a few other incidents . . . they didn't get as much media attention. Sometimes my emotions get the better of me."

I run my tongue over my front teeth. "Really."

He gives me a surprised glance. "What?"

I purse my lips. "Um, impulsive sex with a stranger the night of the wedding rehearsal?"

His eyes widen, then darken. "Right." Our eyes meet and hold. Heat shimmers between us and my insides roll over. We're both remembering that night. Images flash through my mind like a porn movie—JP's beautiful, hard body, his hands on me, his mouth on me, his eyes hot and appreciative as he gazes down at me . . . I shift on the sand. I want to have that again.

I almost whimper.

He looks away. "Well, I sure as hell didn't tell Grandpa about that mistake."

Mistake. My heart squeezes. But I know it was a mistake.

"Grandpa was pissed that I was with Théo's ex."

I don't really want to hear about JP and Théo's ex. Emma. I resist the urge to imitate gagging and say, "I think I like your grandpa."

"He'd probably like you too."

Our eyes meet and hold for another heated moment, then I drop my gaze to Byron and stroke him again.

"Anyway, living here actually makes it easier to be part of the Wynn family. There's a lot less attention."

"Hmm."

He picks up a handful of sand and lets it sift through his fingers. "Why do you sound so . . . skeptical?"

"I think you like the attention."

He laughs. "Why do you say that?"

"You have an image to uphold. That bad boy who doesn't give a shit about anything."

He's silent for a moment. I've probably pissed him off. Finally he says lightly, "Yep, that's me."

"I don't believe you stole your brother's ex."

"Huh?"

"You let people think you did that. But I don't think you did." I meet his eyes challengingly.

"Okay, fine. She told me they'd broken up."

I nod. He gives off the air of not giving a shit, but he wants his grandpa to be proud of him. He wants to live up to his grandpa's accomplishments. He loves his brother and hates that he hurt him. And . . . he really likes Byron.

"I still shouldn't have been with her," he adds. "Even if they *had* broken up, which turned out to be not true."

"Did you . . . really care about her?" A sharp pain pierces behind my breastbone.

He doesn't answer for so long, I say, "Sorry! You don't have to answer that question. None of my business."

"I thought I did at the time." He shakes his head and sifts more sand. "But basically I was just being an asshole." He pauses. "You and Martinez . . . at the wedding . . . you weren't seeing each other anymore."

"No." I frown. "I told you, we used to go out. He left town and I didn't hear from him for months."

"You didn't actually tell me that."

"What?" I frown.

"You said he came to see you and apologized. I thought that meant you worked things out and you were seeing him again."

"No." I shake my head slowly. "He dumped me with barely a goodbye. Then he started a stupid fight. Why would I go back with him?"

He shrugs.

"That's why you seemed so . . . angry at me?" I tip my head to the side. "Did you think I slept with you when I was seeing someone else? Seriously?" My mouth falls open.

He doesn't answer right away. I study his profile—his strong nose and chin, his sculpted lips, his hair falling over his forehead. The pissed-off set of his jaw. "I wasn't angry at you."

"Oh. Seemed like you were."

"If I was angry about anything, it was that you left the wedding early when I thought we were going to fuck all night in my room." He jumps to his feet and dusts the sand off his butt, smiling. "Oh well. Let's get back."

His words hit me in the chest.

That's what this is about. Sex. Or lack of.

Anger churns hot in my belly as I stand too.

The walk back to his place is silent, but I barely notice because my mind is whirling.

The truth is—I'm disappointed, too, that we didn't finish what we started that night. Because it was amazing.

And hot. And fun. I was pissed off after the fight and I stormed out and . . . and okay, I've been regretting it ever since.

I can't tell him that now. Because now . . . we're just friends. And I'm seeing someone else.

And he's an asshole, to be annoyed because I left before falling back into bed with him.

My stomach hurts by the time we arrive back at his place, but I think I've got my shit together. So much for being friends, though.

"So, Wednesday's moving day, huh?" he says in his living room. Byron flops down on the floor, and yeah, he's leaving a trail of sand, but it's not that bad.

"Yes." I lift my chin, determined to do this for Byron. "I'll bring him over."

"Sure. Just let me know." He smiles. "It'll be fine. Don't worry."

"I know."

"Here's my schedule." He hands me a computer printout. "These are home games; these are away. I made a note of when we're leaving and getting back for the next month."

I scan it and nod. Then we set his alarm system with my own code, and he shows me how to use it so I can get in and out when he's not there. "You trust me with access to your place anytime?"

He gives me a long, level look, and says, "Yes. I trust you."

My heart bumps. I look over at my dog. "Okay, Byron! Let's go."

He jumps up, tail wagging. I pick up the leash. "Thank you again for looking after him."

This was a mistake. I mean, I'm sure Byron will be fine. But will I?

13

TAYLOR

Dad carries a box into my apartment and sets it on the floor. He straightens and looks around. "Not bad."

"Could be a lot worse, right?" I, too, gaze around the space. The super gave me the keys to my place a day early and Dad's helping me bring some things over before the big move tomorrow. "They painted it for me, so it's nice and fresh." I actually like the color—a warm greige that will look great with the furniture I'm bringing. "It's small, but I don't need that much room. At least I have a bedroom; I looked at some studio apartments that were all one room. And it's going to be nice to be so much closer to work. No more stressful commutes in bumper-to-bumper traffic."

"You're being a trooper about this." He curls an arm around my shoulders and kisses my temple. "I know this was a shock."

"Well . . . the splitting-up part was. I figured you were going to ask me to move out, though." I smile wryly. "It's time."

"We wanted you to get a good start to your career. We know it's different these days. It's hard for kids to save up, and buying a place is out of reach for so many."

"Well, luckily you helped me out with my school expenses, and it won't take me that long to pay off the loans I have." Again, it could be worse. I know kids with tons more debt than I have.

"You let me know if you need anything at all," Dad says. "I'll help however I can."

"Thanks, Dad." I pause. "Are you doing okay?"

His eyes shadow. "Yeah. I'm okay. Not how I pictured life at this point. But that's okay."

"You and Mom were going to retire and travel."

"I can still travel. It'll just be different."

"What about retirement?"

"Think I'll keep working a bit longer," he says gruffly. "Probably good for me to stay busy."

It doesn't sound like this was Dad's choice. I'm so curious, but reluctant to ask more questions. I don't want to be mad at my mom, but . . . she seems to be doing fine, whereas Dad . . . he's obviously sad. "Yeah," I agree. "And one big change at a time is enough."

"You're a smart girl." He gives me a fond smile and heads back out to get another box.

He brings in more cartons while I unpack things and put them away. Then he gets out his tools and helps me install the blinds I bought for the bedroom window and a curtain rod for the living room curtains I picked out. "I'll come back and help you hang your pictures when you figure out where you want things," he says.

"There's a drawer in the kitchen that sticks. D'you think you could look at that?"

He takes care of that for me too, then drives us back to the house for my last night living under my parents' roof.

It's Halloween and I'm moving.

I took the day off work, since the end of the month fell midweek and we have to be out of the house today.

My parents are helping out by paying movers and letting me take whatever furniture I need, so I have my bedroom set, a sofa and love seat and tables from our family room, and other miscellaneous stuff. Mom's here now, buzzing around cleaning now that the place is nearly empty.

Determined to be cheerful about this, since Lacey and Théo are helping me, I'm wearing a witch hat (it's really nice, with black silk flowers and feathers) along with my old jeans and a black T-shirt.

Lacey laughs when she sees me. "That's perfect."

"What are you saying, Lace?" I touch my hat. "You saying I'm a witch?"

"Nothing wrong with being a witch. I wish I were a witch. With magical powers."

"Good point. I'd just twitch my nose at this stuff and it would magically appear in my apartment."

"Twitch your nose?"

I jump at JP's instantly recognizable voice. "What are you doing here?" Seeing him has my pulse fluttering and my belly flip-flopping.

"Came to help. Nice hat. But you won't have to use magical powers. I brought more help." He nods at the three very tall men standing with him.

One guy steps forward, hand outstretched, wearing a friendly smile. "Hi, it's nice to meet you. I'm Stanley— wanna see my cup?"

I take his hand hesitantly, taken aback by his greeting. "Uh . . ."

"Ignore him—he's an idiot," JP says. "And his name is John, not Stanley, for Chrissake. John Dutchyshyn."

"It's a joke," John mutters.

I can't help but smile.

"And you definitely don't want to see his cup," the dark-haired man says. "Hi, I'm Abdel."

"Hi, Abdel. Thanks for coming."

"And this is Ethan Copp," JP says. "We call him Copper."

The big blond man smiles and lifts a hand.

"This is Taylor," JP continues. "She's the one moving today. And Lacey, my sister-in-law."

"Nice to meet you." Lacey grins.

"I, uh, didn't know you all were coming," I say.

"We finished practice and I roped them into it. Théo told me you're moving today. The more bodies the better, right?"

"Right!"

I don't even have that much stuff and the movers are taking the biggest items, but yeah, having all these guys will make it go quicker.

They load boxes and bags into vehicles, and all I have to do is run around giving directions and try not to stare slack-jawed as these guys heft boxes and bulge their biceps. Because . . . wow.

Byron is at my heels the entire time, not letting me out of his sight. He knows something's going on and he doesn't like it.

It's not long before everything is loaded up.

I gaze around the house, which is nearly empty now. An intense sadness sweeps over me. The house I grew up in and loved so much looks so sad now, cold and vacant.

Because it's not the house that makes a home . . . it's the people. And I'll still have my mom and dad and sister; it'll just be different.

A hand touches my shoulder. I turn to see JP. "You okay?" he asks in a low voice.

I meet his eyes. Concern shines there. I feel that tug . . . my body reacting, being pulled toward his. Why is he such an asshole sometimes, and so nice others? It confuses me and knocks me off balance.

"I'm okay," I finally answer, lifting my chin. "It's the end of something, but it's the beginning of something too. Starting my life on my own, independent."

"Right." His eyes are warm with compassion, and they crinkle up a bit at the corners with a hint of a smile that looks almost like . . . pride.

Byron is pacing, disturbed by all the commotion, strangers in the house carrying stuff out. I drop into a crouch and wrap my arms around him. "Hey, buddy, it's okay. It's going to be okay."

"Should we take him to my place first?"

I bite my lip, my throat thickening. I don't want to give

him up. But I have to. I nod, press my face to his silky head, then stand.

"He's still your dog," JP says in a low voice. He lifts a hand as if he wants to touch me, then drops it to his side. "He'll be living at my place, but he's still yours."

My throat squeezes and I nod. "Thank you."

"I'll meet you at my place. Lacey and Théo can take charge at the apartment until we get there."

"Okay."

"I'll come over later," Mom says. "To see if you need help with anything."

"Call me first. I might be okay. No need for you to drive all the way there for nothing."

"You sure?" She gives me a long, searching look.

"Did you see those guys?" I wave a hand, smiling. "They have muscles on their muscles."

The corners of her mouth lift. "Yes, they do. Okay, I'll check in with you."

We hug. I take one last look at the house, push down the sadness, and straighten my shoulders.

Once more, Byron and I make the drive to JP's place. He seems to know where he is, which is good. JP is already there, waiting in the lobby for us. He relieves me of some of the paraphernalia I'm carrying, taking the big doggy bed and a large bag, leaving me with Byron's leash and another bag. In the elevator, I tell Byron to sit, and he does, looking happy, tail waving on the floor.

"He thinks you're going to give him more treats," I remark to JP.

He grins. "I am."

Inside, he tosses Byron a cookie, which Byron catches

and crunches. I pull his food and water bowls out, set them on the kitchen floor, and unpack the food and treats I brought while JP takes Byron's bed into his bedroom.

"This is his water bottle," I explain, showing him the collapsible dog dish. "For long walks when it's hot. Poop bags. Brush and comb. And this is the number for our vet . . . It's not exactly close, but I'll find another one. Just in case of emergency."

I hand him the typewritten list of instructions he needs for feeding, walking, and grooming Byron, showing him the dog food and treats. He listens and nods solemnly, although his eyes twinkle.

"Okay, we'd better get to the apartment," I say. "I should be helping."

I kneel and throw my arms around Byron. "'Bye, buddy. I'll see you soon." I squeeze my eyes tight as they sting with tears. He licks my face.

I try not to feel sad as I drive from JP's condo to my apartment. It's not very far, which is good, as I'll be able to see him often. Byron, I mean. Not JP.

JP

I meet up with Taylor in front of her new apartment building.

"We went over my schedule, so you know I have a couple of home games coming up, tomorrow and Sunday."

I glance at her as I lift a box out of her trunk, catching her as she surreptitiously wipes a tear. Fuck, this is torture, seeing her upset. Me taking him is better than having to give Byron up to a shelter or something, but she's still so sad. Her love for that dog shows what a big heart she has. "We have a skate in the morning, but I'll be home in the afternoon before the game. I'll let you know the practice schedule; we might have a day off Friday."

She nods.

"If you want to come see Byron Wednesday night while I'm out, that's fine."

"Okay. Thanks."

I'm doing my best to be her friend, since that's what she wants. Even though there's still enough electrical energy between us to power the ExCorp Center.

It doesn't take long to unload her things and carry boxes from one room to another. The apartment is tiny and old-fashioned, but it's clean and freshly painted. Lacey puts things away in the kitchen while Taylor unpacks her clothes and makes her bed in between directing where she wants her furniture placed. I go help her with the bed, fitting pale green sheets over the mattress, then shaking out a big white duvet with sunflowers. She's determinedly cheerful in her ridiculous witch hat.

"I'm sensing a theme here," I say, nodding at her bed.

She frowns. "What?"

"Sunflowers. I notice you have a bunch of sunflower things in your kitchen, too."

"Oh. Yeah. They're my favorite flower."

"Ah." Somehow, this isn't surprising. She's . . . sunshine.

When the movers have left, Théo produces a case of

beer that he stored in the back of the refrigerator earlier. This is greeted with enthusiasm by Dutch, Abs, and Copper. Even Lacey and Taylor crack one open.

"I can order pizza," Taylor says. "I feel I owe you guys food."

We all look at each other and shrug. "Sure."

"I have no idea what's nearby." She grabs her phone and spends a few minutes frowning at it as she swipes the screen trying to find something close.

"This is my favorite place." I show her my phone. "I think they'll deliver here. Let me order."

"No! I want to buy everyone pizza as a thank-you."

"You can pay me back."

She puffs out a short breath. "Fine."

Hiding my smile, I order several large pizzas, then look around for anything else I can help with. There are a couple of lamps in the corner of the living room, so I set them on tables and plug them in. Taylor throws herself down onto the couch and exhales a deep sigh. "I think we're mostly done."

"You want these pictures hung?" I ask, pointing to the frames propped against one wall. More sunflowers, really nice images on black backgrounds, framed in black.

"Um, sure."

"Got a hammer and nails?"

She bites her lip adorably. "Nope."

I laugh. "You better get yourself a set of tools. No worries—we can do it another time."

"I'm too tired to decide where I want them, anyway. And my dad said he'd come help with that."

I take a seat too, on a chair so I'm not too close to her.

Keeping my distance is much better. But I'm not pleased when Abs and Dutch sit on the couch with her between them.

"Thanks for your help, guys. You don't even know me, so I really appreciate it."

"Japester owes us," Abs says with a grin.

"Japester?" Taylor grins and shoots me a look.

"Nickname," Abs says.

"Japester. Okay. I guess your nickname is Abs?" she says to him.

He pats his flat belly and grins. "It's because of my six-pack."

I snort.

"And your nickname probably isn't Dutch because you're from the Netherlands," she says to Dutch.

He laughs. "Nope."

"Théo, what was your nickname when you played?"

"I was The Win Man."

Lacey collapses into giggles. "The Win Man? Oh my God."

"Usually shortened to just Win Man." Théo smirks and adjusts his glasses.

Taylor's beer is empty. I get up and move over to the little kitchen and pull two more out of the fridge. After popping the caps off, I walk over and hand one to her.

She gives me a surprised little smile. "Thanks."

"What about me?" Dutch waves his empty in the air.

"Get it yourself." I sit back in my chair.

"Okay, sure. I see how it is." Grumbling, Dutch rises.

"Hey, bring me one too," Abs calls.

Taylor's smiling, and something warm expands in my

chest. I like seeing her smile. Way more than seeing her cry, that's for damn sure.

"Is that speaker plugged in?" she asks, pointing at the Bose speaker on top of a bookcase.

"Yeah." I nod. "I plugged it in."

She picks up her phone and moves her finger over the screen, and music begins to play through the speaker. "There."

"So, Taylor," Dutch says. "If I said I'd like to score on you tonight, would you think I was being too forward?"

Taylor laughs nervously.

"Ever kissed a guy with no teeth?" he asks.

Her eyes fly open. "Um . . ."

"Because less teeth means more tongue."

"Oh my fuck, I can't believe I brought you guys here." I blow out a breath. "Ignore him, Taylor."

She laughs. Looking at Dutch, she says, "But you appear to have all your teeth."

"Yeah, I wear my fake ones out in public."

"Don't even think of showing us," I warn him.

"I didn't plan to." Dutch looks affronted. "Anyway, there are other reasons you should consider dating me."

What the hell? Is he coming on to her? He can't do that!

I narrow my eyes at him, but he doesn't appear to get the warning.

"I'm good on the ice," Dutch continues. "But I'm *great* in bed. Also, I have a long stick."

Taylor bursts out laughing, unoffended by his inappropriate comments. "Good to know."

"His stick isn't that long," Copper says dismissively. "And it's curved."

"Aren't all sticks curved?" Taylor asks.

"No!" Dutch jumps in. "The blades are curved. Not the shaft."

"Uh-huh." Copper lifts an eyebrow.

"A player's stick is like his fingerprint," Abs put in. "No two are alike."

"A stick's a stick," Taylor says, her tongue in her cheek.

I smile.

"No way!" Dutch leans forward. "There are so many differences. Curve, thickness, roundness, stiffness . . ."

Both Taylor and Lacey crack up. Taylor meets my eyes, hers dancing, and I have to smile.

"It's true," I concede, even though I hate that some other dude is making her laugh. Not to mention flirting with her. "Also the size of the knob."

They laugh more and I relax a little. "And the way they're taped," I put in. "I like to leave the tip bare."

"Just the tip." Dutch smirks to more laughter.

The pizza arrives. We all eat and drink more beers, the guys continuing to be inappropriately entertaining. When they start taking their leave, Dutch says to Taylor, "Well, Taylor . . . if I can't score, can I get an assist?"

She laughs. "You definitely get an assist for helping today. I can't thank you guys enough."

I'm still a tad annoyed about the dirty, flirty stuff, but I can see that Taylor's not even a little interested, and even Dutch is just kidding around. It's actually cool that she likes my friends, idiots that they are.

14

JP

My body hurts everywhere as I lean against the elevator wall riding up to my condo. I tug at the knot of my tie, still dressed in my game-day suit, then roll my shoulders back to ease some stiffness. When the elevator opens, I limp off, my foot and my hip protesting.

I'm okay. Got checked out after the game. Just took some hard hits, one into the boards that fucking should have been a penalty—I hope DoPS reviews it and that asshole Marzetti gets suspended. There also was the hit at center ice—I laid it on Brown, and it was clean, but we both felt it. And the puck I took in the foot standing in front of Mac, our goalie, when their D-man took a slap shot. It dropped me, but I managed to walk it off in the tunnel and get back in the game.

I open my door. Lights are on. I leave the foyer light on so Byron has a little light, but the living room lights are on too. I prowl in to check out what's going on.

Taylor. Asleep on my couch.

I don't move. Don't make a sound. I just want to study her. Her gorgeous hair is spread all around her, her mouth full and soft, long lashes fanned on her soft cheeks. She's on her side, wearing a pair of cropped leggings that leave her calves and feet bare, and one smooth shoulder is revealed by a pink tank top.

Byron's on the floor next to her and he comes padding toward me, looking like he's smiling, tail waving. I smile and crouch down to greet him, rubbing his ears. "Hey boy," I whisper. "You happy to see me?"

I'm getting used to being greeted when I get home. No wonder people love dogs—he's always happy I'm here, and it's kinda nice.

I straighten and survey the big coffee table, and my forehead tightens as I take in the assorted pieces of paper cut into shapes, along with markers and glue. There's also a half-full bottle of water and an empty package of what looks like cashews.

The TV's still on, but the volume is down. Jill Atkins at *SportsCenter* is talking. That's the channel our games are on. I smile as I realize Taylor must have been watching the game.

It's been a couple of weeks since she moved into her apartment and Byron came to live here, and most of the time she comes over I don't see her. I almost always know she's been here, though. Sometimes I can smell her scent . . . the warm, fresh scent of flowers and vanilla that takes me back to the hotel suite and her in my bed there. And it makes my dick stir. Even if I don't smell her, she's usually done something—washed Byron's dishes along with some of my own, tidied up his toys, or brushed him.

Pretty sure she's avoiding me.

I fucking hate that.

On the other hand, it's probably better, if we're just going to be friends. I'm trying to be a good boy, on the ice and off. She has a boyfriend, and I'm not completely confident in my ability to resist the temptation that Taylor unwittingly presents.

But here she is, curled up on my couch, all sleepy and sexy and fuck yeah, tempting as sin.

Guess I have to wake her up.

I let myself indulge a few more minutes, imagining the ways I could wake her . . . kissing her . . . sliding my hands under her shirt . . . easing her onto her back and slipping my hand inside her stretchy leggings . . . then moving over her and pressing her into the couch cushions and . . .

Heat builds beneath the collar of my dress shirt.

Fuuuuuck.

I clench my jaw, step around Byron, and move to the couch. I crouch down next to it and touch her arm. "Hey, sleeping beauty."

Her eyes flutter, then pop open wide. She stares at me and her lips part.

Jesus. I want to kiss that lush mouth so fucking bad. I can't help but stare at it, more heat accumulating around my neck, sliding down my body, my groin tightening.

"JP." She scrambles to push up to a sitting position and shoves her hands into her hair. "What are you . . . Oh my God, I fell asleep. I'm so sorry."

"Don't apologize. It's fine." I want to touch her so fucking bad I can't stand it.

This is me, practicing self-control.

She's studying me, her gaze moving over my suit and tie.

Then she gives her head a shake as if to clear fog away. "I'd better go home."

It's a weeknight and she has to work in the morning. I wish she didn't. I wish I could ask her to stay. In my bed . . .

She has a boyfriend. My gut burns.

She sits up and leans over to tidy up all the stuff on the table.

"What were you doing?" I ask. "Arts and crafts?"

Her lips twitch. "No. I made a vocabulary game. For my kids."

Her kids. That's so cute. "Cool." I want to know more about what she does. She fascinates me. "What do you do with it?"

She shows me the folder where she's glued pictures of different things . . . an apple, a car, a ghost, an umbrella. "I can do a lot of different things with this. Simple things like asking the child to point to the apple . . ." She touches her finger to the apple. "Or more complex instructions, like point to the apple, then the banana. Or I can ask them, 'What do you do with an umbrella?' to get them talking about it. Or, 'Categorize all the things you eat . . . apple, banana, sandwich.'"

"That's how you improve their speech?"

"Right. Depending on what the child's needs are." She puts the folder into a leather messenger bag and begins shoving in the other things she used as well. Then she grabs her water bottle and the empty cashew bag and carries it all to the kitchen.

I follow at a safe distance.

"Come here, Byron!" She pats her thigh.

Byron jumps up and trots over to her. She bends down

to kiss him right between the eyes and rub his back. "'Bye, buddy. I'll see you soon."

She straightens and meets my eyes. "He seems to be doing fine."

We've communicated through texts about him. "I told you he's fine." Then I pause. "But I know he misses you." I don't want her to think Byron's forgotten her.

She smiles. "I miss him too. Sorry for not getting out of here sooner." She grimaces. "Good game, by the way." Her eyebrows pull down. "Are you okay after taking that shot?"

She *did* watch the game. "I'm fine." I shrug. "A little sore here and there." That's putting it mildly. "I'm gonna jump in the tub and let the hot water soothe all my bruises and bumps and sore muscles." The jetted tub was the first thing I had installed after I bought this place and I love it.

She bites her lip. "Sounds like you're hurting."

"I'll be okay. Nothing broken."

"So you're off to Canada tomorrow?"

"Montréal and Toronto. Then Chicago. Back late Wednesday night. Or early Thursday. Which is Thanksgiving."

"Right." She nods. "I'll come see Byron every day."

"You can stay here if you want." This is the first long road trip we've had since Byron moved in. "There's a guest bedroom. Help yourself to anything you need."

Her eyes widen and her expression turns thoughtful. "Oh. Okay. I might do that."

"I was going to text you and suggest it, but since you're here . . ."

"You're sure you don't mind a stranger living in your place?"

"You're hardly a stranger." Jesus.

Her cheeks get pink. We're both remembering that we've been pretty damn intimate, for strangers. She doesn't feel like a stranger.

"We're friends," I add. "Right?"

"Right." She gives a firm nod. "Okay, I'm out. Good luck on your road trip."

"Thanks. But I'll walk you to your car."

"You don't have to do that. It's safe here. I think."

"Of course it is, but still . . . it's late."

"I've walked myself to my car every other time I've been here."

"Just let me do this." I swallow a sigh.

Her lips tighten, then relax. "Fine."

I ride down the elevator with her, trying not to limp, and accompany her across the lobby and out to the visitor parking area. It's a cool November evening, the strong breezes whipping the fronds of the palm trees around.

"You're limping," she says in an accusatory tone.

"Yeah. A bit. It's nothing, really."

"Killer." One corner of her mouth lifts and she climbs into her car.

Smiling, I lift my hand.

She waves too, and backs out of her spot.

I glumly return to my condo. But at least I'm not alone. Byron's there waiting for me, his tongue hanging out of his mouth, looking for all the world like he's grinning. He's a great companion. I rub his head before trudging down the hall to the master suite, pulling my suit jacket off as I walk.

WHEN I GET BACK FROM CHICAGO, BYRON'S SUPER EXCITED to see me, bouncing on his front paws and giving sharp little barks. I rub his head, grinning. "Hey, dude, I missed you too." It's two o'clock in the morning, but I grab his leash. We make a quick trip outside into the cool, quiet night. He waters a shrub and we return to the condo.

Taylor's not here, but I can tell she has been. There's a big plant on the floor in front of the window. I discover she did my laundry, finding folded T-shirts and boxers on my dresser. And my kitchen fridge has been cleaned out and organized.

I shake my head as I dump the contents of my duffel bag on the bed. She doesn't have to do this shit for me. But I have to admit, I kind of like it.

I'm sore and tired, and I want to hit the sack right away. I can sleep as long as I want in the morning, since it's a day off for us. Grandpa and Chelsea are hosting the family for Thanksgiving dinner later, which should be tons of fun. Not.

But before I go to sleep, I send Taylor a text.

> Thanks for the stuff you did. Is the plant for
> Byron?

I don't wait for her to reply since it's the middle of the night. I'm out in seconds.

In the morning, I find her reply, with a smiling emoji.

> Yes, for Byron. He likes some greenery in his space.

> He better not pee on it.

Another smile emoji.

> Pretty sure he won't do that.

I should stop texting her, but I don't want to. I sit on my bed.

> Are you having Thanksgiving dinner with family today?

Or is she having Thanksgiving dinner with Anthony? And maybe *his* family? Ugh.

It's a minute before her reply arrives:

> Yes. With my mom and Shirley. :(

Clearly she's not happy about this. I get it. This is the first Thanksgiving with her family split apart. I gnaw on my bottom lip, wishing I could do something to make it better for her. It's a sucky feeling, being helpless to fix things.

> That'll be nice.

Lame.

> I'll be trying to stay out of trouble with the Wynn family.

You can do it.

I grin.

Thanks. You're probably the only one who thinks so.

Say hi to Theo and Lacey. And Everly.

Will do.

I lower my phone and stare across the bedroom, my chest tightening.

I have to get over this stupid crush.

TAYLOR

Shirley's little cottage-style house is cute and homey. She's a nice lady. She and Mom have only been friends a few years, though, and I was away at school much of that time, so I don't know her all that well. It's good that Mom has a friend she could move in with, I guess, at least until she can find her own place.

The place smells like roasting turkey when Mom opens the door to let me in. "Hi, sweetie!" She greets me with a big hug, then I hand over the bottle of wine and the flowers I brought—my favorite sunflowers mixed with orange and gold chrysanthemums and autumn leaves.

"I'll put these in water," she says, smiling. "Thank you."

"Those are lovely," Shirley adds. "Welcome, Taylor."

"Thanks for inviting me." There's a brief pregnant silence as we all recognize how weird this Thanksgiving is for us.

It makes me sad that we'll never have another family Thanksgiving like we used to—with Mom and Dad, Amy and her husband and the kids, and maybe someday the man I'll bring into the family. Whoever that is will never know what it was like for us to all be together, the fun we all had.

But I can't dwell on that. This is a time of year to give thanks, and I've been really focusing on that, being positive, recognizing all the things I have to be grateful for. I have a great job and a good boss. I may spend a little too much of my own time writing reports and preparing for clients, but I want to do well and I love helping people. I still have my mom and dad and sister. I have great friends, including all those hockey dudes who came and helped me move and then entertained me with their trash talk. I have Byron, and I'm grateful that I have JP to take him in and look after him. I have a home, which is more than some people have.

I lift my chin and accept a glass of wine and take a seat in the living room, ready to get to know Shirley better. Mom fusses around in the kitchen—apparently she's doing the cooking—but it's open to the living room, so she can still participate in the conversation. Shirley asks about my job with sincere interest, and then tells me about her work as a physician assistant, so we have our medical professions in common.

We watch some football, which I'm only mildly

interested in. "I'd rather watch hockey," I confess to Mom and Shirley. "But it's a day off for hockey."

"How's Byron doing?" Mom asks. "That hockey player . . .JP? He's looking after him okay?"

I nod. "He's doing great. I go over quite a bit, since JP travels."

"That's so nice of him to do that," Shirley comments, eyeing me shrewdly. "He must like you."

My face heats. "Actually, we don't really like each other much." This isn't a lie; I'm wildly attracted to him, but he annoys me. Well . . . okay, there are *some* things I like about him. "But I'm grateful to him for taking Byron."

We eat a delicious meal with way too much food, the turkey and dressing and veggies familiar to me because they're Mom's recipes.

"I'm not much of a cook," Shirley offers at one point. "Thankfully your mom's a great chef."

Mom smiles at Shirley and they share a look that catches my attention and . . . puzzles me.

"I made dessert, though," Shirley says with a laugh. "Okay, I bought it, but I'm sure it's good . . . apple pumpkin pecan pie."

I laugh. "Wow. It's got everything in one."

"That's right."

It's delicious too.

When we're done, Mom and Shirley wave me out of the kitchen while they put away leftovers and clean up. I sit in the living room for a bit, then get up to use the bathroom. I stroll down the hall and peer into the first room I come to—a bedroom, pretty much empty. I keep going, peek into what is clearly the master bedroom, much more lived in, then find the bathroom behind the only other door.

I frown as I use the facilities, then wash my hands. It's a two-bedroom house and only one bedroom is being used.

My stomach twists up and my body stiffens. I stare at my own image in the mirror over the sink as thoughts whirl through my mind. I feel like the world just shifted.

Absently I keep drying my hands on the small towel, trying to breathe. What am I supposed to do? Ignore what I suspect? Ask my mom outright? Do I ask in front of Shirley or wait until we're alone? Drop some hints? I don't know. *I don't know.*

It can't be what I think it is. Mom and Dad have been married for over thirty years.

I close my eyes, a little dizzy. Wow. This is . . . wow.

I hang up the towel and hesitate again before opening the door. I suck in a long breath and blow it out.

Sucking my bottom lip, I make my way back to the living room. I walk over to the couch, but I can't sit down. I pace, then turn and find my mom there. Our eyes meet.

I stare at her. "Mom . . ."

"Sit down," she says gently. "I was going to tell you."

I swallow, my heart lodged in my throat. I slowly lower myself to sit on the edge of the couch, clasping my hands. Mom sits near me.

"You and Shirley . . ." I flick a glance to the kitchen. She's there and she's listening, a compassionate expression on her face as she dries a saucepan. "You're not just . . . friends. Are you?"

"No," Mom says quietly. "We're in love."

15

TAYLOR

I$'$S EXACTLY WHAT I SUSPECTED, BUT HEARING MOM SAY IT
. . . my heart contracts and my breath quivers as I inhale
sharply. I gaze at her. I don't know what to say. A million
questions pile up in my brain, but I can't put them into
words.

She reaches out and takes my hand. "I know this is a
shock." She looks at me searchingly. "All of this has been
hard for you. Probably more so than for your sister because
you were still living at home with us."

"Did you cheat on Dad?" I close my eyes. I can't believe
that's the first question that bursts from my lips.

"No," she answers immediately, firmly. "I developed
feelings for someone else and I told him."

"It's true," Shirley adds softly.

I can't look at Shirley. I don't know if I can believe her.

Dad . . . oh my God. Poor Dad. A jagged knife rotates
in my heart, thinking of how he must feel.

"I . . . I can't . . ." I stand, not sure what I'm doing.

"Don't run away, Tay," Mom says. "Please. Talk to me. I know this is a shock, and I'm sorry . . . but I'm so very happy . . ."

"You're happy. Well, that's good. I guess that's all that matters." Her face tightens at my sharp words. "Was it all a lie? Your life before . . . before this? Did you ever love Dad?"

"Yes! Of course I loved him. I married him; we had a family together. I'll always care for him, as the father of my beautiful girls. But things . . . changed."

"Changed a hell of a lot, I guess."

"I'm bisexual, Taylor." Her bluntness makes me blink. "I've always been bi. And it's true, I loved your father. But we grew apart . . . fell out of love—"

"Did *he*?" I ask. "Because he doesn't seem very happy about this."

Her mouth tightens, then droops. "I'm sorry."

I shake my head. "I have to go."

She closes her eyes briefly. "Okay. You go. Talk to your dad. Think about it. We'll talk again, when you're ready."

My throat feels like a fist is squeezing it, so I just nod again, grab my purse and my jacket, and open the door. I pause, look over my shoulder, and choke out, "Thanks for the dinner."

Mom and Shirley both stand there, Shirley's arm around Mom's shoulders in a comforting gesture, and they share a look.

Wow. I stumble out to my car. Just . . . wow. I thought my life had been disrupted before . . . this really messes me up.

JP

I can't drink much, since I'm driving home from Grandpa and Chelsea's place in Santa Monica, but that's probably a good thing, because otherwise the sniping Dad and Uncle Mark are doing with Grandpa and Chelsea might make me lose it.

Everyone feels the tension, I know. The room is thick with it and Mom's face shows her discomfort. Somehow the rest of the family found out Everly's been dating the mayor, and none of them are very pleased that she's going out with an older man. Riley and Everly have never been exactly close, but when Grandpa says to Everly, "I guess it's understandable that you'd date anyone you can, since your biological clock is ticking," I think they're both going to explode.

"Maybe she's more than just a baby maker, Grandpa!" Riley shouts at him.

Everly shoots Riley a surprised and grateful glance. "Yeah. Maybe I don't even want kids."

"What?" Grandpa glares at her.

"Also, I don't need a man to justify my worth," Everly adds.

"Oh for Chrissake. Here we go with the feminist bullshit."

Even I can't take this. "Grandpa," I say in a low, warning tone. "You don't want to go there."

"I suppose you're a feminist too?" he says to me.

"Damn right." I lift my chin.

Chelsea lays a hand on Grandpa's arm and leans in to say something in his ear. He rolls his eyes. "My grandsons can't be feminists."

We all exchange glances.

"I am," Théo says.

"Me too," Harrison, his own son, adds.

"And me." Asher grins.

"It just means that we think men and women deserve equal rights," I tell Grandpa. "And women have the right to decide whether they want children or not."

"Which means controlling their own reproductive health," Riley adds.

Oh, here we go. I nearly grimace. This is a touchy subject in the family.

"Or who they're going to date," Everly adds, leaning over to bump my fist with hers.

Grandpa sighs.

"So, who's going to win today, Cowboys or Chargers?" I ask loudly.

"How can you even ask that?" Théo jumps in to help. "We have to cheer for the Chargers."

We start a debate about the game that is more heated than it would normally be, because most of us just don't care that much about football, but it distracts Grandpa from his sexist views.

So yeah, this family dinner is about as much fun as a tornado in a trailer park. I need to get my ass out of here before I say something I'll regret.

I'm so fucking proud of myself. Ha.

I have a good excuse for leaving early—I need to get back to Byron. I'm so damn grateful for that dog right now.

I turn the music up loud as I drive home, tapping my hand on the steering wheel. I'm wired and tense, and I'm doing my best not to stress over the traffic. Next year I'll host Thanksgiving dinner at my place and everyone can come to me. Okay, that's crazy thinking; as if I could cook a turkey. I remind myself I'm not really in a hurry to get home. Byron will be fine.

That makes me think of Taylor, of course, and how her family dinner is going, such as it is, after our texts this morning.

I know I shouldn't think about her, but I almost enjoy torturing myself with it. Seeing her in my home, knowing she's been there and done little things for me, is both sweet and painful. I can pat myself on the back for how I've behaved, keeping my hands off and my mouth shut, but the virtuous feeling doesn't quite make up for the fact that I'm fucking frustrated and miserable.

I want her.

I wanted her the first time I saw her, but that was all physical. Okay, maybe not *all* physical. There was something about her smile that told me she was more than just a hot lay. And now that I've gotten to know her better . . . I absolutely know that. She's *so* much more than that. She's sweet and kind and fun.

I let out a billowing sigh as I park underground, then stride through the concrete structure toward the elevator. Maybe I should just bring some other chick home so we can bang our brains out and that'll make me feel better.

I let myself into my apartment. I left the foyer light on

so Byron wouldn't be in the dark. As I lock the door behind me, I expect him to come clicking over the hardwood floor to greet me, but there's silence. Frowning, I stride through the condo to look for him. I stop dead in my tracks in the living room at seeing Taylor on my couch, in the dark, Byron sitting next to her, her arms wrapped around him.

His eyes focus on me. He sees me. His tail wags. But he doesn't move.

One corner of my mouth lifts. He's where he wants to be . . . with the woman he loves. I can relate. Well, you know what I mean.

Taylor lifts her head. "Oh . . . you're home. What time is it?"

"I don't know. Eight?"

"You're back earlier than I thought."

"I had to get out of there before I said something that would get me ejected from the game."

"That good, huh?" Her smile is crooked.

I advance into the room, playing with my keys. "What are you doing here? You're supposed to be at your mom's."

She bends her head, but now that I'm closer I see her face is flushed, her eyes swollen and glassy.

"What's wrong?" I lower my ass to the couch next to her, my gut twisting.

"Oh my God." She shakes her head, hair falling down over her face, still not looking at me. "I can't even talk about it. Sorry. I'll go. I needed to see Byron . . ." Her voice catches and my chest spasms. "And . . . I didn't think you'd be home for a while."

"You don't have to go." I lay my hand on her knee.

She's wearing black leggings and I feel her warmth through the thin fabric. "Now, what's happened?"

She presses her head against Byron's and doesn't answer. But she doesn't leave. My chest tightens and worry congeals in my stomach. I wait, even though I'm practically vibrating with the need to know who hurt her so I can go punch him. If it's Anthony, I'm going to fuck that motherfucker's face up.

"My mom," she finally says in a thin voice.

"Is she okay?" My mind races.

She nods. "Yeah. She's . . . she's gay."

I go still. I tip my head back and squint at the ceiling. What did she just say?

"Well, bi," she adds.

I swallow. "Uh . . . bisexual?"

"Yeah." She draws in a quaking breath. "I found out tonight. She and Shirley aren't 'just friends.'"

"Oh." I blink. "Um, wow."

"I know, right? Oh my God."

Well, this is not what I expected, and I have to say, I kind of feel like I just took a butt end in the solar plexus. I have no clue what to say. I search around for about an hour and finally say, "I guess that was a bit of a shock."

"No shit."

I slide my other arm behind her and rub her back in slow circles. "Are you okay?"

"No," she mumbles into Byron's fur. "That's why I needed to see Byron. I needed doggy hugs."

"Yeah, I get it." I pause. "D'you want a drink?"

She hesitates, then nods.

I stand and head to the kitchen and the corner bar. I

slosh rum into two glasses and carry them back. When I sit again, Taylor lifts her head. She releases Byron from the death grip, shoves her hair back off her face, and accepts the glass I hand her, tossing back a big slug.

Jesus.

"Whoa," she says, looking at the glass. "What is this?"

"Rum. Shipwreck."

"It's *delicious.*" She takes another mouthful. "It tastes like vanilla. Sweet."

"Yeah." I sip the creamy, smooth spirit too.

Byron slides off the couch, pads over to me, and lays his chin on my knee. I rub his head.

"Want to tell me what happened?" I ask quietly.

She sighs, then spills everything: the story of how she saw the empty bedroom at her mom's friend's place, and put two and two together, and then her mom came clean. How her mom swore she hadn't cheated on her dad. How her mom claimed to have loved her dad.

"Am I supposed to believe her?" Taylor asks, her voice full of anguish. "My dad's heart is probably broken. He's probably wondering the same thing . . . did she ever *really* love him?"

"Maybe they've worked all that out," I offer gently. "But yeah, if the breakup was her choice, he could be hurting."

She dashes a hand across her eyes. "I hate that. And now that I know it's Mom's fault, I hate her too."

"No, you don't." Even as I say it, I recognize that telling a woman how she feels is not a good strategy. "You're angry with her. You're feeling betrayed yourself because you never knew this about her. But you don't hate her."

"You're probably right." She clasps her glass and stares down into it.

Whew.

"I don't think she would lie to you. If she said she loved your dad, I think you should believe her. And they were together a long time."

"They were waiting for me to leave so they could split up," she says bitterly. "I mean, *she* was waiting."

I slide my arm around her shoulders and pull her into me. "You know that's not true."

She doesn't pull away. Her soft warmth curves into me and my pulse speeds up. "It could be."

"But she *didn't* wait," I point out. "It just happened. She met someone she cares about."

"She was *married*."

"I know, Sunshine. It happens. It sucks." Jesus, when I'm the one offering wise (or not-so-wise) words about relationships, we're in deep fucking shit.

Now she tucks her head onto my shoulder, snuggling into me like she was with Byron, who's now lying on the rug at our feet. "Yeah. It guess. I never thought it would happen with my parents."

"It sucks balls. And not the fun ones."

She chokes out a little laugh. "Thanks for listening to me."

"Anytime." Having her nestled against me, her soft, warm curves, the fragrance of her hair teasing my nose, is making me . . . hard. Pressure builds inside me, pushing at my chest wall. It's wanting. I want her. I want to comfort her every way I know, make her feel good, take her away from all the shitty stuff that's happening in her life and make her happy.

I give her a little squeeze with the arm around her, and she sighs.

"Taylor?"

"Mmm?"

"Can I ask a question?"

"Sure."

"Why didn't you go to Anthony?" I get that she loves her dog, but wouldn't it make sense that she go to her boyfriend for comfort when something so significant has happened in her life?

She doesn't answer. Her fingers drift to a button on my shirt and she rubs it. My abs contract in anticipation, imagining her opening the button . . . and another . . . and another . . . until her fingers are on my bare skin. Barely breathing, I wait for her answer. See how good I'm getting at being patient?

Finally she says, "I'm not seeing him anymore."

My body tightens. My breathing shuts down. My mind empties. "Oh." I take in a shallow respiration and let it out. Then another. "When did that happen?"

"A couple of weeks ago."

I think back. Last time I saw her . . . she wasn't with him. And the time before that. And . . .

Christ.

"Why?" I croak.

She shifts against me in a little shrug. "I wasn't feeling it."

I nod slowly.

"He's a nice guy. It wasn't going anywhere, for me, anyway. I tried." She sighs.

I suck my bottom lip in between my teeth.

A wave of emotion rolls through me, a feeling that's totally caveman—possessive, claiming, protective.

I've wanted her for so long. Since that night at the rehearsal. I've tried to turn it off and tune her out, knowing I couldn't go there, but now . . . there's no reason not to.

Or is there?

I'm not sure how much time passes as I wrestle with myself internally.

I know she felt the chemistry too, when we were together. If it hadn't been for that tool Martinez starting a fight at the wedding, we would have spent another night together . . . and another . . . Hell, we'd probably be married by now.

Whoa. That's crazy thinking.

I know she felt it that night at Théo's place, the night of his birthday party.

I don't know if she still feels it.

Do I go for it? Or wait?

Fuck this being a "good boy." I just want to go with my impulses. I want to do something fucking bad.

Something's changed since she said those words; maybe she senses my turmoil. My arousal. My desire. The air around us is heavier. Hotter. Her body quivers against mine.

I lean forward and set my drink on the table. Slowly. Deliberately.

Then I take her glass and place it next to mine.

She shifts again, lifting her head, her long eyelashes sweeping up as her eyes meet mine. I cup her face, holding her gaze. Heat surrounds us and my skin tingles. "You're beautiful," I whisper. "I'm sorry for everything you're going through."

She gives a tiny nod. "Thanks." She bites her lip briefly. "Thanks for listening. And . . . being here."

I want to be here for her. All the time. I swallow the words and let my gaze roam over her face . . . her flushed cheeks and pink eyes, mascara smudged beneath them. So beautiful.

Our mouths are only inches apart. Her lips part. Electricity sparks around us.

"I want to kiss you," I breathe.

Her eyelashes lower and her chin lifts, bringing her mouth closer to mine and . . . I dive in.

It's a soft kiss at first, even though heat explodes in my belly and sweeps through me. My mouth clings to hers, once, twice . . . and the third time she moans and opens to me. I lick into her mouth, my hand sliding to her neck, around and under her hair, bringing her closer still as I angle my head and deepen the kiss.

She tastes so fucking sweet, like smooth vanilla rum and temptation and longing. A groan rumbles in my chest as we kiss again and again, deeper, hotter. Her hands are on my shoulders, gripping me, curling into my shirt. My head spins and my dick thickens even more, my body straining toward her. I drag my hand from her neck down over her clavicle, slowly, until the full curve of her breast fills my hand.

She whimpers and pushes into my palm, her fingers slipping under the collar of my shirt, teasing the sensitive skin at the back of my neck. One hand glides into my hair, the other finds my skin in the opening of my shirt. I kiss her again, then skim my mouth over her cheek, her jaw. Her head falling to the side, I suck gently on the side of her neck, then lick her there tenderly.

Her breast in my hand makes me crazy. I squeeze it gently, her hard little nipple an irresistible enticement. "Taylor." I clasp her waist with both hands and peer into her eyes, glowing in the dark room.

"Yes."

Is she answering my unspoken question? Or just responding to her name?

16

TAYLOR

Oh my God. My heart is hammering, my skin is hot everywhere, and I'm throbbing between my legs.

Yeah, this never happened with Anthony.

JP's mouth is sin and seduction and sex. My body craves more of him. I've never forgotten how he feels against me, inside me, how hard he made me come. I crave that again, with a wicked, aching need. I can't get close enough to him, digging my fingers into his shoulders. When he lifts his head and stares down at me, his blue eyes blazing with lust and a question, I answer him. "Yes."

He watches me.

"Yes," I say again, my voice a breeze. "Please."

His eyes close briefly and his hands squeeze my waist. "I want you so much, Taylor."

"Mmm. I want you too." I brush my lips over his stubbled jaw. He's so handsome, radiating masculine energy and strength.

"Thank Christ." He stands, lifting me with him, then shocks me by picking me up.

I let out a little squeal and clutch his big shoulders.

"Night, Byron," he calls over his shoulder as he strides down the hall with me in his arms.

I press my face against his shoulder, smiling. "Poor Byron."

"Poor Byron my ass. He had you all to himself getting hugs and kisses. Now it's my turn."

I laugh softly. "You're jealous of my dog?"

"Damn right I am." He lowers me so my feet rest on the rug in his bedroom.

I've been in here, when I left his laundry. Just in and out. Okay, being perfectly honest, I stood and stared at his huge bed, imagining him in it, naked, wondering what it would be like to be in that bed with him . . . like that night at the hotel . . .

Now I'm here, in his room with him, and I'm the object of his rapt attention, his hands moving over me, his eyes studying me, *devouring* me. He frames my face with his big hands and I melt inside. "So long," he whispers, kissing my softly. "Wanted this for so long."

"I thought you hated me." I slide my hands around his torso, feeling the power in his big body.

"Yeah?" His mouth grazes mine again. "Maybe I did, a bit. Because you left." Another kiss. "And you were with someone else." Another stroke of his lips on mine. "And then you were with someone *else* . . . and you wanted to be friends . . . and that *pissed me off*." His mouth opens on mine, hot and hard, and I soften against him, my bones liquefying.

I grip his ribs and succumb to the pull of danger and possibility and lust.

Our mouths are fused, tongues sliding. I want more, more . . . all of him.

"I don't want to be fucking friends," he gasps long moments later.

I smile at how that sounds. "You don't want to be friends who fuck?"

"Ha. Not what I meant. At all." His hands close around the bottom of my sweater, a big, loose turtleneck. He drags it up and over my head. I lift my arms to help and his eyes burn into my skin as he surveys me in front of him in jeans and a black lace bralette.

"This." He strokes his index finger down the center of my chest. "I remember this. Can't stop thinking about this." He cups my breasts and bends his head to kiss the side of my neck. Sizzles slide down my skin, heat pooling low inside me. "So damn beautiful."

Air burns in my lungs as my eyes fall closed, heat suffusing me. His big, callused hands move over my skin, leaving a trail of sparks, over my ribs and my stomach, around to my back, then down to grip my ass through my jeans.

I find his shirt buttons and work them open one by one, panting as he caresses and kisses me. Finally they're all open, and I part the shirt so I can get my hands on his chest. "I remember *this*," I murmur, leaning in to kiss one pec.

His hand curls around the back of my skull and I keep kissing my way over sleek, hot skin, pushing his shirt back off his shoulders. Then I go to work on his pants, unbuttoning, unzipping . . .

"Hold on, Sunshine."

My heart flutters at his name for me.

"Take off your jeans."

I shimmy out of the tight denim, aware of his heated gaze on me. I stand before him wearing the bralette and a black lace thong.

"Holy fuck," he groans, standing to shuck his jeans. "Turn around."

Slowly, I pivot, glancing over my shoulder.

"That ass." Now naked, he moves up behind me and palms my butt cheeks. "Perfect." He squeezes. "I remember this ass . . ." He lays a kiss between my shoulder blades, his lips warm. His hands dip lower, between my thighs. "This pussy . . . I remember how you taste . . ."

My legs tremble and he lifts me, turning me toward the bed, then bends me forward so my front is on the mattress. He nudges my legs apart with his knee and his fingers continue their exploration between my legs, petting me, stroking me, sliding through wetness, grazing over my clit and making my body shudder hard. "So wet. That's hot."

I make a strangled noise into the duvet on his bed. My insides clench hard. I need more of his touch . . . I need to come.

He bends over me and bestows a string of slow, open-mouthed kisses up my spine. He sweeps my hair out of the way and ends at my nape, using his teeth lightly in a claiming love bite that sends shivers of delight down my back. A moan trickles from my lips, my eyes closed against the barrage of sensations.

"You smell amazing," he murmurs near my ear. "God, I just want to consume you."

A thrill races through me. "Do it."

His hands grip my ass, then he gives one cheek a little smack. Shock reverberates through me, but my pussy gets even wetter. "Everyone thinks you're such a sweet, nice girl."

"Th-they do?"

"Yeah." He swats my other cheek and heat flashes inside me. "Everly warned me away from you."

"What?" I push up on my elbows and turn to look at him over my shoulder.

His big hand lands on the center of my back and pushes me down. "She thinks I'm not good enough for you. She's probably right. But goddamn, I want you."

"I'm n-not that good," I stammer.

"You are." He kisses my shoulder. "You are sweet and good and beautiful. But I know . . . in the bedroom . . . you're as bad as I am."

My belly clenches and a tiny whine falls from my lips.

"I didn't tell anyone that," he growls, nipping again at the tender muscle at the top of my shoulder. "They were pissed at me for going after another guy's girl."

I make a noise of protest.

"But I didn't tell them *you* came to my room. I didn't tell them you spent the night and we banged our brains out."

I want to laugh, but the sound comes out choked. "Should I thank you?"

"Yes." He swats my butt again. "No." He drags his hard cock over the crevice between my cheeks in a depraved caress, rubbing it up and down, lower into the liquid accumulating, then back up. "I'm gonna get a condom. And then I'm gonna fuck you."

He pauses.

He's waiting for me to object. My heart squeezes. "Yes. Do it."

"Don't move." He fondles my butt, then moves away.

My breath comes in scant puffs and I'm vibrating with desire. Excitement pulses through my veins. I'm hyperaware of the softness of the duvet against my bare skin, the scent of his detergent or fabric softener, the faint sounds of a drawer sliding open and closed, the crinkle of a condom wrapper, his feet padding in heavy steps toward me.

I quiver in anticipation. Then his hands grasp my hips and lift them. The bed is high, but not quite high enough for him. I scramble onto my knees and push my fists into the bed as the head of his cock prods at me. I gasp as he pushes in, intense and distending.

He lays a palm on my lower back and rubs a small circle. "I'll go easy. Sorry."

"No. It's good. So good." I push back against him invitingly, but he takes his time, easing into me. My body accommodates his girth.

"Yeah. So damn good. So tight and hot around me, holding me."

I squeeze my inner muscles, just because I can, and he groans and taps my ass again. "Careful, or this'll be over way too quick."

"We don't want that," I wheeze.

He's fully seated in me, thick and pulsing, the hair at his groin rough against my ass. His hands curl around my hips as he holds me still, then he moves again, sliding slowly out and back in.

Pleasure pours through me, lighting me up, my body a hot, incandescent glow.

As he moves faster, I bend my arms and fall to the bed again, my head turned to one side, my ass in the air in a decadent pose. His hips smack against me, shaking the bed, jolting my body in a pleasing way.

"Christ," he mutters. "Watching my cock fuck you . . . so damn hot."

I imagine the view he has, and my face burns. I'm glad he likes it. I push back up onto straight arms to peer at him over my shoulder. His face is taut, his expression absorbed. He meets my eyes, his burning hot.

"Beautiful," he mouths.

I need to come. I find my clit and circle it, sensation buzzing through me. I'm so close already, it doesn't take much. I grab that feeling, the twisting tightness low inside me, grab it and focus on it and press into it, JP's cock stroking in and out, rasping over a sensitive spot that sends me twirling up and up and up . . . a swelling, twisting, then bursting feeling swamping me. I cry out helpless, my thighs shaking.

His hands tighten on me, his thumbs digging into my butt cheeks. "Gorgeous," he groans. "Coming on my cock, all sweet and hot. My turn now . . . aw, fuck." He slams against me again and again and again, drawing out my climax almost unbearably. I want to collapse onto the bed, but he's holding me up, fucking me into oblivion, and then he goes still and taut against me. I feel his cock jerking inside me in potent pulses. I whimper again and slide my fingers into my mouth to stop the noises that want to spill out of me.

He shouts his release, guttural noises of satisfaction and pleasure, and I love it that this feels good for him too.

"Jesus," he gasps, his hands gentling on me. "Are you okay?"

"I think so."

"I'm sorry."

"Sorry?" My eyes pop. "Why?"

"That was rough. I got carried away. I don't want to hurt you." His hand trails down my back.

I twist to look at him. "You didn't hurt me. I loved it."

Our eyes meet, the impact nearly physical, a link of mutual understanding. "Good," he says gruffly. "Be right back."

He slides out of me, the disconnection unsettling. I let my weak body flop down and roll to my side, knees drawn up. My breath is still uneven, my nerves still overstimulated. Wow. Just . . . wow.

JP is back in seconds, lifting me into his arms while he somehow yanks down the covers. He deposits me back onto the bed and climbs in with me, pulling the sheet and duvet up over us and tucking me against him. I sigh with pleasure, every nerve ending in my body suffused with contentment. I give my butt a little wriggle against his groin and he lets out a low rumbling noise. "Careful there, sexy. You could be getting fucked again any minute."

"Ha," I scoff. "As if you could get it up again that fast."

"Are you kidding me?" He tilts his pelvis against me, and damn, his cock is half hard. Still? Or again? "I'm good for more than just a one-timer."

I burst into giggles. "Good one."

"Thanks." He rubs his face against my hair. "Damn, baby. You're so hot."

His arms are big and strong around me. I feel safe and secure. I feel like I'm where I belong.

"I never had sex with Anthony," I blurt out. *Fuck.* I close my eyes.

He goes immobile momentarily, his hand stilling where it's caressing my stomach. Then he relaxes and lets out a soft laugh. "Good to know."

"Not that it's any of your business," I add hastily.

"True." He kisses my shoulder. "Still . . . good to know."

He said he'd wanted me for so long . . . but he thought I was dating Manny . . . and then I *was* dating Anthony. Deep inside me, it's not a surprise. I feel that tug every time we're around each other . . . I can't stop looking at him, and I catch him looking at me. I feel the heat. It's probably why things never worked with Anthony. Instead of fantasizing about him and wanting to bone him, I was thinking about JP, remembering how hot it was being with him. Even though I thought he was a jerk who stole his brother's girlfriend.

"How was your family dinner?"

"The usual. Lots of squabbling. Grandpa's not happy Everly's dating an older guy. We debated feminism. They took every opportunity to remind me I'm a shithead for stealing my brother's girlfriend."

"But you didn't!"

"It was still a stupid thing to do." His voice is low and rough. "I didn't steal her. Or intend to steal her. But I should have stayed far away from her. She was my brother's ex." He blows out a gusty breath that stirs my hair. "To be honest . . . it kinda stroked my ego that she was interested in me and not Théo. When we were kids, everyone liked Théo. He was smart and hardworking . . . well behaved. I . . . wasn't."

"Shock." I smile and rub his arm. I feel a pinch at the back of my throat, thinking of young JP trying to live up to his big brother's image. I agree that he shouldn't have dated his brother's ex, but I understand this.

"I tend to act on my feelings. Sometimes I don't think things through."

I let that process. "Like when you're playing hockey?"

He huffs a laugh. "Yeah. I've made some mistakes on the ice too. I'm . . . trying to do better."

I shift and turn to face him. He adjusts his arms around me but doesn't let go. Our heads on the pillows, our eyes meet. "How are you trying?"

"That's why I've been coming to yoga class. A way to deal with stress and pressure."

I nod. "That's good."

"I'm trying really hard to think before I act." He pauses. "Which is why I stayed away from you."

I suck briefly on my bottom lip. "I get it." The whole time I'd been with Anthony, trying to forget about JP, he was exercising his self-control to stay away from me. I swallow down a wave of sadness that we wasted time.

"I should probably *still* be staying away from you," he adds.

I blink. "Why?"

He strokes a fingertip down my cheek and over my

bottom lip. My heart skips a beat. "Because you're a good girl and I'm not a good guy."

"That's not true."

He snorts. "Yeah. It is."

His eyes shift away, but I see a hint of vulnerability in them. Now it's my turn to touch his face, brushing my fingertips over the stubble on his jaw. "I don't think you're such a bad guy, JP Wynn. I think you're . . . complicated."

His gaze slides back to me, glowing with a blue flame. "Thank you." He leans in to kiss me, and it's soft and warm and . . . lovely. Softness fills my chest and I rub my palm over his cheek, and then the kiss turns carnal and deep. Fierce.

I'm here for it. Our mouths and tongues meet and slide, hands exploring, and he moves over me to kiss his way down to my breasts. Cupping them, he admires them, then slowly pulls one nipple into his mouth. My head goes back as bliss spears through me. "These are gorgeous," he mutters. "All of you is gorgeous, but your tits are amazing." He plays and sucks and nibbles until I'm a writhing mess of sensation beneath him, my hips lifting with an unrelenting ache that needs to be satisfied.

And he does satisfy me.

When we're lying in the dark, wrapped in each other's arms, I'm drowsy and filled with a delicious languor.

I always believed in love. A big, beautiful, *everything* kind of love that glows and grows and never ends. I wanted to find love like that. I've tried with so many men. It just hasn't happened for me.

I have to admit my parents' separation has shaken me. If a couple I thought was rock solid and in love for so many years ends up not making it, what is the point of even trying? Does everyone eventually get tired of each other?

Right now, though, this man—I'm so attracted to him. Not only that, I've gotten to like him, despite my misgivings about being with him. Yes, he can be brash and mocking. Yes, he can be quick-tempered, and yes, I've seen him fight. But I've also seen how gentle and caring he is with Byron. How easy and lighthearted he is with his friends. He has a wicked sense of humor that makes me laugh, and despite that cocky attitude he throws off, it genuinely bothers him that he's let down people he cares about. He's trying to be better.

He's a hockey player. He could be traded and disappear at any moment, like Bobby, who used to live in this triplex, and who I may have had a little crush on, and Manny. That is absolutely bad odds for establishing a lasting relationship. But maybe I've been naïve trying to find love and a lasting relationship. Maybe I should just be looking for what I want . . . right now. And right now, I want JP.

17

JP

I'M NOT A FOREVER KIND OF GUY.

Taylor deserves a forever guy. Everly was right to warn me off her. We shouldn't have spent the night together, laughing, sharing stories about our pasts, and yeah, fucking. But goddamn my weak impulse control . . . I can't resist her even though I know I should.

I'm a fucking failure. My goal this year has been to make better decisions and I just failed.

And I'm going to fail again, because Taylor's off work today. We have a practice this morning and then the rest of the day off. Tomorrow Vancouver's in town, but after practice she's all mine for the day.

We part ways in the elevator, where she gets off to go outside to the visitor parking. I smooch her lips. "I'll text you when I'm on my way."

She smiles. "Okay."

I continue down to the underground parking where my car is. After practice, I'll come home and get Byron, then

214

pick up Taylor to head to the beach for a long walk and maybe some sightseeing. Like tourists.

After having Thanksgiving off, everyone's a little sluggish and Uncle Mark doesn't appreciate that. Probably crusty from the family dinner last night that turned into a shit show, he's on the ice barking out commands. "Come on, guys! You're all fat and lazy from too much turducken!"

I exchange a glance with Dutch. Turducken? Where the hell did that come from?

"Let's fuckin' practice!" he yells, lifting his arms.

"He needs to get laid," Dutch mutters.

My eyebrows fly up and my eyes swing over to Uncle Mark. Fuck, I hope he didn't hear that, or Dutch'll be riding the pine tomorrow night.

He doesn't react and I breathe out with relief, pick up a puck, and skate in on net, drilling the puck into the net past Mac.

But moments later, Uncle Mark is yelling again. "Jesus Christ! Are you guys even fucking trying? Come on! We need to get better if we're going to have a chance this year, not worse! Wake the fuck up!"

My gut tightens and I suck on my mouthguard. I look around at everyone else. It's true they're moving slowly today, but I think I've been doing okay. Or maybe I'm a little distracted, thinking about hot sex with Taylor all night. I have to focus. I can do it.

Uncle Mark brings us all in and we gather around him, leaning on our sticks while he gives us shit for a few more minutes. Then we start another drill, Dominic, our assistant coach, blowing his whistle to start us. I fucking move my legs as fast as I can, trying to set an example.

"That's it, JP," Uncle Mark calls approvingly.

Thank fuck.

Everyone else seems to pick up the pace as well. Nobody likes it when Coach is pissed at us and yelling. And goddammit, we *do* want to win. Sometimes it's hard to make the link between working your ass off in a practice and winning more games, but we have to do it. And Uncle Mark is even more motivated because he wants to beat the Condors—Grandpa's team. Both teams can't make the Stanley Cup final. And he wants it to be us.

So do I.

Never mind Grandpa and Théo . . . when it comes to winning, I want it.

I corral my thoughts and concentrate on practicing, doing everything I'm supposed to, working my ass off. I'm sweating and panting by the time we're finally done. It feels good.

Uncle Mark claps a hand on my shoulder as I leave the ice. "Good work, JP."

"Thanks."

I can do something right.

But now that practice is over, I can't shower and change fast enough because Taylor's waiting for me.

Ocean Avenue in Santa Monica and walk to the pier, Byron trotting happily along with us. Despite the chilly breeze, it's busy on the pier, I guess because it's Thanksgiving weekend.

I keep glancing at Taylor. She's been quiet since I picked her up. Cute, but quiet. She's wearing a puffy jacket and a scarf over skinny jeans and Converse sneakers. Big sunglasses shield her eyes.

I reach for her hand, and her head jerks around to look at me. "Something wrong?" I ask, tugging her closer. "You've been quiet."

"I'm fine."

I stop walking, stepping to the side so people can go around us. "When a woman says she's 'fine,' that means she's not fine."

Her lips twitch. "Oh, come on. Give us credit. We can say what we mean."

I lift one eyebrow and wait.

"Gah. Okay, I'm a little freaked out about last night."

"It was that good, huh."

One corner of her mouth lifts. "Yes, it was good. Okay?"

"It was." I lift her hand and kiss her knuckles, keeping my eyes on her face. "Now tell me why you're really freaked out."

She nibbles her bottom lip. "I don't want to be a cliché."

"Uh . . . how so?"

She hesitates again. "I don't know what this is." She waves a hand between us.

"Yeah. I get it. I don't know either." I reach with both hands and gently remove her sunglasses. It's making me crazy not being able to see her eyes. Our gazes lock and hold in amused understanding. "But hey, why do we have to know? This is, like, our first date. Who knows what something is on the first date?"

She laughs. "You have a solid point there."

"Right? Let's just go with it. Let's just have fun."

She nods. "Yes. That's exactly what I want. Let's have fun."

"Excellent."

She takes her glasses back and we resume walking along the worn wooden pier.

"Churros, churros, churros!" a woman calls.

We pass by kiosks and shops, dodge strollers, wait while Byron and another dog check each other out. As we pass by a woman digging in a trash container who pulls something out and eats it, Taylor makes a pained sound in her throat.

"What?" I squeeze her hand.

She grimaces. "That hurts."

"Huh?"

She rubs her chest. "It just . . . hurts. I hate it that people have to do that."

"Ah." I throw an arm around her shoulders and bring her in for a hug. "Yeah, I get it."

At the end of the pier, we stand at the railing. Byron pokes his nose through the wooden structure.

"A seal!" Taylor points down to the animal swimming in the ocean below us.

Byron spots it too, and barks.

The seal pauses and looks up at Byron. Then he barks back.

Taylor laughs with delight.

Byron and the seal keep barking at each other. A crowd

grows around us, everyone laughing and enjoying the impromptu show, especially the kids.

"They're talking to each other!" a boy says, clapping his hands.

"What do you think they're saying?" Taylor asks him.

He tilts his head. I catch his parents' amused looks. "I think the seal wants him to come swimming."

"I think so too. And I bet Byron would like to jump in there and play."

Finally, Taylor reaches down to grab Byron's collar. "Okay, buddy, enough."

He stops, but he looks like he's having a hell of a good time.

We wander to the other side of the pier and again pause to look out over the great expanse of blue, the water a deeper blue, the sky lighter and swept with brushstroke clouds. On a level below us, men are waiting with fishing lines cast into the ocean.

"Have you been thinking about your mom?" I ask Taylor.

Leaning against the rail, she turns to me. "Yes."

"Want to talk more about it?"

"Maybe." She says nothing more.

"I . . . I have no idea what you're going through. My parents are still together. Still crazy about each other, though they've had some, uh, heated arguments over the years. But I can listen."

"It hurts."

I'm getting to know that Taylor has a soft heart. Kids, animals, homeless people . . . and her father. "I see that. I'm sorry."

"I love them," she says quietly. "I thought they loved each other. I didn't realize how important that was to me until I found out . . . they don't. It's fucking me up."

I swallow a chuckle. "I get it."

"I'm an adult, not a kid. It shouldn't affect me this much."

"But it does. And that's okay. You've had stuff dumped on you that you had no idea about. Of course it's going to make you question everything your life is based on."

She nods. "I'm that cliché kid who worries that I'm responsible for their breakup."

"I think that's pretty normal. It's all a big change, and that's hard."

We keep walking. She talks. I listen. I don't have answers to her questions, and I can't make it all go away, but at least I can listen.

She stops in front of a sandwich shop. "Can we get some sandwiches?"

"You're hungry? Sure."

I do a double take when she orders three club sandwiches at the take-out window.

"Hungry?" I raise an eyebrow.

She smiles. "Yeah. Uh, I can pay for them."

"Hell, no." I make the order four club sandwiches, because I love bacon, and moments later we're sitting at a picnic table, eating. I watch in amusement as Taylor feeds the turkey and bacon from half of one sandwich to Byron, who gobbles it down as she eats the other half.

"Is a club sandwich your favorite sandwich?" I ask her.

"Mmm. I don't know. I really love a good grilled cheese." Her grin is cheeky. "It's my specialty."

I laugh. "Yeah?"

"I'm not much of a cook," she confesses. "I also make great popcorn."

"I hope you're not talking about microwave popcorn."

"No!" Her mouth opens in horror. "I mean real popcorn. I make it in an ancient black pot on the stove."

"Okay, good. 'Cause microwave popcorn isn't much to brag about."

"Microwave popcorn is . . . well, I won't say it's terrible, because I love popcorn in any form, but it's not clean food."

"You're into clean eating?"

"Well, I will be when I learn how to cook more." She grimaces. "I'm working on it. I've saved a bunch of good recipes on Pinterest." She tips her head. "How about you? Do you cook?"

"Yeah, some. We get fed pretty well at the arena, and of course they give us good stuff—lots of lean protein and veggies. Over the summer I trained with some other guys in Montréal, and the trainer we worked with gave us great meal plans. It's kind of fun trying new recipes."

"It is. I guess it's important for you to eat healthy."

"Hell yeah."

She feeds Byron a bit of cheese.

"What are some of your favorite foods?" I ask, picking up my bottle of water.

"Like, healthy foods? Or treat foods?"

"Do you really have favorite foods that are healthy?"

"Oh yeah! I love green beans. And roasted cauliflower. And avocado."

"And raspberries." I think about how I gave her my raspberries at the rehearsal dinner.

"Yes." She's remembering too. "I love raspberries."

"I like steak; I guess that's healthy."

She laughs. "Sure. As for treats, well, popcorn, obviously. And I love ice cream."

"What kind?"

"*Good* ice cream." When I laugh, she points at me. "Seriously. There's a place on Pacific Avenue, they use all-natural ingredients and they make popcorn ice cream!" Her eyes get so wide I have to laugh again. "It's amazing! It's buttery and has bits of fudge and cheese."

"What the . . ."

"You have to try it! They have typical things too, like strawberry and chocolate, but they make one with roasted beets. And lavender. And there's one called 'Tall, Dark and Handsome' that's dark chocolate and fudge and a hint of coffee. Oh my God, it's so good."

"You're pretty excited about ice cream."

"Sorry.

"Don't be sorry." Damn, she makes me smile.

"What about *your* favorite foods?" She wraps up the remains of the sandwich she hasn't fed to Byron.

"Well, steak. Prime rib. Hamburgers."

"I'm sensing a theme here."

"Also bacon. Definitely bacon. I don't have much of a sweet tooth. I'd rather eat a bag of chips over candy."

"Oh, I should have said chips too. I love chips."

"Chips and ice cream?" I joke.

She tilts her head. "Hmmm . . . we should try that. Lacey likes French fries and chocolate sauce. Sweet and salty is a good combo."

"That's true. Are you going to eat those sandwiches?" I nod at the other two.

"No." She picks them up. "Should we keep walking?"

"Okay." I shake my head as I get rid of the trash in a receptacle, while she leads Byron out of the picnic area carrying the sandwiches. We stroll back toward the beach.

"Okay, what's your favorite drink?" I ask her.

"Alcoholic, or nonalcoholic?"

"Why do you answer my questions with another question?" I take Byron's leash from her, since her hands are full of food.

She giggles. "You just did it too."

"Yeah."

"Sorry, I didn't realize I was. I guess I like to be clear on things."

"Okay, both."

"Alcoholic . . . I guess Bourbon. Tequila is good too. And wine. That's more than one."

"Lush."

Her lips twitch. "You?"

"Whisky. And beer."

"That's two."

"Ha. How about nonalcoholic?"

"Lemonade. Or water."

I nod.

I blink when she stops and makes a beeline to our left. I halt Byron and watch her approach a woman who's digging in the trash container. With a smile, Taylor hands her a sandwich.

The woman doesn't seem to know what to do. She stares at Taylor, then takes the sandwich and bolts.

Taylor returns, still smiling faintly. She meets my eyes.

My throat feels weirdly thick. "That's what you wanted the extra food for?"

"Yeah." We begin walking again.

"She didn't seem very grateful."

"That's okay. I bet it's kind of . . . embarrassing." She clears her throat. "I can't imagine how desperate for food someone would have to . . . Well." She sighs.

Something shifts in my chest. For a moment, I don't say anything as we walk. Finally, I ask, "What's your favorite TV show?"

"What's with all the questions?"

Our eyes meet and we both burst out laughing, realizing she's just done it again. "Just trying to get to know you," I say.

"Okay, okay. Sorry again. I don't watch much TV, but I like hate-watching *The Bachelor.*" She lists a few other shows, some of which I also enjoy.

"How about hockey?"

"Ah. Right." She slides a little smirk my way. "Yes, sometimes I watch hockey, but only the Condors."

I slap my chest in mock dismay. "Come on! We're way better than the Condors."

"Well, that may be true. But they're my team. They're going to do better this year, with Théo managing them." She laughs. "I still can't believe I know the GM of the Condors."

"What?" I scowl. "How about you can't believe you're walking along Santa Monica Pier with JP Wynn?"

Her smile is brilliant and sunny and reminds me of the first time I saw her. "Oh. Right."

She says it with a wounding lack of enthusiasm that is meant to smack me down. But I only said it in jest anyway, and we both know it. Energy flows between us, a reciprocal sense of understanding and fun. Once again I take her hand.

Then I see a man digging in the trash ahead. I squeeze her hand and point.

She flashes me a smile and when we get closer, she darts over to give him the other sandwich. This time her gesture is rewarded with an almost tearful smile and thanks, the man clasping her hand.

Wow. This woman . . . she fascinates me. Humbles me. There's no way I'm good enough for her.

But I want to be.

18

———

TAYLOR

It doesn't take much for JP to convince me to spend the night at his place again. We stop by my apartment to grab a few things, then return to his condo. After changing and cleaning up, we leave Byron and JP takes me out for dinner.

We drive to a casual brew pub just off East Broadway. I look around the space as we enter, most tables full, the atmosphere vibrant and buzzing with noise. We're seated at a wooden table for two near a window. The long bar has a line of beer taps, and there's a steel tank in one wall with wooden barrels mounted on it.

"I can't believe you brought me here."

He freezes. "Why?"

"I told you my favorite drink is Bourbon, not beer." I'm yanking his chain, but I can see he's not sure how to react. "Just because you like beer doesn't mean everyone does."

Then his lips twitch. "You were chugging down beers fine that night at your place after we helped you move."

226

I grin. "Yeah. I'm just messing with you. This place looks amazing."

"Whew. You had me going for a minute. Thought we were going to have to leave and go to a wine bar."

"What's wrong with a wine bar?" Again, I'm kidding, pretending to take offense.

"Absolutely nothing." He leans forward. "I'd take you to one tomorrow night, but we have a game."

I lift one shoulder and pick up my beer menu. "Some other time."

I stare at the menu, afraid to think very far ahead. "What should I have?"

A server stops by our table and lists some specials. Apparently, their menu changes all the time.

"Um . . . what does that mean . . . 'on nitro'?" I ask, after she names an Irish oatmeal stout "on nitro."

"Nitro refers to the gas used in carbonation," she explains. "Nitrogen versus carbon dioxide. It makes a creamier, smoother beer. You'll notice a difference in the mouthfeel, because it has smaller bubbles."

Wow. A lesson on beer. "Okay, I'll try that."

JP orders the same, saying, "What the heck, I'll try something new."

We also order some chicken drumettes to share while we look over the food menu. "This is a cool place," I say.

"Yeah, I like it. We come here after games sometimes."

I study the menu and have a hard time deciding between pizza, a burger, or fish tacos. In the end, the pizza —with prosciutto, figs, mascarpone and mozzarella cheeses, and a balsamic reduction—wins out. I *have* to try that. JP orders a burger with bacon and blue cheese, which also sounds amazing.

"Can I ask you more questions?" he says, picking up his beer.

I grin. "Can I answer them with questions?"

He laughs and shakes his head. "Man, you're good at that. No. Just answer the questions."

"Okay, ask away."

"What's your favorite sex position?"

I choke on my beer. "Um, wow. Why . . . argh." I shake my head, smiling ruefully. "Sorry. Do I really have to answer that?"

He hoists an eyebrow.

"Oh my God, I can't stop doing it."

"Or you're avoiding the question."

"Or that." I exhale. "Pfffft. Okay, fine. Call me boring, but I like missionary. It's . . . intimate. Face to face."

He nods.

"But I do like, um, well, I don't know what you call it. It's not really doggy style . . . or maybe it is? Because I'm not up on all fours, I'm more flat."

"Let's call it downward doggy."

A laugh bubbles out of me. "Oh my God!"

He grins. "Why not?"

"Okay." I rub my forehead. "Wow."

"What do you like about that position?" He leans forward, eyes gleaming.

"I like the . . . depth."

"Ah. Well, I *am* a hockey player."

I squint. "What does that mean?"

"I like to go deep."

"Bahaha!"

"Also, when we play rough, we hit from behind."

"All righty then. Is it getting hot in here?"

"Just you. You're definitely hot."

"You're definitely dirty."

"I may have been called that once or twice. How about the position where the guy is doing a headstand and you're on your knees and—"

"What? I can't even picture that!"

"I've been working on my headstand," he says modestly. "Just in case."

I slide my tongue over my bottom lip and his eyes darken. "I can't believe we're having this conversation."

"Just getting warmed up for later."

Now I'm *really* hot. I tug at the neckline of my sweater and JP laughs softly.

Our server brings our food, thankfully ending the conversation there.

Or not.

"Actually," JP says, picking up his burger, "I think a lot of those weird sex positions are overrated. I don't like anything that takes away from the pleasure. If I have to focus on keeping my balance and not falling over, having my dick sucked isn't going to be as good."

My face flames, but I can only laugh at his outrageous frankness. "I agree. If it's something I have to work too hard at, it's not fun anymore. Not that I'm a pillow queen," I hasten to add.

"I know that," he drawls.

My belly flips. "What are *your* favorite positions?"

"Hmm." He finishes chewing and swallows. "I agree

with you about missionary. I'm fully in favor of doggy or any variation of it. Girl on top is excellent for the view. Also a fan of having my face sat on."

"Oh." The air is sucked out of my lungs.

"And . . ." He shifts. "Well, how about I just show you."

I stare at him, my inner muscles clenching. He's gorgeous . . . broad shoulders, big hands, sexy mouth . . . I'm melting into a puddle on the wooden chair. "Let's go, then."

He chuckles. "Finish your pizza, Sunshine."

As always, his nickname makes my insides go soft.

"Do you like the beer?" he asks.

Change of subject. Good, good. "I do. It *is* creamy."

We keep the conversation innocuous while we finish eating, although the way he looks at me all thirsty—and not for beer—makes me squeeze my inner thighs together.

It seems a shame to rush out of the restaurant instead of lingering and enjoying the atmosphere and maybe another drink, but . . . oh well. We're on the same page, and JP quickly takes care of the check and then we're on our way back to his place.

Even his car makes me horny; or maybe it's him. Watching him drive the sports car is sexy. Oh man. I'm just so erotically charged right now, everything is sexy. I mean, everything about JP.

"Better take Byron out," I say breathlessly in his condo when my dog comes leaping to greet us.

"I'll do it. Be back in a few." He kisses my forehead and grabs Byron's leash.

After the door closes, I stand with my eyes closed, my heart pumping, my pussy aching.

I tell myself to just enjoy it. *Just enjoy it.*

I force my brain to stop overthinking things, force my feet to move, and carry my bag into his room. I packed something I think he'll like, and I want to be wearing it when he comes back.

I quickly change into the rose-gold satin slip edged with delicate lace. I tug down the covers on the bed and debate climbing in to wait for him there. No, I'll be a little more subtle than that.

I stroll out to the kitchen, and I'm drinking a glass of water from the fridge dispenser when JP and Byron arrive. Byron's all happy and bouncing around. I set down my glass of water and fondle his head when he bounds up to me. "Hey, buddy."

JP stands in the opening to the kitchen eyeing me, slack-jawed. "Whoa."

I glance down at myself, then pirouette. "You like?"

"Fuck yeah." He advances closer, eyes dark and hot. "I love it."

He pins me against the counter with his body and fingers the tiny spaghetti strap on my shoulder. "This is sexy as fuck."

"Thank you." My belly is a flurry of excitement. I set my hands on his chest, then slide them up over his shoulders. His hips press into me and I can feel his erection. I love that.

His hands grip my waist and he easily lifts me onto the counter. His gaze wanders down my body and lingers on my thighs, the lace hem of the slip barely covering anything. Easing my legs apart, he moves between them and bends his head to kiss me.

My entire body sighs with pleasure at the feel of his mouth on mine. I slip my fingers into his hair and open my mouth to him, inviting his tongue in. Soft noises rise in my throat and I squirm on the counter. Big hands curl around my butt cheeks and slide me forward along the smooth, cool granite until my pussy is pressed against him.

"God *damn*," he mutters, sliding his mouth over my jaw.

I wrap my legs around him, trying to get closer . . . closer. "Need you inside me." I tilt my head and moan as he licks my throat.

"Yeah."

Hands beneath my ass, he steps away from the counter and turns. I grasp his shoulders and tighten my thigh muscles on him as he carries me down the hall and into his room. My bones are dissolving, my body pulsing with lust.

I left the bedside lamp on and he deposits me onto the bed, kicks off his shoes, then comes down over me. He finds my mouth again with his and his hands roam my body as we make out in endless, deep, seeking kisses, over and over. He rolls onto his back, bringing me on top of him, hands sliding under my slip to curve over my bare cheeks, squeezing, molding my flesh, then rolls me under him again, pinning me beneath his heavy weight, and I love it.

I love it.

"I HAVE TO SET AN ALARM, UNFORTUNATELY," JP SAYS LATER as he fiddles with his phone, then plugs it in and sets it on the nightstand.

"How early do you have to be at the arena?"

"Oh, not till later. Uncle Mark did away with game-day skates this year. But I have to be in Lakewood by eleven o'clock."

"Lakewood?" I roll over and eye him curiously. "Wait— I guess it's none of my business."

He shakes his head and slides into bed next to me. He pushes his hands into my hair and holds my head, peering down at me. "I'm not seeing anyone else."

"I never . . . Okay, I'm lying—the thought did cross my mind." I bite my lip. Do I want us to be exclusive? I sure as hell am not looking for marriage or long-term commitment; I've already decided that. But the idea of him being with someone else bugs me, and I certainly don't have any interest in seeing any other guy. At all.

His eyes search mine. "Do you want to see other guys?"

"No!"

"Okay, good. Can we agree that as long as we're seeing each other, we're only seeing each other?"

I nod slowly. "Yes."

"Good." He kisses me softly. "Come with me tomorrow."

"Where are you going?"

"There's a learn-to-play program the team runs. Every Sunday, at a few different rinks in the area. Tomorrow is my turn to go to Lakewood."

"Oh." I purse my lips. "Okay. I guess I could come."

"It's not exciting. Some of the kids can barely skate."

"So no fights?"

He laughs. "No fights."

"Damn. But okay, I'll come."

"Bloodthirsty," he murmurs.

"Not really. I'm joking. I actually hate fights. I worry someone's going to get hurt."

"It's part of the game."

"I know. Some people get so excited, guys jumping up and banging on the glass and cheering, but not me."

"Better not come to *my* games, then." He nestles me in against him, his mouth against my hair.

"Why did you fight against Bertelski last year?" I ask sleepily.

He tenses. "Why are you asking that?"

"You're answering my question with a question. But I'm asking because I'm curious. What makes guys fight?"

"I don't know about all guys. I fought him because he was an asshole."

"Mmm. That's all it takes?"

I feel him smile. "He had the puck behind his own neck and accidentally gave it away to Abs. Abs scored immediately, but when he skated away, Bertelski followed him and crushed him into the boards. There was no play going on and Abs didn't even see him coming. Separated his shoulder and he was out for months."

I let that sink in. "Okay, yeah, he was an asshole."

"I just couldn't let that go," JP admits.

I don't like fighting, but . . . somehow this makes me like JP even more.

"What about when you got benched when you played in San Diego?"

"How do you even know about that?"

"I don't know. I think Théo mentioned it." Or maybe I googled it.

He sighs and strokes my arm. "Okay, the truth is, I was on my way to practice. I was leaving my apartment. A bunch of the guys lived in that complex. It was pouring rain and cold that morning, and I spotted this girl walking. It was the coach's daughter. She was drenched and hungover and wearing high heels. She'd spent the night with Tank, one of my teammates."

"Hmmm."

"I offered her a ride home. Of course she begged me not to tell her dad about it."

"So when you got there late, you had no good reason."

"Nope."

"You could've made something up."

"I couldn't lie," he says quietly.

"You never told the truth?"

"Not till now."

Wow. That is some code of honor he has going for himself there. As I lie wrapped in his arms, cocooned in soft sheets, I feel like I'm falling through the mattress, through the floor, down twenty-five stories of his building. I'm falling . . . hard.

19

TAYLOR

After a breakfast of omelets, yogurt, and fruit, it takes us about twenty minutes to get to Lakewood. JP tells me more about the program as he drives.

"The team gives the kids a set of equipment for four weeks to try it out," he says. "There are volunteers who come and help teach for the most part, but the kids think it's cool when some of the players show up."

"I'll bet."

"Dutch is supposed to be here today too."

"Oh, cool. This sounds like the kind of thing Everly raises money for."

"Yeah, sort of, except for the wrong team."

I laugh. "I don't think she sees it that way."

JP parks in the lot outside the recreation complex and hauls an equipment bag and a stick out of his trunk. I follow him inside. I'm wearing one of his sweaters over my leggings because he told me it would be cold in here. He also loaned me a pair of gloves, which are too big, but oh well. I buy a large coffee from the canteen and JP shows me into the arena. Yep, it's freezing in here.

There's a lot of action inside here, people milling around on the rubber floor mats off the ice, parents I guess, and a lot of kids. A *lot*.

I make my way around the boards and take a spot near the glass to watch. The kids are all wearing the same jerseys, either the black or gold of the Golden Eagles colors. As they come onto the ice, I can see some of them are already pretty good little skaters.

Parents start surrounding me, gathered at the glass to watch their little players. There are a few tables and chairs, and some take seats, but most are standing, holding phones and cameras. I can't help but overhear their comments.

"This program is so great!" a mom with blond hair says. "It's really taken off the last few years. Our older son started hockey in it three years ago, and since then it's exploded."

"It is awesome," another young mom agrees. "The Eagles have done a lot to increase youth hockey programs in Southern California."

"Definitely. Oh my God, look! It's JP Wynn!"

I look. Yes, it's JP, on the ice, wearing a jersey and a ball cap, holding a stick and skating smoothly as he says something to a youngster beside him.

"He gives a lot of money to this program," Blond Mom says. "He sponsors all the equipment for the kids."

My eyes pop open wide. JP never said anything about the money he gives the program. He made it sound like he just shows up once in a while.

"I'm sure he *has* a lot of money," a dad puts in.

Mmm. That is probably true. I shift from one foot to the other and pretend I'm not listening.

"Well, sure he does, but not only does he give money, look, he's actually here giving his time. And the kids love him."

They do indeed seem to love him, trailing behind him like he's the Pied Piper on skates.

I watch, admiration growing in me as he helps the kids. Apparently they're learning how to fall, as they all skate forward and then sprawl and slide across the ice. JP demonstrates. Who knew falling down was a valuable skill?

"Is your son going to join up the next phase?" Blond Mom asks the other woman.

"Yes, he is."

"Mine too. They get to keep the equipment if they do that. Such a great incentive."

"For sure. It'd be tough to afford all that hockey gear, especially when you don't even know if your kid will like playing."

I watch the kids. Maybe there are future superstars out there . . . thanks to JP.

My heart expands against my ribs and I take a quick sip of my coffee.

I see a couple of the kids have long ponytails. Hey, they're girls! For some reason I assumed this was all boys, but nope. That's pretty cool too.

It's so motivational. Inspiring. I love helping kids and this makes me want to do even more. And it makes me like JP Wynn . . . even more.

After JP's done, we head back to his place.

"You can take me home if you want," I tell him. "I don't want to interfere with your game-day routine."

"Yeah, I'm pretty superstitious."

"Are you?"

"No."

I laugh. "You must have some things you like to have the same all the time."

"I do like to have a nap. There are studies being done that show it's not really needed, but I love my game-day naps."

"Ah. Okay. Well, I don't want to interfere with that."

"Pretty sure I'll sleep better if you're with me."

I slant him a look. "Are you serious?"

"Yeah. I'd love to have a nap with you."

"I'm not really into sleeping in the middle of the day. Then again . . . I didn't get much sleep last night."

"I know."

His wicked grin makes me smile. "Okay, I'll nap with you, but if there's something I'm getting in the way of, just tell me."

Napping with him sounds . . . lovely. Decadent.

"You never told me that you paid for all the equipment for those kids."

"Oh. Yeah."

"Slipped your mind, huh?"

His lips twitch, eyes focused ahead as he drives. "Something like that."

"I think that's awesome."

"It's nice to give back. Most players do something, but I grew up with that. It was an important thing in our family. Along with lying, stealing, and cheating."

I snort-laugh. "Oh, come on. Your family's not that bad."

"Ha."

Byron's excited to see us back. We both take him out for a short walk to do his business, then back in the condo, JP heads to the kitchen. "Lunchtime," he announces.

I follow, not sure what this involves.

"Salad." He pulls out a big plastic container of greens. "Chicken. Sweet potatoes. Can you grab an avocado?"

Earlier, I noticed the avocados in the fruit bowl. I love avocado. I grab one and reach for a cutting board and a knife.

"You can cut it into chunks," he says, dumping greens into a big bowl. "This is so good—kale, spinach, romaine." He adds chicken and chunks of sweet potato, sprinkles on some pumpkin seeds, and then pulls another container out of the fridge. "Dressing. Vinaigrette."

"Did you make that yourself?"

"Sure. It's easy."

I scoop the avocado flesh out of the skin, then cut it up. JP adds that too, dresses the salad, and serves it up on two big plates.

"This is so good."

He nods. "One of the recipes I got from Bernard in Montréal."

He says the name the French way. I repeat it. "Bear-nar."

He grins. "Yeah."

"Speak French to me."

"Tu es belle. Tellement sexy. Je veux te baiser de toutes les manières."

I sigh. "Lovely."

He smirks.

"Wait. What did you say?"

"Je vais te lécher la chatte. Et téter les nichons."

I narrow my eyes at him. "I think you're talking dirty to me."

"Yes, I most definitely am."

"Well, it sounded very sexy."

"Good." He wraps his arms around me and squeezes. "I told you you're beautiful and sexy and I want to fuck you every way I can. Lick your pussy. Suck your tits."

"Oh." My belly does a flip and flutter. "Um."

"But not now. Right now we're just going to nap. Faire un somme."

"Faire un somme." I attempt to repeat it.

"Oui. C'est ça." He kisses my forehead.

We clean up the kitchen together, then he leads me into his bedroom. With the blinds drawn, it's nearly like night in here. He sets his phone on the nightstand, then strips naked. I stand in awe, watching him reveal that beautiful body to me, one piece of clothing at a time. He climbs into bed and pats the mattress. "Come on, Sunshine."

"Why do I have this feeling if I take my clothes off we won't be sleeping?"

He smiles, his eyes closed. "Don't worry, I'm very committed to my nap."

"Okay." I undress too and slide in with him. His arm comes around me and pulls me into him, spooning. He feels so good . . . His body is about two hundred degrees, firm, strong, hair-roughened. Our legs twine together, and damn if I don't find myself sliding deliciously into slumber.

After our nap, I cautiously let JP go about his routine. He eats a slice of whole-grain bread with peanut butter, then dresses in a suit and tie that makes him so handsome I could weep. It brings back memories of the wedding: him in his tux, me in my bridesmaid dress, dancing, then on his bed in his hotel room . . .

He smooths a hand over his blue paisley silk tie and smiles.

"You look gorgeous," I say in a husky voice.

"Will you stay here?" he asks, moving closer. "I'm sure Byron would like it."

"I have to work in the morning."

"Do you want me to take you home before the game? Or in the morning?"

"In the morning." I should probably go home and do some laundry or something, but I'm weak. Plus, staying with Byron is nice.

"Good. Help yourself to food, or order in if you want." He kisses me, a long, gentle, *hot* press of our mouths. "A new pre-game ritual," he murmurs. "See you after the game."

"Okay. Good luck. Oh . . . is it bad luck to say that? I'm supposed to say 'break a leg,' right? No, that's show business. Uh . . . play well? Oh, wait, I know . . . go get 'em, Killer!"

He grins. "Thanks."

It's only three o'clock; the game doesn't start till six. I have time to do some of the work I brought home—reports I need to finish writing for next week. I find my laptop and look around. The dining table is too high for me, and I can't work for long with the computer actually on my lap. JP has a room he uses as an office. I'm sure he wouldn't mind if I go in there.

As is his whole place, it's beautifully furnished, with elegant dark wood office furniture. I park my butt in the big leather chair. Way too big for me, but it'll do. I find the lever on the side and raise it as high as I can, then scoot up to the desk.

I get to work, but then I need to make some notes. I have a notebook out in the other room, but JP probably has pens and paper in here. I slide open a drawer in the desk and pause, staring.

Not what I expected to see in his office desk—it's knitting needles, a skein of wool in multiple shades of blue, and some knitting. I poke at it, then pick up the needles carefully. I can't tell what it is, but I don't want to wreck it. I once tried to learn how to knit and didn't get far with it, but I know that dropping stitches is not a good thing.

Everly and Lacey both knit. Why would JP have knitting here in his condo? In his office?

I'm super curious, but not likely to get an answer to that right now, so I slide the drawer shut and try another one. This time I find pens and a notepad. Perfect. I shake my head and get back to work.

When I next check the clock, it's nearly game time.

I've already confronted the fact that I'm a fickle

Condors fan because I've watched a few Golden Eagles games lately. But I rationalize it that I'm not an Eagles fan; I'm a JP Wynn fan. Ha. That makes it okay.

I feed Byron, then peruse the contents of the fridge. Oh hey, there's the leftover pizza I brought home last night. That'll be perfect.

With my reheated pizza and a glass of red wine, I sit cross-legged on the big sectional, Byron curled up beside me, and click the remote to find the game. They're just finishing the anthems for the game against Vancouver. I bounce a little in anticipation.

JP takes the opening face-off tonight and the camera zooms in on his face as he bends over center ice. He looks fierce and focused.

The ref drops the puck and the game is on, fast and ferocious, both teams battling hard.

About halfway through the first period, my phone pings. I plugged it in to charge earlier, and I lean way over to grab it from the end table. Mom.

> Hi honey. Haven't heard from you. I hope you're okay. I know this was surprising news and I want to talk more about it. I'll always be your mom and I'll always love you—nothing changes that. Text me or call me when you're ready.

Tears spring to my eyes.

I do love my mom, and her message is . . . perfect. Not angry, not pushy, not passive-aggressive guilt-inducing. She's been the best mom in the world. Whatever has happened between her and Dad, and her and Shirley, doesn't change that . . . she's right.

I message her back.

> I'm not quite ready to talk . . . but I will be.

I've lost my focus on the game and to my disappointment, Vancouver has scored. Damn.

Oh right, I don't really care who wins this game.

My phone pings again. Expecting it to be Mom, I blink seeing it's Lacey.

> Hey, where you been, girlfriend?

She's texted me a few times over the long weekend, and I haven't replied.

> I'm a bad friend, sorry. I've been busy.

> Whatcha up to?

Hmmm. What do I tell her?

I don't reply right away, watching as JP and Number 76 —who is that?—get a two-on-one against Vancouver and JP shoots at the net . . . and misses. The crowd roars its disappointment and I express a loud "Bah!"

> I've been at JP's most of the weekend.

> Oh. Is he on a road trip?

I hesitate before typing the two letters and hitting send.

> No.

What is going on?????

Then another text from her arrives.

Is Byron okay?

I smile.

Yes he's fine.

OMG!

Then my phone rings. I roll my eyes. Should have known.

"Hi," I answer.

I'm greeted with a small screech.

"Calm down, Lace."

"What is going on?"

"I don't even know. It's a long story." I sigh. "I have a lot to tell you."

"Start talking."

I tell her about my mom. And Shirley. And coming here to let Byron comfort me and then most of what happened after that. "I was so upset," I explain. "And JP was so nice to me . . . and I told him I'm not seeing Anthony anymore, and, well . . ."

"Oh my God."

"Yeah. It's been . . . brewing between us ever since the wedding."

"You know . . . he's kind of a player, right?"

"I know."

"He's not a settle-down kind of guy."

"I know that too. And I don't want that." I lean my head back into the couch cushions. "My parents' separating has made me think about a lot of things. If they couldn't make it, why would I think I can? What's the point? So if I feel something hot and exciting for JP, why not go with it? It's not going to be forever. Nothing is."

Silence presses on my ears. "I'm going to have to disagree with you on that," she finally says.

"I mean except for you and Théo, of course." They're deliriously happy now, sure, but there are no guarantees, even for a couple who seem so perfect. I don't tell her that, though.

"Of course." She pauses. "I don't like hearing you say that."

"Say what? That I'm giving up on love?"

"Yeah." Her voice is tinged with sadness. "That's not you, Tay."

"Sure it is. So don't worry about me and JP."

I can tell I'm not convincing her.

"Okay," she says slowly. "Can I tell Théo?"

"Sure. It's not a secret."

"Maybe the four of us can go out sometime."

"That would be fun." I think. Or would it be too . . . serious? Too couple-like? Well, I'll let JP deal with that.

"I'm sorry about your mom," Lacey says. "That must have been quite a shock. You never knew that about her?"

"Nope. Not at all. Why would I? She was happily married. At least, I *thought* she was—"

"Wait, she *was* happily married. Don't let this taint your whole past. She wasn't lying to you."

I let out a whoosh of breath. "That's what JP said too."

"Huh."

"Huh what?"

She chuckles. "Sounds like JP is a smart guy."

"He's been really . . . supportive."

"Is that a euphemism?"

Now I laugh. "No. I mean that."

"Well, that's good."

"It's hard not to question everything I knew, though."

"I'm sure. Why don't we have dinner one night next week? You can tell me more and talk it all out."

"That would be great."

"You want to invite Everly? Or just the two of us? Would it be weird, with JP being her nephew?"

I think about that. I like Everly. She's very sensible and smart. "No, let's invite her too."

"Okay, I'll do a group text and we'll set something up." After a beat she says, "Be careful, Tay."

I know what she means. "I'm fine."

20

TAYLOR

CHRISTMAS IS RAPIDLY APPROACHING.

JP and I have been spending a lot of time together, but we won't be having Christmas together. My mom and Shirley are going to spend the holiday with Shirley's family—her mother and brothers and their families—so Dad invited me to go with him to San Diego to visit Amy and Jeff. We're going to drive down Christmas Eve and come back the day after Christmas. I'm excited to see my sister, and super excited to see my two little nieces.

But this makes me think that if I'm not going to see my mom at Christmas, I should at least talk to her. We've texted a bunch of times, but I haven't seen her since Thanksgiving. JP's brought it up a few times, and it's true that she and I need to talk things out. So I text her and ask if I can come over and bring her a Christmas gift.

Her reply comes immediately.

I would love that. I have a gift for you too.

Her quick and heartfelt response chokes me up a bit.

So Saturday afternoon, I'm going to her place. JP is away on the last road trip of the year before the Christmas break. I wish he were here so he could come with me, but this is something I have to do myself. It's my family, and my issues that I have to deal with.

Mom greets me with a huge, emotional hug. I can tell she's nearly crying. She holds me tight for a long moment, and I hug her back. She's my mom and I've missed her. I love her.

Taking my jacket, Mom says, "Shirley's gone out shopping."

I nod, appreciative of her effort to give Mom and me time alone. We settle into comfy chairs near a cute Christmas tree, with mugs of hot chocolate and a plate of cookies on the coffee table.

"I'm so glad you're here," Mom says. "I've missed you. I hate thinking that you hate me."

"I don't hate you." I look down at my mug. "Why didn't you ever say anything about . . . this?"

She pauses. "It's not that easy. First of all, I was happily married. You're my daughters. There was no reason to tell you. Also . . . I've had bad experiences telling people I'm bisexual. I've only ever had one relationship with a woman before Shirley, back when I was in college. My friends were weird about it. They made me feel like I was just experimenting and dismissed it. At eighteen years old, *I* even wondered if that's what it was. After that, I only had relationships with men. But whenever I'd tell a man I was seeing that I was bisexual, or that I'd had a relationship with a woman, they turned it into something . . . sleazy. So I stopped telling people."

"Did Dad know?"

"Yes. That was part of the reason I loved him so much—he accepted that part of me, and listened to me when I explained it. With him, I felt like I could be honest. He never felt threatened by it." She meets my eyes and holds my gaze steadily. She knows I've worried about how Dad feels through all this. "I want you to know that I was absolutely, one hundred percent in love with your father."

I nod. "That's good." My throat thickens and I swallow. "Is Shirley . . . bi?"

"No." Mom shakes her head. "She's gay."

"Does *she* understand your bisexuality?"

Mom hesitates, and I look up sharply to study her face.

"We've had a few conversations about it," Mom says carefully. "She worries that because I was in a heterosexual relationship for so long, and I have children, that I'll want to be with a man again. I've tried to reassure her it's not like that. Just because I've been in relationships with men doesn't make me any less bisexual. It's who I am."

I nod slowly. Okay, great. I wasn't sure how I felt about Mom being happily involved with someone else; now I'll worry about her and Shirley.

"I don't know if things will work out with Shirley long term. I love her, but we have some things to work through." She pauses. "I want you to know that she's not just the only woman I've met who I'm attracted to and want to have a relationship with . . . she's the only *person*. I truly never anticipated that my feelings for your father would change."

She pauses. "What bothers you more? My bisexuality? Or the fact that I fell out of love with your father?"

"It's not your bisexuality. That was a . . . surprise, for sure. But . . . I've come to realize that it doesn't matter who you're with; it's still heartbreaking that y-you and Dad . . ." I can't go on.

"I know." She reaches out a hand and covers mine, squeezing it gently. "I know. This isn't something I ever thought would happen."

"It makes me question everything . . . our family, the whole foundation of our lives."

"I know. I'm so sorry. But I'll say it again: we *were* a happy family. I wasn't lying or hiding anything from you. That foundation is solid, sweetie. And I'll always be your mom. I'll always love you."

"Like that book you read us when we were kids."

"Love you forever." She smiles.

"Yes. And I love you too."

"When do I get to meet this man *you're* seeing?"

"You did meet him." I pull back and swipe my fingertips beneath my eyes. "The day I was moving out."

"Phhht. That wasn't really meeting him. I do remember he's very handsome."

"He is." My insides warm and soften. "And . . . I like him."

"Bring him for dinner sometime." Her eyes shadow. "Unless . . ."

"No, that would be fine. I just . . . things aren't serious with us."

"Hmm. Okay. Does he have teeth?"

I choke on a laugh. "Yes, Mom, he has teeth."

She grins. "Just asking."

"Should we open our presents?"

"Yes. Let's do that."

I bought Mom some expensive bubble bath and bath salts in her favorite jasmine scent, knowing how much she loves to soak in the tub and read a book. I unwrap her present to me, a heavy box, and find a beautiful set of bright yellow Fiesta dishes—plates, bowls, and mugs. "Oh! I love them!"

"I thought they'd look nice in your kitchen, with your sunflowers."

"Thank you, Mom."

I set the box on the floor and lean over to hug her again.

I SPENT MOST OF THE WEEKEND AT JP'S CONDO, WITH Byron, so I went home Sunday evening to watch the game there. The Eagles were in Vegas, and flew home right after the game, meaning they got back in the middle of the night, and I have to work Monday morning.

Monday is busy, packed with appointments. Kids are out of school, so we're booked up, meaning no time for notes or progress reports or calling doctors to discuss care plans, but that's okay—we'll catch up after the holidays. The kids I see are all wound up about Christmas, but it's so much fun. Right now I'm saying goodbye to Sophia, a four-year-old girl who was born with profound hearing loss. When she was eighteen months old she received a cochlear implant, and after years of working with her, her speech and language skills are almost within normal limits. She's going to start kindergarten next year and we're all so happy with her progress. I haven't personally been involved with her that long, but she's such a sweet little girl that I may have fallen a bit in love with her.

"We don't need to see her back for six months," I tell Sophia's mom. "We'll assess for school readiness at that point, and we'll have the summer to work on things if need be."

"I can't thank you enough," Mrs. Estevez says.

I pick up Sophia. "Did you go see Santa the other day?" I already know she did from her mom, who nearly cried telling me about Sophia sitting on Santa's lap and being able to talk to him and hear him, such a typical kid thing to do that so many take for granted. I got a little choked up about that too. Things like this are why I love my job.

"Yes! I asked him for a princess tent play castle."

"Oh, that sounds wonderful. Next time you come, you can tell me about it."

"If he brings it," Mrs. Estevez adds.

"I have to be good," Sophia agrees.

"I won't see you for a while. I hope you have a wonderful Christmas."

"Merry Christmas, Taylor," Sophia says, giving my cheek a smacking kiss.

My heart swells and I give her a squeeze before setting her down. Warmth spreads through my chest, a feeling of satisfaction and affection. We don't always have positive outcomes, so I take the ones I do have and enjoy the hell out of them.

I leave the office a bit late but with a sense of satisfaction.

I text JP to tell him I'm on my way home. He probably slept all day after the road trip, but hopefully he's up for going out for dinner or something. Or we could just stay in and make something together. I haven't seen him since they left on Thursday, and I miss him.

I've missed him so much.

The last few weeks have been amazing. When I'm with JP, I'm plunging into a chasm of emotions. I like so many things about him. He makes me feel so many things. I want to be there for him when he's hurting and laugh with him when something's funny. When I'm not with him, I'm thinking about him, reliving sexy times with him, worrying about him . . . missing him.

Gah! I can't fall into this trap. It's all a big hoax—love. I've learned that. I want nothing to do with that.

Sure, things are great now. At least, I think they are. But I thought things were great for my parents, for *thirty-two years*. Still, these feelings inside me keep getting bigger and stronger, and I don't seem to be able to stop them. I'm trying. But, damn, I'm so happy with him.

I miss him when he's away, but I'm trying not to. I have a full life—friends, career, family (although it's messed up), and Byron. I have yoga and my book club and walks on the beach. I'm not sitting around crying because he's on a road trip.

I get JP's reply to my text when I'm home, saying that he'll come over in a while.

I tap my response.

Okay.

Then I move over to my little Christmas tree in the corner, the one JP helped me pick out and decorate, to turn on the lights. It's small, but I love how it sparkles. Then I change into leggings and a sweater. I still have gifts to wrap, for Amy and Jeff and the kids, for Dad, and for JP.

I picked up gift bags and wrapping paper at the dollar store on the weekend, so I start some Christmas music on Spotify. Sitting in the middle of my living room floor, I set about wrapping, starting with JP's gifts so they're done before he gets here. Contentment settles inside me, here in my own place, wrapping gifts, with sparkling lights in front of me, Christmas melodies and the scent of the little pine tree filling the air. It will be a different Christmas this year, but that's okay.

Maybe I should bake cookies. Then I laugh out loud. That's getting carried away. I probably don't even have the ingredients I'd need to make cookies.

I arrange the gifts under the tree, then head to the kitchen to inspect the cupboards. Eep. Pretty empty. Since I was at JP's all weekend, I didn't shop for my own groceries. But I've got a box of penne pasta and a can of tomatoes, so along with a few other ingredients I put together an easy pasta sauce.

I sit down and watch the news, waiting for JP. A volcano is erupting in Hawaii. There was a shooting in Encino. The California Highway Patrol is doing a bang-up job of arresting drunk drivers over the holiday season.

JP and I talked about that the other night. Drunk driving, I mean. When we were out at a Christmas party one of his teammates had, he would only have a couple of drinks even though others were pushing him to have more. I love that he's responsible that way. I told him the next time we go to a party, I'll be the designated driver.

Finally the buzzer sounds. It's JP and I let him in the front door of the building, then open my apartment door for him. My belly flutters with excitement. When I see him, my heart leaps and my whole body hungers for his touch. A smile breaks across my face. "Hi." I step into him and throw my arms over his shoulders. He smells so good. I press my nose to the side of his neck and breathe him in. I love the feel of his big body against mine.

He pulls me up against him, squeezing the air out of me.

"Hey! Need to breathe, here."

"Sorry." He loosens his grip and gives me a wry smile before swooping down to kiss me.

"You must have missed me." I lay my palm on his cheek and smile back at him, my body buzzing with joy and lust.

"So damn much."

"Come in." I slide my hand into his big one and swing the door closed behind us. "Are you hungry? Did you eat?"

"Yeah, I could eat something."

"I don't have much in the house, but I'm making penne all'arrabbiata."

"Sounds good."

Now he's here, that feeling of contentment settles even deeper inside me, even as I recognize how dangerous it is to feel this way.

JP

She's so beautiful, her golden-brown eyes, long eyelashes, smooth skin . . . and that mouth . . . Fuck, I missed her.

I crush her to me again, desperate for her.

A growl rises in my throat and I pull her closer, tilt my head, and deepen the kiss, devouring her. God, I want her. I *need* her.

"Mmm."

I lick into her mouth and she opens for me, melting into me. My blood fizzes in my veins, my groin throbbing. Moments later we finally separate, staring into each other's eyes.

She smiles. "I'd better cook that pasta."

After we eat, we move into the living room to exchange gifts.

"You go first," he says.

"No, you."

I growl, then sigh. "Okay." I first open the smaller gift in a bright red gift bag. I pull out the black T-shirt and hold it up in front of me to read DROP AND GIVE ME ZEN on the front. I shout out a laugh. "Perfect."

She beams at me. "Open the other one."

I unwrap the large, flat package. It's a customized, framed black-and-white image of a hockey player composed of different hockey terms, with WYNN and 13 on the front of the jersey. I hold it in both hands and stare at it, my heart expanding hard against my sternum.

I lift my gaze to meet hers. She's biting adorably on her bottom lip. "This is . . ." I stop and clear my throat. "This is fantastic. Thank you."

Her eyes light up. "Do you really like it?"

"I fucking love it."

She lets out a breath. "Oh, good."

I set it down carefully, hold out my arms, and say gruffly, "Come here."

She flies over to me and I crush her in my embrace, pressing my face to her hair, breathing in her scent. "Fuck, Taylor. What am I gonna do?"

"Hmm?" She pulls back, still smiling, but her eyebrows tug together. "Do about what?"

I close my eyes. "Nothing." I kiss her, thoroughly and hotly, until she's breathless and squirming. "Okay, your turn."

"I like opening presents," she says happily, picking up a box wrapped in gold paper. "Almost as much as I like giving them. You didn't wrap this, did you?" She eyes the perfectly folded corners, neat tape, and pretty ribbon that were done at the shop.

"Uh, no."

She laughs. "That's okay." She carefully opens the paper, then the box inside. She stares at the gift, then lifts it up. A delicate yellow-gold sunflower with a diamond center hangs on a shiny gold chain. Her fingertips fly to her lips and press there. "Oh my God."

I wait, rubbing my jaw, swallowing. I had it custom made for her because I couldn't find exactly what I wanted.

She swipes at her eyes. Jesus. I hope that means she's happy.

"Th-thank you. This is so beautiful."

"Oh good. I thought it was pretty. Not as pretty as you."

She reaches for me to hug me, wetting the shoulder of my shirt with tears. "Thank you. I love it." She opens the clasp, hands the necklace to me, and gives me her back so I can fasten it around her neck.

"There's one more gift. We were, uh, kind of on the same wavelength."

She turns back to me, wiping moisture from her cheeks with her palms. "Oh."

I hand her another gift, a small flat package, and she pulls the paper from it.

"It's uh, maybe overkill." I rub my hands on my jeans.

She smiles. But then she starts crying again when she sees the square piece of dark wood with sunflowers painted on it and the words YOU ARE MY SUNSHINE.

"Too much?" I ask. Jesus, I didn't mean to make her cry this much.

"No," she sobs, setting it carefully on the coffee table. "It's perfect. And you're about to get very lucky."

I catch her as she launches herself at me again and plants a huge kiss on my lips.

I already am lucky.

LATER, IN HER BED, BOTH OF US DROWSY AND SATED,

Taylor's cheek on my chest and our legs twined together, she murmurs, "I went to see my mom on Saturday."

"Ah, shit, I forgot about that. I'm such an asshole. How did it go?"

She smiles. "Good. Shirley wasn't there, which I was grateful for. Just me and Mom." Then she sighs. "It's hard when your parent has a new relationship with someone else."

"Especially when it happened so fast. If you'd had time to adjust to your parents' separation and their relationship ending, it probably would have been easier to accept someone else. A woman your father's dating, or a new partner for your mom."

"Yes . . . that's true. Anyway, we talked about a bunch of things. I think I feel . . . better."

"Good."

"Thank you for pushing me to do it."

"I didn't push you. Just . . . nudged."

She snuggles into me. "Thank you."

"For what?" I pass a hand over her hair.

"Just for being here. For listening. You're a good listener."

She's thanking *me*? I haven't done anything. Listening is about all I can do, and it doesn't seem like much. "Thanks."

21

TAYLOR

Dad and I are in his car, driving down to San Diego on Christmas Eve. I eye Dad sideways from the passenger seat, assessing how he's doing. He's always been lean, but he lost weight after the separation. Doesn't look like he's lost any more, though. His eyes are kind and warm as he smiles at me. "So how are you doing, Tater Tot?"

I laugh. "Daaaad. Don't call me that."

He chuckles too. "I'll never stop calling you that. Someday you'll have kids and they'll love it."

I roll my eyes. "I'm never having kids."

"Phhht."

"Nope. Not falling in love, not getting married, not having kids."

He frowns. "You love kids."

"Yeah, I do." I pause. "But I work with them every day. I won't miss not having my own."

Dad shoots me a curious glance, like he's not sure if I'm joking or serious. "Where'd this come from?"

I lift one shoulder, not looking up.

"Have you talked to your mom?"

He knows that I found out about Mom and Shirley, and that I was having a hard time with it.

"Yes. Just the other day. I went over to give her a Christmas present and we talked. Things are okay. It's going to take me some time to . . . process things. I still feel like she's to blame for this."

"I don't want you to blame anyone," he says quietly, staring straight ahead, his jaw set. "There's no one reason our marriage ended. There's no one reason people get married. No one reason we stayed together thirty-two years. Relationships aren't just one thing; they're a million things, a million moments, some little, some huge. And there's no one reason a marriage ends. So don't look for someone or something to blame."

My heart constricts. I don't want to make this all emotional and weird, though. "Okay," I manage to say. "I . . . She says she really loved you."

He swallows. "Yeah. And I believe her."

"Did you doubt it, though? You must have questioned it . . ."

He clears his throat. "Honestly, I didn't. Your mom and I had a lot of wonderful years together. I believe she loved me."

Wow. Dad is so strong. So . . . decent. He's a good man. "Are you really doing okay?"

"I really am. Don't worry about me, Tater Tot."

I huff out a small laugh.

"It's hard, not gonna lie," he says. "But sometimes doing what you have to do to be happy is hard. It takes a lot of strength, but that's what tough times teach us . . . how strong we are. I'm going to be just fine."

"Okay, good."

"It's not because of us that you think you'll never get married, is it?"

I sip coffee from the travel mug I'm holding. "If you two couldn't make it, who can?"

"Don't think like that. Lots of people make it. And you have so much love in you."

"Thanks, Dad." I'm choking up again.

He's right. I've always felt that way. I love dogs. I love kids. I love life. I love . . . *love.*

I've been telling myself I don't care about love, but it's not true. I still want it.

I think . . . I want it with JP.

Especially after last night. We talked about my visit with my mom, and he was so supportive and understanding. We opened our gifts and he couldn't have given me anything better. I touch the golden sunflower nestled between my breasts and almost tear up all over again.

And he made me see stars . . . no, not just stars. He made me see the sun, the moon, the planets . . . with his usual generosity, he gave me everything, and I tried to give it all back to him.

Dad and I talk more as we drive, the Pacific glinting blue and silver on our right as we cruise along the highway that hugs the coast. We talk about his business, the house he's going to make an offer on, funny stories from the kids I work with. And when we grow quiet, I think more about what he said earlier. About the moments. A million little moments.

The look on JP's face when he opened my gift to him. His nervousness when I opened mine. Those were moments . . . small but weighty. Fleeting but momentous.

Relationships are hard. I guess. It's been a while since I had one, and I don't know if my two college boyfriends even count as that. What I feel with JP seems . . . different. Bigger. Important. It feels like . . . everything I ever wanted or needed or even imagined having.

When I used to believe in big, beautiful forever love.

JP

In my own defense, I've been a little distracted, thinking about Taylor. That must be why I decided at the last minute to bring Byron to Grandpa and Chelsea's place for Christmas dinner.

I don't even want to go. At Thanksgiving, I vowed I would be the one to host so I could get totally shitfaced and not have to drive anywhere, but that's not happening. Maybe with a little more time, I could have gotten someplace to cater a turkey dinner, but I'm sure as shit not cooking a turkey myself. I don't even know how to cook a turkey.

Byron's happy to jump into my car. He probably thinks we're going to the beach or to see Taylor. "No such luck, buddy," I tell him glumly. "I need you tonight to distract my family from giving me shit, okay?"

He looks like he's smiling back at me. I give him a thumbs-up.

Christ. I'm talking to him like he's a person. The same thing I used to tease Taylor about.

I went over to Mom and Dad's place this morning to exchange gifts. Théo and Lacey were there too, all cute and in love. I can't believe it, but they make me miss Taylor.

Byron's pretty excited when we get to Grandpa's. He has no idea where we are and he bounds around the house checking things out, sniffing crotches and searching out food. Everyone loves him, so that's good.

"Oh, a dog!" Chelsea exclaims. "Come here, boy! What's his name?"

"Byron."

"Such a good boy!" She gives him love and attention, which the dude enjoys. I don't blame him. Isn't that what we all want? "Is this the dog you're looking after?"

"Yeah."

"We need children," Mom says. "Les enfants. Christmas is so much fun with children. Why do we not have any grandchildren here?"

"We do." I point at myself, then Théo.

"Tu te crois malin," she says, basically calling me a smart-ass. "I mean babies. You and Théo need to get going on that."

"Up to you, bro," I tell him. "Not happening here."

"Oh, come on." Lacey winks at me. "You and Taylor could have beautiful babies."

"Oh!" Mom looks at me hopefully. "Are things getting serious with you two? I wish she was here! I want to meet her!"

I take the drink Chelsea offers me. Man, I need this.

Luckily, Harrison arrives, so Mom's distracted by greeting him. And he brought a woman. Jesus, it's Christmas dinner with the Wynn family—is he insane? He introduces her to us.

"Hi, Jackie, nice to meet you." I shake her hand. She looks like every other woman Harrison has dated—beautiful, slender, long blond hair.

When Harrison gets to Grandpa, Grandpa smiles at Jackie and says, "Hello, Jenny!"

Harrison frowns and says in a low voice, "It's *Jackie*, Grandpa."

Grandpa apparently doesn't hear him, and says to Jackie, "So nice to see you again."

I exchange a look with Théo. None of us have ever met this woman before . . . has Grandpa?

Nope.

"You haven't met Jackie before, Grandpa," Harrison says, shooting Jackie an apologetic glance.

Grandpa frowns. "She was at the wedding with you."

Harrison's face turns scarlet. I smirk, betting he probably wants to drop through the floor. "That was Jenny. This is Jackie."

Grandpa frowns and gives Jackie an up-and-down look. "She looks just like Jenny."

"He's not wrong," I murmur to Everly.

She chokes on a laugh. "Nope."

"Well, at least you're not dating your brother's girlfriend," Grandpa says to Harrison.

Zing. Yes, I felt that burn.

Just why I didn't want to come. That's probably the first of many.

We're all distracted at that moment by a loud bang and sizzle in the corner of the living room. The women scream and the men shout.

"What the hell?" Grandpa yells.

My gaze falls on Byron just lowering his leg at the tree. Smoke drifts around him.

"Fire!" Riley cries.

"Oh my God!" Mom and Chelsea squeal.

"It's fine, it's fine!" Dad shouts.

"Oh my Christ." I rush over to Byron and spy the puddle. "Byron!"

His head goes down.

2 2

———

JP

"Isn't he housebroken?" Everly asks.

"Of course he is!" Wait, I'm shouting at her. I don't need to shout at her. "He must just be confused because this is a different place. This tree is real. Mine is fake."

I drag him away by the collar. Chelsea rushes up with a roll of paper towels, which I take from her. She doesn't have to clean up my dog's messes.

Wait. He's not *my* dog.

Whatever.

Chelsea stares at the tree, now dark. "Oh dear." She bites her lip, gathering up the wet tree-skirt.

The tree is a masterpiece of design, wound with shimmery silver ribbons, laden with gold and silver ornaments, flowers and feathers. Without the million little white lights, and a wisp of smoke drifting around it, it still looks nice, but . . . "Sorry," I mutter.

"Not your fault." She pats my arm. I appreciate her

manners. She probably wants to stab me and kick Byron outside.

After I clean up the mess, I sit in a chair in the corner of the room, still gripping Byron's collar. He sits happily on the floor, leaning against my legs. Hard to be mad at the guy.

"Well, it's not Christmas unless something bad happens," Everly says. She turns to her brothers, Noah, Asher, and Harrison. "Remember the year you guys snuck into my room and stole my training bras and panties and hung them on the tree?"

They all laugh. "Yeah, that was good."

"You weren't laughing when I hung your tighty whities there too."

"That was an unusual tree," Chelsea says, smiling. "I laughed so hard."

"Then there was the year I tried a new potato recipe," Mom says. "Théo refused to eat it. He was so upset that it wasn't just plain mashed potatoes, he had a temper tantrum and locked himself in his bedroom. We ate Christmas dinner without him."

Lacey cracks up at that, leaning into Théo. "He really doesn't like changes to his routine."

Mom laughs too. "No, he does not."

Théo rolls his eyes. He knows it's true.

Everly brings me another drink and takes a seat in the armchair near me. "Try this."

"Eggnog?"

She nods. "With a kick."

I take a sip. "Whoa! That's good."

"It's the Kraken."

"Huh." I swallow more. "Never been a huge fan of eggnog, but this is goddamn delicious."

She's got one of her own. "We're going to need a lot of this."

She's not wrong. We toast each other.

There are multiple conversations going on around us, including as usual an argument between Dad, Uncle Mark, and Grandpa. But at least it's about hockey, not over money and theft and lawsuits.

First they're comparing points. The Golden Eagles are ahead in the standings, but the Condors are doing surprisingly well this season. Then they move on to arguing about goalie interference challenges.

"There should be a two-minute delay-of-game penalty for an incorrect challenge," Grandpa says. "There are too many of those."

"I don't like the idea," Uncle Mark says.

Théo speaks up. "Coaches are using it incorrectly."

"Is *your* coach?" Uncle Mark demands.

Théo grins. "No."

"It's supposed to be used when the refs completely blow a call," Dad puts in. "But when it's close, they challenge it for other reasons, and that has to stop."

I reach down to pat Byron, and discover he's gone.

Shit.

I jump up and sweep the room with my gaze. Then I spot him . . . in the dining room, paws up on the sideboard where Chelsea laid out a bunch of appetizers and goodies. He's scarfing down . . . something.

I shoot across the room, shouting, "Byron! No!"

All heads turn to follow me. I skid to a stop and survey

the empty box of chocolates on the floor, then the nearly clean antipasto platter on the table. Except for the black olives. He turned his nose up at the olives.

"Oh sweet Jesus." Memory of Taylor warning me about how he likes to eat strange things slams me. I groan.

"Oh mon Dieu," Mom says delicately from behind me, setting her fingers over her mouth.

"Chocolate is bad for dogs!" Jackie says. "It can kill them!"

I close my eyes. I think this is true.

I gaze in horror at Byron, whose head is down in shame. He walks his paws out in front of him slowly, lowering himself to the floor. Jesus hopscotching Christ. Have I killed Taylor's dog?

I drop to a crouch in front of him and rub his ears. "It's okay, buddy. Sorry I yelled. Are you okay?"

He turns big brown eyes up to me. I look up at the others. "Should I take him to the vet?"

"It's Christmas Day. I'm sure vets aren't open," Mom says fretfully. She crouches and runs a hand over Byron's head.

"There must be an emergency hospital for animals or something." Shit. I have no idea what to do. My heart races, pulsing in my ears. My hands go clammy.

Everyone is gathered around now, all wearing expressions of dismay.

Christ. Taylor's going to kill me. Literally. If something happens to her beloved dog on my watch, she'll never forgive me. Why the *fuck* did I offer to do this? I should have known! I can't be counted on for anything. "Stay alive, buddy. Please. Stay alive." I know it's stupid, but I can't help it—I have to talk to him.

Everly takes charge, grabbing her phone and pulling up Google. "Okay, there's an emergency animal hospital not far from here. Should I call?"

"Yeah!"

She makes the call and explains the situation.

"How much does he weigh?" she asks me, lowering her phone.

"I have no idea!"

"Lift him up," Asher says helpfully.

"Christ." I pick up Byron. "He's heavy."

"I have my bathroom scale." Chelsea scurries away and returns with the scale.

I try to set Byron on the device, but he's not having it. So I pick him up again and step on with both of us. "I can't see it," I say, my arms full of dog. "What is it, Ash?"

"Two . . . seventy?"

"How much do you weigh?" Everly demands.

"Two-oh-six."

Ash snorts.

"What? Close enough."

"He's sixty-four pounds," Everly says into the phone. She listens, then lowers the phone again. "How much chocolate did he eat?"

Harrison grabs the mangled box. "This is . . . ten ounces."

Everly relays this through the phone, but there are more questions. "What kind of chocolate? Dark? Milk?"

"Jesus! It's chocolate!" I'm sweating and losing patience.

Mom pats my arm. "Calme-toi."

"It was different kinds," Chelsea answers. "From La Rochelle." She names an expensive chocolate place. "Never mind, that doesn't matter. It has dark, milk chocolate, and white chocolate."

Everly listens, nodding. "Okay. No, he seems okay right now."

At that moment Byron starts making disgusting noises. We all stare at him helplessly as he heaves and retches and heaves and eventually horks up a repulsive mass of food all over Chelsea's expensive Kashmir carpet.

"Oh, he just vomited," Everly says calmly into her phone.

Harrison makes a gagging noise and bolts.

Everly's listening, nodding and pacing. "Okay, thank you," she finally says and ends the call. "Okay, they said for his weight and with it not all being dark chocolate, he should be okay, especially if he just vomited. That's what they would get him to do if we took him in. So they said to keep an eye on him. He could also have diarrhea—"

"Great," I mutter.

"He could also pee a lot and seem restless," she adds. "If he has tremors or a seizure or an elevated heart rate, you need to take him in right away."

I feel around and find Byron's heartbeat. Christ, I don't know how fast a dog's heart is supposed to be.

Chelsea arrives with more paper towels, and once again I clean up a mess. I have to admit I'm feeling like Harrison, my stomach roiling. I keep swallowing as I clean the carpet. Man, what a wuss I am.

"I'll pay to have the rug cleaned professionally," I tell Chelsea.

"Don't be silly. It's fine."

"I think I'm going to take him home." I check out Byron. He doesn't look as happy as he did earlier. "No fun being sick, huh, buddy?"

"But we haven't eaten!" Chelsea protests.

"I know. I'm sorry. I shouldn't have brought him. It's been a disaster."

Her lips twitch. "I've learned to expect that."

I share a wan smile with her. Chelsea is . . . okay.

"I'll make you a plate," she says. "Dinner's ready. You can heat it up at home."

"That would be great."

A few minutes later, she hands me a huge platter piled with turkey and dressing, potatoes and veggies, tightly wrapped in plastic. I know Byron's not feeling well, because he shows no interest in it whatsoever.

I keep an eye on him as I drive home. He's lethargic, rather than restless. So is that okay? Or is that worse?

When I get home, I take him for a short walk, then give him fresh water in the kitchen. I grab my phone to google "dog eats chocolate" and scroll through several results. It's all pretty much what Everly said.

I sit beside Byron on the couch and stroke his back. "Sorry, dude. This is my fault. You don't know any better."

What the hell am I going to tell Taylor? He'd better be okay when she gets back tomorrow. My imagination runs wild, picturing telling her that Byron's dead and I killed him. I almost feel like puking again, thinking about that. It would be the worst thing that could happen to her, and after her parents splitting up and having to move out, she sure as hell doesn't need any more bad news.

This is what she gets for hanging around with me.

23

TAYLOR

"Do you want to see Byron?"

I asked Dad to drop me off at JP's instead of my place, which we have to basically pass by anyway, and when we get there I realize he hasn't seen Byron since we moved out.

"Yeah, I would." He puts his car in park. "Haven't seen the mongrel for a while. I'll get to meet this hockey player you're seeing, too."

Eeeep.

I've texted JP so he knows this. I have a key, so we head right up and I knock on his door.

He opens it and my heart sighs at the sight of him. He's wearing soft, faded jeans and a navy long-sleeved Henley. He looks . . . tired. Huh. "Hi."

"Hey, Sunshine." He curls an arm around my neck and kisses my temple. Then his gaze shifts behind me to my dad.

"This is my dad, Carlos. Dad, this is JP Wynn. Dad wanted to see Byron."

"Hope it's not any trouble," Dad says, extending a hand to JP.

They shake hands, sizing each other up.

"Not at all. Come in." JP steps aside and we walk into his condo.

Dad checks the place out, nodding, apparently satisfied.

Byron's on the couch. He lifts his head and his tail moves, but he doesn't come bounding to greet me. I frown and speed right over to him. "Hey, Byron, my boy." I caress his head and look up at JP. "Is he sick?"

"Um." He swallows. "Yeah."

"What's wrong?" Panic has my heart lodging in my throat. I cup Byron's head in both hands and peer at him.

"He got into some food last night. I took him over to Grandpa and Chelsea's place."

"Oh no." I turn to JP. "What did he eat?"

"Er, he got hold of a box of chocolates."

"Oh no!" I stare first at JP, then at Byron, in horror. Chocolate can kill a dog! "Are you okay, my guy?" I rub his head again.

Dad crouches down beside me. "He seems quiet."

"Yes."

"We called the vet," JP says, his voice rough. He fills me in on the details. "So I've been keeping an eye on him. I think his stomach doesn't feel well. Besides the chocolates, he also ate a bunch of cheese and salami and bread." He clears his throat. "He's had some diarrhea. But none of the other signs they mentioned."

"Oh my God. You poor pup."

"How the hell did that happen?" Dad stands and gives JP an accusatory stare.

"I *told* you he likes to eat weird things!" I say.

"Yes, you did." JP holds his hands up, palms out. "I take full responsibility. It was a dumb idea to take him. We're a big family and there was a lot going on, and I took my attention off him for a few minutes."

I'm . . . upset. My dog! How could this have happened? For a few seconds, I'm pissed at JP. He should have watched him better!

But I can see how distressed JP is, how he's beating himself up over this. I take a deep, calming breath, then move over to JP. "It's okay. Byron's okay." I think I'm telling myself as much as him.

"I feel terrible about it," JP says. "I'm so sorry."

Dad returns to Byron and gets a hand lick. "Miss you, Byron."

"He misses you too," I say.

"Guess it's a good thing I'll be able to take him at my new place," Dad says.

I sense JP tensing. "I'm sorry," he says again shortly. "But yeah, it's probably a good thing."

Right. Byron won't be living here anymore.

I don't think I like that.

I remember the first day I brought him here, how dismayed I was about him living in a high-rise condo without a yard. But he's been fine. JP takes good care of him, despite what just happened, and I'm around too and . . . I don't know what to say about this. I rub the faint ache in my chest, watching Dad interact with Byron.

I turn back to JP and meet his eyes. "It's okay," I say again quietly.

Dad doesn't stay long, and I hate the tension between

him and JP. Clearly Dad blames him for not looking after Byron and that's not going to help JP's guilt at all. Also, I want Dad to like the man I . . . care about.

Okay, the man I'm falling in love with. I've thought about it a lot the last couple of days, when I wasn't playing with my nieces or visiting with Amy and Jeff and Dad. I'm falling in love with JP.

It's scary and yet right. I guess I can tell myself that I don't believe in love anymore, but . . . somehow it snuck up on me.

After Dad leaves, JP assuring him he'll get me home, JP throws himself down onto the couch and sprawls out, resting a hand on Byron's back. "Jesus. Your dad hates me."

"No, he doesn't."

"I don't blame him. You should hate me too."

I sit next to him. "Byron's going to be fine. You look worse than he does."

He scrubs a hand over the dark stubble on his jaw. "I didn't sleep much last night. I was afraid he was going to die if I didn't watch him. Man, I'm a shitty dog sitter."

"No, you're not." I lay my cheek on his chest, arms around his waist.

"How can you even say that? And I didn't tell you what else happened last night."

"Uh-oh."

"He peed on Chelsea's designer Christmas tree and shorted out the lights."

My head jerks up. "No!"

"Yes."

I give Byron a slitty-eyed look. "Byron! Why would you do that?"

"Duh. It was a tree."

I laugh. "Oh my God. That's so awful. I'm sorry."

"What are you sorry about? I'm the one who took him there."

"He's my dog. He doesn't usually pee in other people's houses."

"It was a tree. He pees on trees."

"Well, yeah. But still. Oh, Byron."

He looks back at me with big, sad eyes.

"Yeah, I know, you're not feeling well. You did that to yourself, you rascal." I stroke his fur again.

"How was *your* Christmas?" JP reaches out and takes my free hand. "Did you have fun with your sister?"

"Yes! And the munchkins. I have pictures." I jump up to grab my phone and show him all the pics I took. I scroll through them quickly, not wanting to bore him, but he stops me a few times and asks questions, wanting to know which little girl is Penelope and which is Mia. There are even a few of me with the nieces that Dad took using my phone, and a selfie I took with Amy, heads together, big smiles.

"You two look alike."

"Yeah, apparently we do." I set down the phone. "It was great to spend some time with them. Amy and I managed to get a little alone time so we could talk about Mom and Dad. And you."

"Me?"

I smile and smooch his lips. "Of course you. I missed you."

"Mmm." He kisses me again. "Missed you too, Sunshine. Although I was pretty traumafied last night, thinking that I'd killed your dog."

"Traumafied?"

"Yes." His lips twitch. "Seriously, I think I would have packed up and emigrated to Kazakhstan if he didn't make it. I could never face you again."

"Oh." My heart squeezes, both at the thought of Byron so sick and JP being so . . . "traumafied." "Are you . . . going to miss Byron?"

He frowns and doesn't immediately answer. "Maybe."

I give his broad chest a little shove. "Yes, you are. You love him."

"Eh. I'm kind of used to having him around now."

I can't stop my smile. He does love Byron. Look how upset he is about Byron being sick. "When Dad reminded me that he'll be able to take him again, I realized that I'm going to miss him too. This house he's looking at is in Mar Vista, which isn't that close. But, Dad misses him now, so . . ."

"Hmm. We may have a custody battle on our hands."

I laugh, but it's not really funny.

I want to tell him how I feel about him. I'm bursting with it, bursting with love and affection for him . . . also lust. Maybe I can *show* him how I feel about him . . .

I shift so I can kiss him, my mouth lingering on his. He makes a happy noise, his hand coming up to cup the back of my head. He tilts his head and kisses me back, deeper, his tongue sliding into my mouth.

"Missed you, Sunshine."

"Missed you too, Killer."

I feel his smile before he kisses me once more, lifting me onto his lap. His hands slide under my sweater and my skin reacts, tingling everywhere. My belly flips and my breasts ache where I press them against his chest.

I want to feel his skin too. I slide off his lap, off the couch, and onto my knees between his thighs. I skate my hands up under his tee, enjoying the ridges of his abs, the firmness of his pecs. I brush over his nipples and he groans. Leaning lower, I press a kiss to his stomach, a slow, open-mouthed kiss, letting my tongue brush there. I kiss him again, working open the button of his jeans.

His cock is hard and straining behind his fly. I press there before I undo the zipper, and JP makes another low noise of pleasure. I kiss the soft skin I reveal as I lower the zipper and part his jeans. "I love this place on a man."

His hand is gentle in my hair. "What place? My dick?"

"Well, yeah, that too. But this place . . ." I tug the elastic of his boxer briefs lower. The head of his cock is already poking above them and it springs up. I wrap a hand around his shaft and move it so I can kiss him below his navel. "Right here." I lick him there. "It's so soft and sensitive and . . . low enough to hint at what's beneath it . . ." I trace my tongue over the trail of dark hair, then kiss lower and lower, until my lips meet the neat thatch of dark hair.

"Christ." Now both his hands are in in my hair.

I curve my hands over the square, masculine bones of his hips, so different from mine, then nuzzle his groin, nipping at the thin skin with my lips, teasing him by kissing and licking all around his cock. His hips lift, his body hot and trembling, and finally I kiss the head of his cock. My tongue laps delicately, still taunting him. His fingers tighten on my skull, but he's not pressing me to do more than I want.

"That feels so good." He lets out a rumbling groan. "Please . . . suck me."

"Mmm." I want to. I open my mouth and take him in, swirling my tongue around to get him wet and slippery so my lips glide over satiny flesh. Smooth and hard, I love the feel of him filling my mouth, the weight of him on my tongue, the male essence of him tantalizing my taste buds and filling my head with his scent.

It's heady and wild, making me so wet and aching.

He releases me to shove his jeans lower and now I can access his balls. I cup them tenderly, sliding my mouth up and down.

"Is it weird doing this in front of Byron?" he chokes out.

I lift my head and meet his eyes, smiling. "You want me to stop?"

"Fuck no."

"He's a dog. And he's asleep."

I resume my blow job, relishing everything about it until JP's body tenses. His hands are back in my hair and he holds me up off him. "Gonna come, baby."

"Good." And I suck him more, and more, faster, clasping the base of his cock tighter, until he shouts as he releases in my mouth. I swallow him down, savoring him, so turned on I could almost come myself.

He hauls me up on top of him, his hands shaking, his breathing fast and ragged. "Jesus. I love that."

"Good." I kiss his cheek.

He returns the favor by carrying me into his bedroom, stripping me out of my clothes and worshiping my body from head to toe, eventually focusing on where I need him most . . . his lips and tongue gliding and sucking, his big hands cradling my butt and holding my pussy to his face. Sensation slides down my legs, weakening them, and coiling heat spirals up inside me until I burst into a million pieces of light and heat.

MUCH LATER, WE'RE NESTLED IN HIS BED, EVEN THOUGH IT'S only seven o'clock. I don't have to work tomorrow. We just ordered in food, though it's not here yet, and checked on Byron, who's doing fine.

"I know you're beating yourself up over what happened with Byron."

He sighs. "Yeah."

"Don't do that."

"Okay."

"Seriously." I shift and prop myself up on an elbow to look at him. His gaze drops to my bare breasts. I smile. "You keep doing that. Remember what Arya says in yoga class?"

His eyebrows pull together. "What?"

"About being nonjudgmental. Including toward ourselves. You're too hard on yourself when you screw up. That causes you stress you don't need."

He gazes back at me. "You're right."

"I do it too," I confess. "That's why I didn't want anything to do with you after the wedding."

His forehead creases. "What were you beating yourself up over? I thought you were pissed at me for getting in a fight."

"I felt like the fight was my fault." I bite my lower lip. I still feel guilty about that, even though it was Manny who instigated things.

"How was it your fault? You said you weren't with Martinez then."

"I wasn't. But . . . he saw us leaving together when we were going up to your room . . . and . . ." I stop. I haven't ever told him this. "And I wanted him to know what we were doing."

JP goes very still. "What?"

"I know. I felt terrible. I hate fighting. I was so afraid you were going to get hurt, and Lacey and Théo's wedding was ruined, and it was all my fault."

"Wait. Back the fuck up." He sets me away from him and stares at me. "You wanted him to know we were going up to my room to fuck?"

"Well . . . yeah."

"You were using me to make him jealous? That's what that was?" His voice rises.

"No! I wanted to go with you! But Manny had—"

He interrupts me, and honestly I don't blame him, because I sound really lame right now.

"Fuck! I pissed off my entire family because you were trying to get back at a guy who dumped you?"

I flinch and jerk away from him, my heart kicking against my ribs. *"What?"*

"What is *wrong* with me?" He gets out of bed, looking away, not meeting my eyes, hand on his jaw. "Goddammit. I can't keep doing this."

"Doing what?" My mouth hangs open.

"I keep screwing up, making the same mistakes over and over."

"What mistakes?" Then I feel like I've been slapped. "Are you thinking I was using you like Emma was?" Heat burns through my veins and I throw back the covers and jump out of bed. I'm naked, but so what.

"Huh?" His shoulders hunch as his head jerks around.

I march over to him and poke my forefinger into his chest. "I am nothing like her!"

He stares at me.

Tears threaten. I swallow, my throat strangled. Does he really believe I was using him to make Manny jealous?

"No," he says slowly. "You're nothing like Emma. That's not what I meant."

"Well, that's what it sounded like!"

His head moves from side to side. "No."

"I get why you feel like I was using you. Believe me, I've been over and over that. It's why I feel guilty. But I wasn't using you. The night before the wedding, when I came to your room . . . that had nothing to do with Manny."

Some of the tension eases from his rock-hard jaw as he watches me. Listens to me.

"I was . . . attracted to you. I wanted to be with you. And it was the same the night of the wedding. I just . . . didn't mind if Manny saw us together. I never thought he was going to start a fight with you. And that's on him."

His shoulders slump. "Fuck. You're right." He slides a hand around the back of my neck and pulls me up against him, pressing my cheek to his shoulder. "You're right. I'm an asshole."

Now I'm shaking even more, with relief. "Yeah, you are."

His soft laugh ruffles my hair. "I get frustrated when I think I've screwed up again."

"It . . . hurts that you think being with me is screwing up."

His chest expands against me and his arms wrap tightly around me. "I don't think that. I was wrong. I didn't screw up. You're honest and real and you don't play games. I lost my temper because . . ." He tenses. "I hated to think you only wanted to be with me to get back at someone else. That already happened to me once."

Oh. Oh God. I can tell how hard that is for him to admit. My heart softens. He blames himself for hurting his brother by going out with Emma, but the truth is, he got hurt too, when he found out she didn't really care about him. I hate that . . . but I hate her more, for hurting him.

"I'm still here," I say gently, laying my hands on his face, holding his gaze steadily.

"Yeah." He closes his eyes, and covers my hands with his, then brings each palm to his mouth to kiss. "I don't know why. Like I said, I'm an asshole."

"Yeah. Sometimes you are."

"Thank you for calling me on it."

I smile and kiss his mouth. "Anytime, Killer."

24

JP

Tonight, our first game after the Christmas break, we're playing in Nashville.

Yep, that means me and Manny Martinez on the ice together again. He pissed me off in that preseason game we played against the Predators, but that was months ago. Hopefully he's over Taylor now. I just want to play hockey.

I've been doing so well. When we played Boston, that shit-disturber LeHane was on my ass all night. He's a fucking pest, and his whole role on the team is to annoy the opposing team and try to draw penalties. I've gotten sucked into it in the past, but not this year.

The guys who are like that know me. They know my temper, they know they can get to me with chirps and dirty hits behind the play, trying to get under my skin. I was doing pretty well at ignoring LeHane but when he stood in front of Mac, our goalie, hassling him, my anger started growing. I didn't let it take over, though: I channeled it for good and laid a crushing hit on him on our next shift together. Totally clean, but he had to pick himself up off the ice, shaking his head. That sent a message.

Martinez is not that kind of player, so there shouldn't be problems tonight. I just want to play good hockey. The Preds are in a different division, but we need every two points we can get. Right now, we're on track for a playoff spot and we need to stay there. I've been scoring goals; in fact our entire line has been hot lately, getting more minutes, getting recognition from Uncle Mark in the dressing room and when he talks to the media. I don't want to let down the team by taking dumb penalties or letting someone mess with my game.

I tape my stick before the game, part of my routine. You want to know something weird? Every Wynn family hockey player tapes his stick the same way. We have different preferences when it comes to the actual stick—length, lie, weight, curve, flex—but taping is something I learned from my dad, who learned it from Grandpa. This is weird, because usually hockey players have pretty individual preferences when it comes to taping sticks, but it's kind of a family superstition or something that we all tape our sticks the way Grandpa did—white tape on the knob and shaft, the first piece twisted into a rope that's wound around the handle exactly five revolutions, creating grips. White tape over that starting from the top. Then black tape on the blade, leaving the tip bare. Heh. I remember the discussion that night at Taylor's new apartment when she moved in.

The precision and care needed to get it perfect helps me get in the zone. I've got earbuds in and I'm listening to "All Night" by Walk the Moon, part of a motivational playlist I put together that I've been listening to. The steady beat has my head moving. I feel great.

I've had this feeling for a while now. Like everything is going right. Things have been relatively peaceful with my family. The team's been playing well and I've been contributing. And . . . Taylor.

I have to say, I like it when she's there when I get home. I like it when she's in my bed all night. I really like it when we have days off together and we can have morning sex and coffee in bed, and take Byron for long walks on the beach, and cook dinner together or hang out with my friends or with Théo and Lacey. I like . . . her.

I like her a lot.

I catch Abs looking at me and realize I'm smiling like an idiot. He knows better than to say anything to me, though, because interrupting a player's routine is a total dick move. We like to trash-talk and play pranks and joke around, but a guy's game-day routine is sacrosanct.

I go through my own warm-up that I learned last summer from Bernard. It hits every body part, starting with ankle hops and marching, ending with side shuffles and high-knee running.

In the dressing room, the mood is light, music pumping out "Wow" by Post Malone. I have a routine for how I get dressed too, like most players. I always put my jersey on last.

Uncle Mark comes in for a few last-minute reminders. "Their goalie's playing well," he says. "We gotta get pucks on him. Get traffic in front of him." He tells us who's starting and we all clap.

I hit the ice at a run and it feels great, the ice smooth, my blades sharp. I love that feeling. I take a spin, then head to the bench since I'm not starting and pull off my helmet for the national anthem.

The game is intense. We get off to a flying start, moving our legs, keeping our game north-south. Martinez lays a few hits on me, most of which I manage to absorb or evade. I'm good at that. The first couple weren't an issue—I had the puck along the boards, so of course he was going to hit me. Then he comes after me after I pass the puck to Dutch, driving me into the boards from behind, snapping my neck back. I didn't even know it was him at first. It was dirty and right on the numbers and he should be going off, but no whistle sounds, and I can't fucking believe it as I haul myself up off the ice to catch up to the play. Jesus Christ.

Now I'm pissed.

Luckily I'm not hurt, but I'm pissed.

On the bench I vent to Frenchy (Louis Ouellet). "What the *fuck* was that? I can't believe that didn't get called."

"I know." Frenchy shakes his head. "Asshole."

Benny, our head trainer, claps a hand on my shoulder behind me. "You okay, Japester?"

"Yeah, yeah." I roll my head around. My neck might be sore later, but I'm okay.

Both goalies are going to be stars of this game, because both teams are fighting hard. They're standing on their goddamn heads, though, blocking shot after shot, and it's the third period before we finally manage to put one past their netminder.

We celly like we'd just won the Cup, jumping on each other and pounding one another's backs. Thank fuck.

We're up by one with about six minutes left in the game. One goal's not good enough. Still lots of time for them to tie it up. We're changing on the fly, and I leap over the boards and chase the puck deep in the Nashville end where Copper dumped it before heading off. Their defense is on it, though, and I'm slammed into the boards. By Martinez. Again.

Dutch takes the puck and passes it to Bergie.

"Fuck!" I yell at Martinez. "Hit me like that again and I'll drop you, motherfucker."

Bergie passes cross ice to Johnny, then to me. I don't have a lane, so I pass it back to Bergie on the blue line. He takes a one-timer. The goalie makes the save and smothers the puck. The whistle blows.

Martinez skates up to me and circles me. "Frustrated, man? Not getting enough of that sweet pussy?"

"What the fuck are you talking about?" I growl, turning to face him. I glide closer to him, my blood heating.

"Taylor. Just remember . . . I was there first." He smirks. "She likes to share that sweet pussy. So tight and—"

He doesn't get out the rest of what he was saying because I've dropped my gloves and punched him. He drops to the ice immediately, blood running down his face. I'm on him, but he's not even fighting back, and that pisses me off even more. I've been fucking played.

The linesmen are there right away, pulling me off. A bunch of Preds arrive and surround us menacingly, quickly followed by my teammates. My chest is heaving, adrenaline slamming through my veins. "You're the fucking pussy," I spit out at Martinez, then hate myself for using that sexist slur. "You fucking douchebag prick!" I can't even think of insults bad enough for him. For what he just said.

"Enough," the linesman holding me back says. "You're out of the game."

"What the fuck?" I glare at him. "He said—" I stop dead. There's no way in hell I want to repeat what he just said with cameras on us and possibly microphones picking it up.

I am so fucked.

"Last five minutes of regulation time," the ref barks. "You're out." He drags me across the ice.

Meanwhile, Martinez is getting attention for the blood dripping down his face. He didn't even drop his gloves! Rage billows inside me, hot pressure that makes me yank myself out of the linesman's grip and try to go at Martinez again. This time my own teammates rush at me to grab me and hold me back.

"Jesus, man, calm the fuck down," Dutch says in my ear. "What the hell?"

I take in a shuddering breath. Yeah, I've lost it. I've totally lost it, and no amount of compartmentalizing or deep breathing or thinking calm thoughts is going to help me right now. I skate over to the gate, jump off the ice, and stalk down the tunnel to the visitors' dressing room.

"How's your hand?" Benny asks with unruffled composure.

I shake it out, only realizing now that the knuckles are grazed and throbbing.

"I'll get you an ice pack."

I drop to the bench in front of my cubby, toss aside my helmet, and let my head fall forward.

Then I hear it. A roar from the fans, so loud it almost drowns out the goal horn. Fucking Nashville scored.

I close my eyes, my heart still trying to pound its way up into my throat.

Benny hands me the ice pack and I hold it on my knuckles. "Thanks," I mutter. "They just tied it up, didn't they?"

"Yeah."

Shit, shit, *shit.*

I'm stuck here listening and fuming as the game goes into overtime. And we lose.

The mood in the room is grim afterward. The guys are pissed and Uncle Mark is yelling at me. "What the fuck were you thinking? We were up by one goal! There was only four minutes left in the game, goddammit!"

I know. I *know.*

The air in the room is heavy. I can see everyone trading glances.

"Oh, for Chrissake." Uncle Mark rubs his face. "We'll talk about this tomorrow."

I nod miserably. I know I screwed up, but come on! I'm supposed to let him get away with that? "He was on me all night," I say. "You guys saw it. He was trying to get a rise out of me."

"It worked," Frenchy says dourly.

I take a deep breath. Can't argue with that.

Jordan Zorby, our communications director, is organizing media interviews and tells them I'm not available. I should probably face the music, but I'm glad I don't have to tonight. After showering and changing into our suits, we all board the bus back to the hotel. Once there, Dutch says, "Come on. Let's go get a beer."

Like I want to go and be chewed out for losing my shit.

Then I catch Dutch's eye and he's not looking at me like he's judging me; he looks like he's concerned about me. "Okay."

We head out toward Broadway. Nashville is usually one of my favorite places to visit, but tonight I'm just cranky. Kitty's, a bluegrass place, is packed, but some bills trade hands and we soon have a table and a waitress with a big smile and bigger hooters standing next to us to take our drink orders.

"Okay, what happened?" Dutch asks once we've all got beers in front of us and the flirty waitress has departed.

A live band is playing, so I have to lean in and shout to tell them what happened. "You guys saw it, right? He was riding my ass all night."

"He was." Copper shakes his head. "Dickhead."

I draw in a slow breath. "He said something about Taylor."

Everyone makes identical "Ooooh" noises.

"What did he say?" Dutch asks.

"Never mind."

"Did he insult her?" Copper demands.

I glower into my beer. Steel guitar and banjo whine before the singer starts in about good corn liquor. That's what I should be drinking. I lift my hand and the waitress hustles right over. She's been watching us like a hawk.

"A round of your best corn whisky." I manage a smile for her.

"Did he insult her?" Copper asks again.

"Yeah."

"He can't do that." Dutch scowls and narrows his eyes. "She's a sweetheart and doesn't deserve that."

Dutch flirted mercilessly when he first met Taylor, and still does, but I know it's all in fun. The guys all like Taylor. He narrows his eyes. "Just wait till the next time we play them. He's a dead man."

"Fuck yeah," Copper agrees.

"Yeah, yeah, the code, yadda yadda. We don't settle things that way anymore." My effort to be reasonable is half-hearted.

"In fact, I kinda want to go find him right now," Abs muses, cracking his knuckles. "We could beat the crap out of him."

"Off the ice we'd get arrested for assault." I shake my head. Holy crap, I'm the voice of reason here. We're in deep shit.

"Is he that hung up on her?" Dutch asks.

"I don't get it." I shrug. "He could've had her. He moved to Nashville and barely said goodbye to her."

"Guess he regrets that."

"No shit. But why is he taking it out on me? I didn't steal her from him." I catch their glances and my gut goes stone cold. "No! I did not! Why are you looking like that?"

"We heard what happened at Théo's wedding."

"They were broken up then! I didn't even know they'd ever been together." I meet their eyes resolutely. "It's the truth. I didn't move on her until I knew she wasn't with anyone else."

They all nod.

"What about you?" Dutch asks slowly. "Are *you* that hung up on her?"

"Me?" I open my eyes wide. "Nah." I drop my gaze to my beer. "Just having fun."

"Uh-huh."

"Seriously." I shrug, trying for casual.

"Didn't look like it, the way you reacted."

I'm not falling in love with her. I know better than that. I make bad choices all the time, as I've so clearly displayed tonight. She doesn't need that. Like Dutch said, she's a sweetheart and I can't be relied on to do the right thing. After all the stupid things I've done, I sure as hell would never expect someone to be serious about me.

"I don't think Martinez is that hung up on her," Copper says slowly. "I think he was just trying to get under your skin."

"I already figured that out."

"He just said that because he knew it would get to you."

I fill my lungs with air and let it out. "You're right. I knew that. But when he said it . . . I lost it."

"Understandable." Dutch lifts his chin. "That dickwad knew exactly what to say."

"It won't happen again." As I say it, I realize what a huge mistake I've made.

I can't get involved with someone to the point where I lose it during a game. I can't care that much about someone. I can only care about hockey and playing my best and working on self-control and managing my emotions.

Christ . . . look what just happened. I lost a game because of my temper. Because of . . . Taylor.

I'm not blaming her. Not at all—don't even think that. I'm blaming myself. Totally.

I've lost control of my emotions because of her. I got all riled up because of her. I'm feeling shit I've never felt before, and I can't. I just can't.

Things only get better the next day, when the Department of Player Safety slaps me with a one-game suspension, which is automatic for instigating a fight in the last five minutes of regulation time. I know that rule, but it was the last thing I was thinking about. And that's on top of the two minutes for roughing, five for fighting, and ten-minute misconduct I got.

Dad's on the trip with us and after we land in Tampa Bay, he searches me out in the hotel to have a word with me. I can feel the waves of disappointment rolling off him.

"Look, I know I overreacted," I tell him. "I've had time to think about it and calm down." Sort of. "I'm sorry. I'm trying to do better."

"There are times we need to do things to send a message. That wasn't one of them."

"I know. Believe me. Uncle Mark and I already talked about this."

Uncle Mark has calmed down from last night, but he's still pissed that my penalties lost us the game.

"It won't happen again," I add glumly. I have to make sure of that.

Tonight I'm watching the game from the goddamn press box with Brando, who's out with a bum ankle. I've got a cardboard cup of coffee in my hand and it's all I can do to keep from crushing it, my fingers flexing with anger and frustration, wishing I were down on the ice. Wish they had something stronger than coffee in there.

Dad passes by on his way to the visiting management box and stops to speak to Brando about his ankle. To me, he's Dad; to Brando, he's the team owner. Brando even calls him Mr. Wynn. I still feel Dad's displeasure. But hey, no one's more pissed at me than I am at myself.

I watch Sokolov from the Lightning get possession of the puck and skate in on net. He fucking undresses Johnny and scores a goal that has the arena exploding. The coffee cup dents in my hands and my teeth grind together.

Brando and I exchange unhappy looks.

"Bad turnover," he says mildly.

"No shit."

We lose again, three–one, not a great way to start off after the Christmas break. We're going home and I know what I have to do to make things better.

25

TAYLOR

"WHAT THE HELL WAS THAT FIGHT ABOUT?"

I know that's not a great way to greet JP after he's been away for a few days and I missed him, and he probably feels like shit about getting suspended, but I was so furious when that happened. I was watching the game and I actually jumped up off the couch and stood in front of the TV with my heart lodged in my throat.

"You punched him in the face for no reason!"

JP's face is rigid, his jaw set. "Yep. No reason at all."

I pause and narrow my eyes. "Are you being sarcastic?"

He shrugs. "Sometimes you just gotta have a good throw down."

I toss my hands up in the air. "No, you don't! What the hell, I thought you were trying to stay out of fights!"

"Well, I failed. As usual." His bitter tone makes me flinch. "And apparently you're pissed about that."

I blink. I kind of am, but . . . "I don't like it when you fight."

"It's part of the game."

I close my eyes. "I'm sorry, I shouldn't have started this conversation as soon as you walked in. I was upset about the fight, but I'm not that mad. Come in. I'll get you a beer."

"I can't stay."

I've turned toward the kitchen, but I swing back around. "What?"

"I can't stay. I'm meeting the guys. I just came to talk to you because I didn't want to do this over the phone."

My heart stops beating, then lurches into an uneven rhythm. My breath sticks in my throat. "Do what?"

"Break up with you." His mouth is a thin line, his chin jutting.

I stare, my jaw loose. "B-but why?"

"I don't want to be a dick, but . . .well, I guess I am. Sorry. I shouldn't have let things get this far with you. I'm not cut out for relationships."

I try to swallow, but it hurts. My eyes burn. My head is a vast, empty space. Maybe clouds are floating through there, but that's it. This can't be happening.

I try to marshal my wandering thoughts. In fairness, I wasn't looking for a relationship either. I knew this would end at some point. Better now, than thirty years from now. Right? I swallow.

Only . . . I'd just started having stupid, hopeful thoughts about a future with JP. I'd just come to see that even though I kept telling myself I didn't care about love, I really did still want it. I wanted it with JP.

I'd felt so close with him. The gifts he gave me were so sweet. We fought and we apologized and we made up.

How stupid could I be? I should have known that was crazy.

I draw a long breath in through my nose, my throat quivering. I'm afraid to speak because my voice will come out shaky. Finally I nod slowly and manage to say, "Okay. I get it."

He glances at me. It's quick, but enough for me to see the misery in his eyes before he looks away. "Good. Okay, then. Yeah. Good."

I pause. I still have a million questions zinging around inside me, but none of them matter, I guess. He's done with me.

It's okay. I knew it would happen.

JP looks like someone's jabbing the butt end of a stick into his kidneys. "You're an amazing woman," he says hoarsely. "With the biggest heart. You deserve to find someone good enough for you."

I lift my chin, even though it's wobbling. "Yes. I do."

"Don't worry, I'll still keep Byron. I know your dad is taking him soon, but this doesn't change anything about that. I'll look after him until then."

I nod numbly. Right. Byron. "Thank you." The words squeeze out of my constricted throat.

"Bye, Sunshine."

As my apartment door closes behind JP, I feel the crack —a sharp burning in my chest as if a fissure just opened up. I literally gasp, and I slap my hand over my mouth. I can't breathe, can't speak. Pain shudders through my entire body.

I make it over to the couch and sink down onto it. Oh my God. I need Byron. I need hugs, I need doggie kisses, I need . . . comfort. Now I don't have JP and I don't have Byron. What am I going to do?

JP

Our next game is a home game, Friday night. I take my game-day nap, this time alone. This time I don't get a goodbye kiss when I'm leaving. (Byron's slobbery dog-breath kisses don't count.) This time Taylor won't be waiting for me when I get home.

That's okay. It's for the best.

I go through my usual taping routine at the arena, listening to music. The team didn't end on a high note before the Christmas break, but what's done is done. I have to learn to forgive myself and put my mistakes behind me, not brood about them forever. That's not how to move forward. Tonight I can start over. I can show everyone I'm better than that last game. I can control my emotions.

And I do.

The game is shit.

Actually, we win, but not thanks to me.

Most guys get reamed out by the coach after a bad game. Not me. I get reamed out by the coach *and* the team owner.

This is what it's like to be a Wynn.

"What the fuck was that?" Dad demands, sitting in

Uncle Mark's office, the soundproof door closed. "You looked like a robot out there."

I lift my chin. "Yeah. Mission accomplished."

"What?" He squints at me, then glances at Uncle Mark.

"Grandpa told me that passion is great, but it can also be a curse."

They both stare at me.

"Seriously," I continue. "He told me you have to control your passion. Otherwise it can destroy you."

"Your grandfather is nuts," Uncle Mark says.

"It made sense." I frown. "He said the best players control their emotions, rather than let their emotions control them."

"Yeah." Dad nods, rubbing his chin. "But they *have* emotions. You looked like a machine. Doing all the right things. But you had no passion."

I think about that. He's probably right. But that's good. Passion—desire, hunger, thirst, whatever you want to call it —is trouble. On the ice and *off* it. "Yeah. I've been working on controlling my emotions all season."

"I know you have been," Dad says.

"You do?"

"Sure. We've been watching you. You've seemed a lot more . . . not exactly laid back, but not wound quite so tight."

"Must be the yoga," I joke. "Or maybe the knitting. Everly taught me how to knit."

I wait for the trash talk.

It doesn't come.

"But controlling your emotions doesn't mean playing with *no* passion," Uncle Mark says.

They're both looking at me like they're worried about me. What the hell is that about?

"Life is better with no passion." I attempt a smile. "Easier to stay out of trouble."

"That's fucked up, Jean Paul."

Oh, shit. I'm in trouble when my dad is calling me by my full name.

"What's going on with you?" Dad rubs his chin. "Are things okay with you and Taylor?"

I jerk with surprise. "Uh. We broke up."

Dad and Uncle Mark exchange loaded glances.

"What happened?" Dad folds his arms across his chest.

I shrug and avoid his eyes. "It's better not to be involved with someone. Like I said, I've been working hard to do better. Stay out of trouble."

"What does she have to do with that?"

"Oh fuck no." Uncle Mark scowls. "Was *that* what that fight with Martinez was about? Jesus! I forgot about what happened at the wedding."

They both level me with condemning looks.

My gut cramps up. Then a wave of heat submerges me, and I can't breathe.

It's all too fucking much.

I'm a Wynn. I have to be the best. And I can't be. I just can't.

The pressure is suffocating. I can't do anything right. I play with too much emotion or I don't play with enough. I find a woman who's warm and kind and caring, but I can't care about her because it fucks up my game.

"He said crap about her," I burst out. "I had to hit him."

The air in the room goes silent and heavy.

"I see," Uncle Mark says slowly.

Dad covers his eyes with his hand.

"I know, I know. That's why I broke up with her. I can't be losing my shit like that over a woman."

"You know he probably didn't mean it," Dad says. "He was just trying to get to you."

"I know that! And it worked! Fuck." I drop my head.

"Will it happen again?" Uncle Mark asks.

"No! Like I said, that's why we broke up."

"So if Martinez insults her to your face again, you won't deck him?"

"I . . . I . . . " I close my eyes. "He better not."

"Jean Paul. Are you in love with her?"

I roll my eyes, curling my hands into fists. "Why?"

"Look," Dad says. "It's understandable that someone insulting the woman you love would upset you. But it's going to upset you whether you and Taylor are together . . . or not. People say stuff to you. The best chirps go for a guy's weakness. They ever tell you your mom likes butt play?"

My jaw slackens.

"Ha." Uncle Mark grins. "One time some asshole told me he saved money on car insurance by riding my mom."

Dad and Uncle Mark both guffaw.

"Not even funny right now," I mutter.

"The point is, guys are always going to go after you for something if they think it'll throw you off. You gotta ignore them, whether it's about your mom, your girlfriend or your damn dog." Dad pauses. "Breaking up with Taylor isn't gonna fix that. Actually . . . "

"What?" I frown, my mind unable to make sense of what they're saying.

"I think you were playing better when you were with her."

I think my head's going to explode. "I have to go." I stand. "Are we done?"

No other player would get away with such disrespectful behavior, and this just makes me hate myself even more.

But Uncle Mark nods, and Dad says, "Yeah. But I'm here if you need me, Jean Paul. As your dad."

When I get home, I know Taylor has been there. Don't ask me how, I just feel it. Maybe a hint of her scent. Or it could be the Christmas present sitting in the middle of my coffee table that wasn't there when I left.

I sit down and eye it. The tag reads, "To JP, From Byron."

I glance at the dog. He's watching me eagerly, as if he's waiting for me to open it. "You got this for me, huh, dude? Good doggo."

Slowly I pick up the square wrapped gift. I loosen the shiny red ribbon and peel off the paper. Then I open the white cardboard box. Nestled in tissue is a mug. I pull it out.

I smile. A color picture of a happy Byron adorns the mug. I fucking love it. I didn't want to admit it when Taylor was asking me about that, but I really am going to miss the mutt.

Trust me to fall in love with a dog who's not even mine.

Then I turn the mug around and see the words on the other side:

JP,

Thanks for
picking up
my poop.
Love, Byron

Fuck!

My nose burns and my eyes prickle.

I drop my head forward, holding the mug in both hands, squeezing my eyes shut.

I have never felt like such an asshole in my life.

TAYLOR

My office is closed until Monday, so I don't have to go to work. I'm grateful in one way, but it might be good to have something to distract me from my wrecked heart. I know that's dramatic, but I don't care.

Lacey and Everly and I get together Saturday for lunch to exchange gifts since we didn't do it before the holidays. Everyone was busy with Christmas parties and such. I haven't told them that JP and I broke up and I'm not looking forward to it, but I do kind of feel a need for some girl support.

We meet at Bistro del Rey. Seated at a square table near the window, we have views of the marina, wispy clouds streaking the pale blue sky above the boat masts and palm fronds fluttering in the breeze.

We exchange hugs and settle into chairs, arranging our purses and gift bags.

"First up is cocktails!" Lacey says. "Let's see what they have."

I smooth my hand over the white linen tablecloth and pick up a menu. "Oh, I see what I want." They have a cocktail called Sunflower—lemon, grapefruit wedges, gin, and Bourbon. "This was made for me." Except my throat closes up and my chest aches, thinking about JP calling me Sunshine. Buying me beautiful sunflower gifts. My bottom lip pushes out, but I firm it up and swallow hard.

Once we've ordered drinks, we take our time with the lunch menu.

"You look tired, Taylor," Everly says. "Busy Christmas? How was your trip?"

"My trip was awesome." I play with a fork. "It was so much fun to see my nieces, and my sister of course."

"You don't sound like it was fun."

I sigh. "Okay. I might as well just get this out. JP and I are no longer seeing each other."

Stunned silence presses against my ears. I look up at my friends and see their wide eyes and parted lips in identical expressions.

"What happened?" Lacey touches her throat.

"I'm not even sure. We had a fight, just before Christmas, but I thought we got over that."

"What was the fight about?"

"I, uh, told him about how I wanted Manny to know I was with him at the wedding. He freaked out because he thought I was just using him to get back at Manny."

"Ohhhh." Lacey grimaces.

"I explained it to him, and he apologized and it was fine. And then after what happened with Byron—"

"Oh my God!" Everly claps a hand over her mouth. "Is Byron okay?"

"Yes, he's fine."

"What happened?" Lacey sits up straight, looking back and forth between Everly and me.

Everly tells the story, since she was there, and honestly even though it could have been tragic, she's so funny and it's such a ridiculous story, she has me and Lacey cracking up.

"You ladies are having fun." Our server arrives with our drinks. He smiles as he sets them in front of us.

"Yes." Lacey wipes a tear from her eye. "We are."

I can't believe I'm laughing when I feel so shitty. "I love you guys."

"Oh, hon." Lacey sobers. "Okay, back to you and JP . . ."

"He felt terrible about Byron." I sip my drink. "Oh my God, this is good. This is going to last about two seconds." I take another taste. "He's so hard on himself. He makes a mistake and he beats himself up over it forever."

Everly nods slowly. "Yeah. You're right."

"Anyway, he came over to my place and said he was breaking up with me because he's not cut out for relationships."

Lacey winces. "I did warn you about that."

Everly frowns at Lacey. "That's not really helpful, Lace."

Lacey's eyes widen. "I'm just trying to . . . shit. You're right. I'm sorry. That wasn't helpful at all."

"I know you tried to warn me." I sigh. "I should have

listened. I thought . . . we could just have fun. I gave up on finding love after my parents split up, but . . . it found me."

Lacey tips her head to one side. "You're in love with him."

My bottom lip quivers. "Yes."

Both women reach out to squeeze my hand.

"He's an idiot." Everly huffs out a breath.

"Men," Lacey says. "What are you going to do?"

"I don't know." I finger my sunflower necklace. "He gave me this for Christmas." I show them, and they peer at it and oooh and aaah. "And a sort of painting that says 'You are my sunshine.'"

"Aw." Lacey actually tears up. "That's so sweet."

I sniff. "I know. I can't believe he turned around and broke up with me."

"He'll figure it out," Everly says. "I know he will."

"How do you know that?"

"Because I'm going to kick him in the nuts and help him."

I laugh. "Don't do that. You don't have to get involved."

Everly appears unconvinced. "We'll see."

"Maybe Théo should talk to him." Lacey's eyes brighten. "JP helped Théo when I left him."

"I don't want people interfering. I just want him . . . to be happy. Maybe he does need to talk to someone, though."

"You're a better woman than I am." Everly lifts her Negroni and drinks. "I'd want to kick him in the nuts."

"I'm so glad I have you both." I lift my glass and touch the rim to Everly's, then Lacey's. "The crazy thing is, I didn't want to fall in love. After what happened with my parents, I realized love doesn't last for anyone, so why even try. Dammit, I don't know how this happened."

"I do." Lacey smiles. "It's because you're you. And you're full of love. Which is why *we* love *you*."

"Stawp. You're going to make me cry again." I blink away tears. "Enough crying. Let's get drunk."

"I'm in." Everly lifts her glass.

26

JP

We practice Saturday morning. I eat lunch at the arena with the guys, then head out to do some shit. I have suits to pick up at the dry cleaners, food to buy, and I need new socks. Exciting stuff. I'm about to go home when I get a text from Théo.

> Get your ass over here.

I smile grimly, remembering getting a text like this last spring, when Lacey took off back to Vegas.

I send him a reply.

> Okay, okay. Meet me at Time Out. When can you be there?

I know he's talking about a sports bar in Manhattan Beach. I sigh. Does he just assume I have nothing else going on? Fine, I have nothing else going on.

Half an hour

Okay.

When I walk in a while later, he's already there, drinking a beer. I high-five him. "You won."

"Won what?"

"The race to get here first."

He laughs.

I pull the stool out from the high-top table and slide onto it. "What's up? Lacey leave you again?"

"Fuck off."

The pretty waitress appears. "Hi there." She looks at me. "What can I get you?"

I order a craft beer and she disappears. I look at Théo with a cocked eyebrow.

"This is about you and Taylor."

I roll my eyes. "Great."

"What the fuck did you do?"

I heave a gusty sigh. "Taylor talked to Lacey, right?"

"Yep."

Then I drop the smart-ass 'tude. "She okay?" I finger a paper napkin on the table.

"No. She's not."

My insides spasm painfully and my chest throbs. I keep staring at the napkin.

"Be glad it's not Everly here, because she wants to do some damage to your lucky charms."

I choke. "What?"

"Your twigs and berries."

"Come on!"

"Bits and pieces."

I scowl.

He laughs. "Big Joe and the twins?"

"Slightly better."

The waitress brings my beer with a gratifyingly flirty smile.

"Okay, seriously, what's going on?" I pick up my glass.

"You broke up with Taylor."

"Yeah." I take a big gulp.

Last time he and I met here, we confessed some messed-up stuff, feelings we'd had about each other our whole lives that had impacted our relationship. And our relationships with others. So I'm guessing Théo is after more bro talk.

"Why? You don't care about her?"

It takes me a while to find words. "I do care about her," I choke out. "Too much. I can't do that. It fucks up my mind."

"Hmmm." He sips his beer. "I'm trying to see things from your point of view, but I can't stick my head that far up my ass."

"Asshole." I drink my own beer.

"Look. You gave me shit when I screwed up with Lacey. I'm here to return the favor."

I nod. This is what I expected. "Go for it."

His lips twitch. "Tell me why you really broke up with her."

I sigh. "Because of that fight with Martinez."

He looks at me like I'm speaking Cantonese.

"I punched him because he insulted Taylor."

His expression lightens. "Ah! Okay, now we're getting somewhere."

"Don't you see?" I glare at him. "I've been trying so hard to stay out of trouble. To control my emotions on the ice. She's got me all fucked up and confused, and then I go and lose it because of her. It cost us *two* fucking games! Dad and Uncle Mark are pissed at me. Hell, the whole team is pissed at me." I shake my head bitterly. "I can't go losing my shit over a woman. I need to stick to my goal. But I keep fucking up." The words come out rough and scratchy. "I keep dating women I shouldn't. I keep losing my temper on the ice. I keep doing stupid shit like letting Lacey's dog piss on the Christmas tree and eat poison. I nearly killed her dog. And I insulted her by implying she's just like Emma."

"What—and I can't stress this enough—the *fuck*?"

I snort-laugh.

"Seriously, man? *Emma?* You think Taylor is like Emma? As Mom would say, esti de câlice de tabarnak!"

"Ha. Mom has never in her life said that."

"Pretty sure she said that the time we tried to ski off the garage roof and you broke your wrist. Never mind that." He glares at me.

"I don't think she's like Emma." I rub my forehead. "It was a misunderstanding. I apologized."

"Thank fuck for that."

"But see? When I do the wrong things, it's the wrongest thing of all the wrongs that ever wronged. It was best to end things with her."

He laughs. Fucker.

Théo tips his head back and looks at the ceiling. "Everyone fucks up. It's how you learn."

"Why don't I learn, then?"

"You don't learn because you don't *let* yourself learn. You don't let it go. You keep whipping yourself. You know you have to let shit go when it comes to sports. You screw up, make a turnover, a bad pass, miss a shot . . . you have to let it go."

I pause. "I know that."

"Then do it! Let it go in your private life too." He pauses. "I forgive you, JP."

His blunt words set me back. I stare at him.

"I forgive you for what happened with Emma. Now fucking forgive *yourself.*"

I can't even speak for a minute, reeling. Then I manage, "That's not what this is about."

"Isn't it?" He frowns.

I let his words play over in my head again. I've heard this before. After I nearly killed Byron, Taylor reminded me that not being judgmental is part of dealing with stress. Including judging myself.

Oh Jesus.

He's right.

I'm still pissed at myself for what I did to him. .

"Fuck," I mutter.

Last time we sat in this bar, I confessed to Théo. I told him I felt I could never be as good as him, so I just tried to be badder. My whole life I've embraced that bad boy, that cool guy who hides his feelings under a cocky smirk, who lets his bitterness get in the way of making good decisions, who takes the blame for shit he didn't do. And yet . . . way down deep inside, I don't want to be that guy. I want to be better. And I've been trying. I'm not perfect, but I've been honestly trying. But I can't get past the secret, hidden fear that I *can't* be better.

Now I've lost the best woman I've ever met—a woman who apparently likes me despite all my goddamn flaws, a woman who makes me a better man because I want to be worthy of her, a woman who forgives me when I screw up —because I can't forgive *myself*.

She doesn't judge me or blame me. Even when I screw up, she's still sweet and loving and forgiving.

"Let it go." He holds my gaze. "It's all okay. Love you, bro."

A giant fist is squeezing my throat. Christ, I think I'm going to cry. "Love you too," I choke out. "What am I going to do?"

Théo's lips turn upward at the corner. "About Taylor?"

I give my head a shake. "Yeah." I had something so perfect and amazing . . . I had sunshine. Now everything feels dark. I need that sunshine back. "I don't know."

"You have to be honest."

"Yeah."

"With yourself first of all. Do you love her?"

I swallow. "Yeah."

He nods. "Then you have to tell her that."

My jaw drops in alarm.

"Yep."

I suck in a breath. "Okay."

"It's good if you can do something to show her you love her. Like groveling."

"Groveling?" I grimace. "Like get down on my knees and beg her to take me back?"

"Pretty much."

"Ugh. I think it's too late. I wouldn't blame her for not taking me back."

"Well, at least ask her to forgive you. At least be honest with her, so that if things really are done, you both know the truth."

I nod slowly. "Yeah. Okay. This is my worst screwup yet because I hurt her. I don't know how to make it up to her, but I'll figure something out."

"Okay, good. We're having a New Year's party—Lacey and I. You can come. Taylor might be there."

My heart slams into a rapid rhythm. "Right. Okay."

WE PLAY SUNDAY, THEN WE PLAY NEXT TUESDAY, WHICH IS New Year's Eve. I've been playing, but Dad and Uncle Mark are right—I feel like a zombie. I hate it.

I took a stupid tripping penalty on Sunday, but that was it. Staying out of trouble. That's me.

I haven't scored either.

Dutch, Abs, and Copper want me to go to a big New Year's party after the game that apparently one of the Lakers is throwing in his mansion in the hills. They promise me lots of gorgeous women, booze, drugs, and a swimming pool.

I'm not into it. Even if I was, I have other plans— Taylor. Since I met with Théo, I've been hard at work on my project. Monday is an optional practice and I bail on it because I'm busy. But things aren't going well, and I need help.

I call Everly. "You working today?"

"I'm taking off at noon."

"Come by my place. I need you."

She laughs in a nasty way that makes me frown. "Okay."

What is up with that? Oh right. My lucky charms. This might be dangerous. Oh well.

27

TAYLOR

I DON'T FEEL LIKE PARTYING THIS NEW YEAR'S EVE. IT'S A big phony holiday anyway. It's just another day.

But I'm dressed in a cute Little Black Dress. I've kicked off my heels and I'm padding around Lacey and Théo's house in bare feet, moving to the music Lacey has playing, holding a glass of champagne, a big smile fixed on my face.

It's not a huge party. Some of the Condors management is here—Théo's assistant GM Scott Jermey and their coach Dave Martin, along with their wives. Wyatt Bell, who lives in this same building, is here, and team captain Jimmy Bertelson and his girlfriend. Some of the Wynns, but not all, are here, including Everly.

Everly and I are going to share the bed in the downstairs spare bedroom, so we don't have to drive home tonight. All the champagne, whee!

"Having fun?" Lacey stops near me and clinks her glass against mine.

"Sure." I force a smile.

"I have to tell you something."

"What?" I eye her curiously.

"That fight JP got in with Manny the other night . . . he did it because Manny insulted you."

My chin nearly hits the floor. "What?"

"Yes." She nods, shooting a furtive glance toward Théo. "That was why JP hauled off and punched him."

I move my head slowly from side to side. "Oh my God. *What did he say?*"

"I don't know. It doesn't matter. JP told Théo."

I inhale and exhale. "Wow."

"It's kind of romantic."

"He got kicked out of the game, suspended for the next game, and they lost both those games!"

"That's how much you mean to him."

"*Then why did he break up with me?*"

"Uh . . . oh hey, I need to check on some food."

Watching Lacey dash away, I shake my head.

Manny said something to him, about me . . . and JP punched him? I press a hand to my stomach. That would be just like him . . . getting himself in trouble trying to protect someone else. It was never about him. It was protecting another player, covering for the coach's daughter . . . defending me.

Damn. It was my fault that he got in trouble. No wonder he broke up with me.

I guzzle some champagne to ease the tightness in my throat and head to the kitchen for a refill. I move to stand next to Everly at the island in the kitchen and grab a bottle, refilling my glass until the fizzy drink overflows. Oops.

The kitchen is crowded. Why do parties always end up

in the kitchen? One of life's mysteries. I pop a spinach puff into my mouth.

"It's ridiculous," Everly says. "No other team sport tolerates fighting."

"It's part of the game." Wyatt Bell smiles from the other side of the island.

Man, he has a sexy smile. If I weren't already in love with JP, I'd . . . Wait. That totally makes me seem like a puck bunny. I had a little crush on Bobby Ponomarenko when he lived in this house. Then I dated Manny. Then I dated JP. No good has come of any of it.

"Hockey should be about skating, speed, and skill," Everly says.

I give her a thoughtful look as I sip my champagne. I'm pretty sure I've heard her defend fighting in hockey. Why is she arguing about it with Wyatt?

"What does your father think about fighting in hockey?" Wyatt asks with a glint in his eye.

"Please. Don't bring him into this. He's a dinosaur. Of course he thinks fighting is necessary."

"It does have its place. Cool things down when the game is getting out of control. Send a message to the other team—and your own team—that bullshit won't be tolerated."

"How about sportsmanship and controlling your temper?"

I watch the back-and-forth with interest. Everly's getting pretty heated, while Wyatt seems to be baiting her . . . and enjoying it.

"It's a complicated issue," Wyatt says.

"It's not complicated. It's simple—don't fight."

He laughs.

"How do you explain to your kids that it's okay to beat someone up on the ice, but not off the ice?"

"I don't have kids." He shrugs.

I sense Everly grinding her teeth.

"That I know of," he adds.

Now Everly actually growls.

"Kidding!" Wyatt holds up his hands. "It was a joke. Hey, we know what we're getting into when we drop the gloves."

"I don't think you do. Men think they're all invincible."

He laughs again and lifts his glass to his mouth.

"Fighting is actually decreasing in hockey," Théo puts in, stepping up to the island. "This season, there have only been point-two fights per game."

Everly grins at her nephew. "Thank you, Mr. Stats."

"Thirty years ago, it was one-point-three fights per game. So it's changing."

"Yeah." Wyatt nods. "Better these days to ice the most skilled team you can—you have way more advantages than come from fighting."

Everly's jaw drops. "You were just arguing in favor of fighting!"

He gives her a slow, entrancing smile. "I can argue both sides of an issue. I was in the debate club in high school."

"You've got to be kidding me." Everly's eyebrows rise. "A hockey player in debate club?"

Wyatt doesn't take offense. "I'm a master debater, sweetheart."

I crack up, but Everly doesn't seem to think it's funny.

Should I point out that Everly can also argue the other side of that issue? Mmm . . . nah.

Yeesh, serious sparks there. Interesting.

The music, the conversation, and the laughter get louder as the evening progresses. People are dancing out on the patio. Lacey warned me that JP might be here, but it's getting close to midnight and he hasn't shown up yet. I'm ashamed to admit I'm disappointed. I have to get over this.

Sadness washes through me. The bubbly champagne isn't helping my mood. I want to go to bed, but I guess I have to hang in until midnight.

Lacey's going around with another bottle of champagne, topping up glasses in preparation for midnight. Like I need any more.

The doorbell rings as Lacey's filling my glass.

"Someone's late," I comment. And then, somehow, I know it's JP.

The door opens and he walks in . . . accompanied by Byron.

"My baby!" I set down my champagne, hold my arms out to him (Byron), and he gallops toward me and leaps at me. I catch him, stumbling back a step, but I'm okay. "My Byron! What are you doing here?" I let him lick my face and then set him down. His tail waves excitedly. "Um . . . what are you wearing?"

It's a . . . sweater. Different shades of blue, knit into a simple style, but it's . . . crooked. One side is shaped differently from the other, hanging down nearly to his feet, and the neckline is uneven.

I look up at JP. He's standing near me and he's holding a huge bouquet of flowers—sunflowers. But not just any sunflowers: there are golden yellow ones, but also orange and red and brown, and some with all those colors, all with deep chocolate centers. They glow in the dim room.

I lift my gaze to his face.

He's not smiling, but his eyes are intent on me.

"These are for you," he says, holding out the flowers to me. "Happy New Year. I hope the year brings you joy and happiness and light."

I slowly reach for the flowers.

"Do you know what sunflowers symbolize?" he asks quietly, moving closer to hand the bouquet to me.

"Um. No." My heart is hammering against my breastbone. My mouth has gone dry. My hands shake as they take the flowers.

"They symbolize adoration, loyalty, and longevity."

He's close to me now, close enough for me to see his long eyelashes, the darker ring of blue around his sapphire irises, the carved shape of his beautiful mouth.

"Which I think is perfect for you," he says. "Because . . . I adore you."

I can't breathe. I glance wildly around and yep, everyone's watching this unfold.

"You're loyal," he says. "To your family and your friends . . . and even to me when I screw up." He swallows. "As for longevity . . . I would like a chance to have that with you."

My insides are shivering. My tongue feels swollen in my mouth and I can't speak. My eyes probably look like they're going to pop out of my head. I clutch the flowers tightly.

"I screwed up again," he says. "Breaking up with you was the biggest, stupidest mistake I've ever made, because I love you. But this time, I'm trying to learn from my mistake. I'm asking you to forgive me. I'll understand if you can't. But I'm going to try to forgive myself so I can move forward."

I'm blinking fast now, my eyes smarting.

It feels like everyone in the house is holding their breath, even though music is still pumping out of the speakers.

This is really . . . weird. And uncomfortable. But I'm just drunk enough that I don't care.

"JP . . ." My bottom lip quavers. I step closer to him. I glance around. "I love you, too."

He grins.

A cheer goes up around us.

"Oh my God." I duck my head briefly. "What is happening?"

"I wanted to do this in front of everyone so if I crashed and burned, I'd be properly humiliated."

"You're crazy."

"Yeah."

Our eyes meet. We both smile. And I'm lost in it, twirling in a sparkling blue tornado, sucked up in JP's beautiful eyes and warm smile and . . . love. There's nobody else but JP in that moment.

"Can you forgive me?" he murmurs. "I was such an idiot."

"Yes, you were."

"I'm sorry. You inspire me," he says in a low voice that only I can hear now. "I nearly killed your dog and you forgave me. I lost it on the ice and cost the team games . . . and you still supported me."

I swallow, my throat feeling like a puck is lodged there,

still focused on his face. "Yes. Because that's what love is. But you have to love yourself, JP."

He nods. "I know."

"Do you?"

"I've been working hard. Trying to be better. I'm going to screw up sometimes and I know that's okay."

I touch his face. "We all screw up."

I go onto my toes to touch my lips to his. This is met with a round of applause.

"It's nearly midnight!" Lacey calls. "Let's count it down!"

I set the flowers on a table and move into JP's embrace. We watch each other as the others shout, " . . . five . . . four . . . three . . . two . . . one! Happy New Year!"

"Happy New Year, Sunshine."

"Happy New Year."

He pulls me up against him, holding me tight, kissing me ravenously, deeply . . . melting me.

Everyone else at the party is moving around to kiss others. They ignore us, making out in the corner of the room, leaving us in our own little bubble. Eventually I pick up my champagne glass and take a sip, then hand it to him. He does the same, holding my gaze.

I look down at my dog.

"What is he wearing?" I ask again.

"I made it for him."

I blink and roll my bottom lip between my teeth briefly. "It's . . . amazing."

"It was a hell of a lot of work." He passes a hand over his forehead and back over his hair. "Why couldn't you have a Chihuahua? I started it a while ago, but then I had to finish it before tonight. Everly came and helped me."

"Oh." My heart expands, so full of love for him I could burst from it. I'm full of helium, light enough to soar.

"Byron gave me a gift," he says, as if I don't know. "So I thought I should give him something."

"It's perfect." That hockey puck has materialized in my throat again.

"I loved his present," he tells me.

My smile is shaky. "Good."

"And I *am* going to miss him. A lot."

"I know."

I soak in the love and worship I see in JP's eyes and let myself revel in the fact that I can be honest with him, and love and worship him right back.

This is a moment. We've already had challenging moments, and if I've learned anything from my parents and what's happened with them, it's not that forever love doesn't exist . . . it's to appreciate the good moments. To take them and cherish them and keep them . . . and they, and maybe love, will last forever.

28

JP

I'M SO GODDAMN RELIEVED, I'M GUZZLING CHAMPAGNE LIKE I'm Hugh Hefner at a Playboy Mansion party. I'm happily buzzed. I refuse to let go of Taylor, and we mingle with everyone else with my arm firmly around her waist.

"When did you take up knitting?" Harrison asks me with a smirk.

I don't even care. "A month or so ago. It's good stress relief. You should try it."

"Yeah, I don't think so."

"Not secure enough in your masculinity? That's okay. Not everyone is."

He laughs. "Fuck off."

"I'll make you a scarf."

Harrison holds up his hands. "Hey, don't worry about me."

Taylor's smiling so big she could eclipse the sun. Byron looks pretty happy too. He's made a full recovery from the food theft incident.

"We may have a little problem," I tell Taylor eventually.

"What's that?"

"I'm too drunk to drive home." I lean closer and say in her ear, "And I want to get you in my bed and fuck you until you scream."

Her eyelashes lower. "All right then." Her lips twitch. "I'm too drunk to drive too. But I planned that."

"What?"

"I'm staying here tonight."

I stare at her. "Perfect!" I grab her hand. "Which room?"

"Hold up, Killer. I'm supposed to share the room with Everly."

I frown. "No threesomes. Especially with my aunt."

"Eeeew."

"I'm kidding. No, I mean I'm not kidding. You know what I mean."

She giggles. "I know what you mean."

"Well, shit."

Everly must have heard us. "What are you saying about me?"

"I told JP that you and I are sharing a bed."

She narrows her eyes at him. "Don't get all weird."

"*I'll* get weird about it," Wyatt puts in. "That sounds hot."

"You're disgusting," Everly says. Then she sighs dramatically. "Okay, fine, I'll let you two lovebirds have the bed. I'll sleep on the couch."

Now Lacey jumps in. "What? The couch?"

"It's fine." Everly shrugs, also half-cut. "I think I'll be able to sleep anywhere."

"I have an extra room," Wyatt says casually. "You can sleep there."

"I'm not sleeping at your place." Everly waves a hand. "Are you kidding me? You'd probably stab me in my sleep."

"Is that a euphemism?" He arches a brow. "'Cause I bet my stick would feel good in your crease."

My eyes bug out and my hands curl into fists. "Hey, man, that's—"

But Everly is laughing. "In your dreams," she says. "And that's why I'm not staying at your place."

Taylor squeezes my biceps and shoots me a warning look. Okay, I'm not gonna punch the guy, but Everly's my aunt—I have to watch out for her.

Oh hey, she can totally look after herself.

"Okay then, problem solved." I pick up Taylor. She squeals. "Good night, all."

I carry her into the bedroom and shut the door firmly behind us.

She's laughing and falls onto the bed. "I don't know if drunk sex is going to be very good."

I follow her down onto the bed. "I'm not that drunk."

"No whisky dick?"

"I wasn't drinking whisky." I kiss her mouth, her cheek, her jaw. She shivers beneath me and parts her legs so I can settle between them. I hitch her dress higher on her hips to allow her to open them wider and press my hard-on against her soft center. She sucks in a sharp breath and wraps her arms around me. "God, I love you."

"I love you too. I didn't want to fall in love, but I did."

"Why didn't you want to?" I inhale the scent of her skin where neck joins shoulder. Intoxicating.

"Because of my parents. I figured what was the point. If they can't make it, nobody can."

I lift my head and peer down at her. "No."

"That's how I felt. But . . ." She strokes the back of my neck and sensation rolls down my spine. "After I talked to my dad on the way to San Diego, I . . . I realized I was falling for you. And I thought maybe . . . we could try. Then . . ."

I kiss her quickly. "I'm sorry. So fucking sorry."

She gives a tiny nod. "I know. My dad told me how a relationship is made up of a million moments. Good ones and bad ones. There are no guarantees . . . but you have to treasure the good moments."

I swallow. "Yeah."

"*You* need to do that." Her expression turns earnest. "You need to enjoy the moments. You're too hard on yourself when you screw up. That causes you stress you don't need. Remember the yoga classes? No judgment? Even of ourselves?"

I gaze back at her. She's so right. "Théo told me the same thing. In hockey, we have to learn to let our mistakes go. Sometimes I can do that . . . sometimes I can't. I'm working on it. Off the ice . . . I need to work on that, too."

"Yes."

"I . . . I've had a hard time, lately." My tongue feels thick as I reveal this to her. "It's a lot of pressure. Being a Wynn . . . means being perfect."

"No." Her eyes are full of acceptance and kindness. "It doesn't. *You* put the pressure on yourself."

I let this turn over in my mind. "Um . . . maybe?"

She smiles, a slow, sweet, seductive smile.

"I could never be as good as Théo. My whole life. So I tried to be different. But that didn't work out so well."

"You *are* different. You are two different people." She digs her fingers into my shoulders. "And I love *you*. I love how you don't want to disappoint the people you care about—your family. Your team. I love how you pretend to be so bad, but you teach kids how to skate, and buy them equipment, and you love Byron. You hated that you hurt your brother. You want your grandpa to be proud of you."

A rough shudder closes over my chest. I can't breathe. Can't speak.

She knows me. She sees me. The real me. The me I want to be.

We kiss again, long, open-mouthed, tongue-sliding kisses full of passion and gratitude, relief and hope. I slowly strip her out of that sexy dress, revealing a black lace bra and panties. She's everything . . . my fantasy, my friend, my ally. She'll support me when I make mistakes—but I vow to never again make a mistake that will hurt her. And I'll support *her*, whatever life brings her. I never realized how incredible it would feel to have someone who gets me so completely, and the fear of opening up and being vulnerable and revealing all my stupid insecurities seems microscopic in comparison to the huge swell of love and joy I now feel.

I kiss her throat, her collarbones, between her breasts. I slide my hands beneath her to unfasten her bra, toss it aside, then cup her breasts and squeeze them, desire rushing through my blood. I sweep my hands over her soft skin, taking the measure of her curves, following their path with my eyes to worship her with my touch, my gaze. My mouth.

I want to taste her, lick her, make her come . . . She falls apart, crying my name, and I rip off my own clothes, grab a condom, and move back between her legs.

I start to rip open the wrapper and she stops me with a soft touch. "We don't have to use that . . . if you trust me."

"Christ. I trust you. Do you trust me?"

She nods. "Yes."

My body throbs, heat mainlining through my veins, my cock an aching spike. I toss the condom over my shoulder and grip my shaft to run it through her folds, so soft and so wet.

I let out a long groan as I ease inside her. Her body closes around me, gripping me so tightly from root to tip as I seat myself fully. I pause, meeting her eyes, and reach for her hands to twine my fingers through hers.

"I want to be good enough for you," I say hoarsely. "I may not be the best . . . but I want to be the best I can be."

"You're not a bad guy if you're trying to be better. That's all any of us can do. Try to be our best selves."

I move inside her, clasping her hands. Sensation pours through me in waves, pressure building. Our eyes lock together and it's excruciatingly intimate and yet . . . essential. I don't care if she sees inside me, because she loves me. And I love her.

"This moment," she says softly. "Enjoy this beautiful moment."

"I want a million beautiful moments . . . with you."

Thank you for reading JP and Taylor's story! If you enjoyed it, please tell your friends!

And the Wynn Family saga continues! Read on for an excerpt from *Win Big*!

EVERLY

———

THEY SAY THAT EVERYTHING HAPPENS FOR A REASON.

But sometimes that reason is you're drunk and make bad decisions.

In my defense, it was New Year's Eve. Who doesn't get drunk and make bad decisions on New Year's Eve? Right?

Not me. I never make bad decisions. Well, not anymore. Not since I was sixteen years old and broke my parents' hearts, destroyed their trust in me, and nearly wrecked a bunch of lives. Since then, it has been my life's goal to never disappoint them again. That means never screwing up, working hard, being perfect. Easy peasy.

I'm lying in Wyatt Bell's bed.

This is totally contrary to my life's mission, on so many levels.

At least I'm alone, thank fuck.

Wyatt Bell. Six feet two inches, two hundred twenty pounds of sex on skates. Plays defense for the California Condors.

I know we made out for a while with our clothes on. It was hot as hell and I was happily oblivious to all the reasons we shouldn't be doing that—chiefly, the fact that I hate him—as my lady parts combusted in a feverish explosion of lust. Wow.

I nearly have to wave a hand in front of my face as scorching heat rises to my cheeks.

A hockey player. On the team my dad owns.

God! How *stupid* could I be?

Anyway, my clothes are still on—a body con, short black dress, bra, and panties. Not like I had a lot to remove, but there's comfort in the fact that I'm still clothed. And alone.

Where is he?

A headache drums at my temples and I lift my hands to rub there, closing my eyes. My mouth tastes like I licked the inside of a dumpster, and my stomach is . . . iffy. I think I have a hangover.

I'm not sure because it's been that long since I had one. I don't get drunk enough to be hungover.

I'm annoyed at myself.

I crack open my eyes. Daylight brightens the edges of the window around the blinds. I have no idea what time it is, but obviously the sun is up. I lift my head, which makes it pound more, and peer at the bedside table. No clock.

I go backward in my mind . . . pretty sure I brought my purse . . . which has my phone in it . . . it has to be here somewhere.

And where is Wyatt?

Welp. Best find out.

I throw back the covers and swing my legs over the side

of the bed. A sick wave washes over me, but it doesn't last long. I think I'll live.

I eye the room. The open door appears to be an en suite bathroom. Excellent.

Feet bare, I pad across the big bedroom to the bathroom. I barely note the gorgeous stone tiles, a massive shower with multiple heads, and the big granite vanity as I take care of business. As I wash my hands, I observe my reflection. Hair standing on end, mascara smudged beneath my eyes, and . . . is that . . . *whisker burn* on my jaw and throat? Dear God. I close my eyes.

Then I draw in a deep breath and tiptoe across the bedroom to the other door. I've never been here before and even though this condo is in the same building as my nephew's, where I've been many times, it's a completely different layout. But I find my way to the kitchen/living area, which I now vaguely remember from last night.

The place is empty.

This is good. Great. I spy my purse on the coffee table and make a beeline for it. I can grab it and get the hell out of here before I have to face Wyatt.

"Morning."

I jump, my feet literally leaving the floor, and whirl around at the deep, gritty voice.

Oh sweet Jesus, he looks just as good the morning after. His dark gold hair is kind of long on top and right now it's tousled all over. Dark gold beard stubble shadows his jaw. His eyes are hazel, and I know from seeing him close up they're more green than brown, with gold flecks in them. I nearly whimper. "Morning," I choke out.

"Want some breakfast?" He stretches and the T-shirt

he's wearing rises and reveals skin between the hem and the top of the sweatpants, which are sitting so indecently low on his hips they should be illegal. Not to mention the, uh, enticing bulge at his groin, which is clearly recognizable. I swallow as I avert my gaze. "Or coffee?"

"No! I'm good. I need to go. Uh . . ."

"Yeah?" He heads to the kitchen and the Keurig on the counter, popping in a K-Cup.

"Where did you sleep?"

He turns and flashes a wicked smile. "You don't remember?"

I trudge toward him, straightening my dress. "I don't remember much. Ugh."

He purses his lips and studies me. "You feel okay?"

I drop my purse on the counter and lean my elbows there. "If by 'okay' you mean feeling like my brain is bleeding out my eyes, my stomach is full of battery acid, and I'm about to die in five minutes, then yes, I feel okay."

He bites down on the smile that tugs at his lips. "That good, huh."

"Okay, I'm exaggerating."

"Here." He opens a cupboard and produces a small white bottle. He shakes out a gel cap and hands it to me, reaching next for a glass, which he fills with water from the fridge dispenser.

"Thank you." I toss the pill into my mouth and swallow it. I guzzle that delicious cold water down until the glass is empty. "God, that's good water."

His lips twitch again. "Sure you don't want coffee? Some toast might help with the battery acid."

I sink onto a stool and rest my head in my hands. I want to leave, but I also want to feel better. "Okay."

"I slept in the spare room." He busies himself at the Keurig again, then the toaster.

"Oh."

"After you passed out, I figured I'd let you sleep it off alone."

I gasp in outrage. "I did not pass out!"

He gives me a look, chin down, lips puckered. "Uh-huh. Anyway, don't worry, I didn't take advantage of your state of inebriation."

"*You* weren't inebriated?"

"Yeah, I was. I admit it." He grins. "Not as much as you, judging from your condition this morning."

"Ugh. I haven't been hungover since I was a teenager. I really don't like it."

"No one does. By your age, you should have learned how to pace yourself."

I frown.

He slides a mug of coffee across the counter. "Do you need milk and sugar?"

"A little milk?"

"Sure." He opens the fridge and pulls out a carton.

I splash a tiny bit into the dark brew and stir it with the spoon he provides, then pick up the cup and sip it.

"What do you want on your toast? I have butter, peanut butter, or . . . well, that's it."

"Just butter." I don't usually eat bread, but I need something in my stomach. "Thanks."

While I eat mine, he makes himself toast, spreading his thickly with peanut butter.

I don't know what else to say to him. Last night we had plenty to say to each other . . . we argued about politics, hockey, and climate change, which he didn't even take seriously! There's something about him, a cocky confidence, that makes me want to poke holes in that self-assurance, disagree with everything that comes out of his mouth, and prove him wrong.

One of the first times we met, we got into an argument about men being "showers" or "growers." Wyatt was trying to tell me there was no such thing and I concluded I needed to do some research on that, which seemed to piss him off.

I enjoy pissing him off.

Judging from the dick print in those soft sweats, he's a "shower."

I normally try to avoid conflict, but there's something about sparring with him that makes my blood sizzle and energy flow through me.

As for kissing him . . . whoa. If I thought my blood sizzled just from talking to him, making out with him had me shorting out and melting down.

"So, looks like JP and Taylor are a thing."

"Yep." I smile, my chest softening. My friend Taylor looked so happy last night, after the guy she loves showed up to apologize for being a dick to her, and did it in style. She and I were supposed to share a room at Théo and Lacey's place, who hosted the New Year's Eve party, so we didn't have to drive home, but after JP arrived and he and Taylor made up, how could I not let them have the room?

Which is how I ended up at Wyatt's place, in need of somewhere to park my drunken ass for the night. And how we somehow ended up rolling around on his bed, desperately kissing and groping each other.

It was hot.

I gulp some coffee.

"I'm happy for them," I say, not letting on how my heart swelled with tenderness watching the scene last night. "They're good for each other."

"Can she keep him out of the penalty box?"

I lift an eyebrow.

JP is my nephew, and don't think that makes me old. My dad remarried and had me when he was forty-eight, right around the time the kids from his first marriage, my half brothers Mark and Matthew, were having kids. I'm twenty-seven, only a year older than JP. JP is also a hockey player, like Wyatt. JP plays for the Long Beach Golden Eagles—the enemy. Awkward, due to the fact that Matthew owns the Eagles, Mark coaches for them, another nephew and my brother play for their farm team, and my niece is the goalie coach for the farm team.

Yep, we're a hockey family.

"Well, I don't think it's up to her," I say, lifting my chin. "But she's good for helping him manage his emotions, so that may be a benefit."

Wyatt shrugs and starts peeling an orange. "If you say so."

My family's a bit messed up for a bunch of reasons, and I'm not very happy with the fact that my half brothers are currently suing my dad for allegedly stealing money from them. I'm not happy with the fact that Matthew bought the Long Beach Golden Eagles as a way to get back at my dad for allegedly stealing their money. And I'm not happy with the fact that Matthew stole Mark from us. Mark was the Condors' coach until Matthew hired him. (I say "us" because even though I don't actually work for the Condors, I do run the Condors Foundation.)

I can criticize my family, but if anyone else does, I'm coming for them. "You're just pissed because he punched you in the face at Théo's wedding."

My family's messed up, remember?

"I was trying to help, for Chrissakes," he says, rubbing his jaw as if it still hurts five months later. "He didn't need to do that." He holds up the peeled orange to me, offering it.

I reach for it. "Thanks." I break it apart. "I don't think he meant to hit you," I add begrudgingly. There was a bit of a brawl on the dance floor and Wyatt had intervened. I wasn't a fan of Wyatt's even then, but he didn't deserve to get whacked in the face.

"Yeah, I know, he told me that." He shakes his head. "Your family is something else."

My defenses go on alert again. Can't really dispute that statement, though, much as I enjoy arguing with Wyatt.

"It's been entertaining since Théo moved in here," he adds.

"Glad you find my family entertaining." Théo is my nephew; JP's brother. Théo is also Wyatt's boss. Oh my God.

He laughs. "I'm not dissing your family, hot stuff."

My eyes fly open. "Hot stuff?"

He leans on the counter, opposite me. "Oh yeah. I always suspected you were hot stuff under that snooty, arrogant front."

My jaw slackens. I blink. I open my mouth but nothing comes out. Finally, I manage to screech, "Snooty? Arrogant?"

He lifts one big shoulder. "You're Princess Wynn, right?"

My eyeballs are no longer in danger of bleeding, they're in danger of popping out and bouncing across the counter. I jump off the stool. "Princess Wynn? Are you fucking kidding me?"

The corners of his mouth lift. "See? Hot stuff. After last night macking down on my bed, I have no doubts about that."

"Aaaargh!" My fingers curl into my palms. "You are . . . *you're* arrogant, too!"

"Good comeback." He finishes peeling another orange. "I'm disappointed, hot stuff."

Heat rises inside me, and now I splay my fingers out at my sides. "You're just a party-loving, woman-chasing . . . jock."

Oh my God. My entire family is jocks. As if that's the best insult I can come up with.

I blame the hangover.

He laughs softly. "Hmm. We disagree. What a surprise, princess. How about we settle this like adults . . . in the bedroom." He cocks an eyebrow, smirking.

I suck in a fast breath and my cheeks flame. "Oh my God. Princess . . ." Heat boils inside me. "You . . . you have no idea." I don't finish that thought, just grab my purse and stalk away from him toward the door. Luckily my shoes are there—black stiletto heels I wore to the party last night.

"Thanks for the breakfast," I call over my shoulder

through clenched teeth. I may hate him, but I was raised to be polite.

"You're welcome."

I jump, because he's followed me to the door.

"And for the Advil," I grudgingly say. "And . . . a place to sleep."

"Next time . . . we'll do more than sleep." He leans in closer, lips curved in a sexy smile.

God. I haven't brushed my teeth. I probably smell like a winery and look even worse. He is not going to kiss me. Much as I might like that . . . because he looks amazing, and I know he tastes amazing and feels even better . . . "Yeah, that's gonna happen . . . *never.*"

He chuckles again.

I make my escape. Yes, I am a living clichéd walk of shame, in my short, tight party dress and heels, making my way to my car parked a couple of blocks away on Pacific Avenue. I have absolutely nothing to be ashamed of, it's just an expression. Except I am a tad mortified that I succumbed to Wyatt Bell's sexy appeal last night and let him feel my boobs and kiss me until I couldn't breathe.

Arrogant. Snooty. Oh my God. My teeth grind together as a stalk down the street.

Princess Wynn. He has no idea.

Win Big

ACKNOWLEDGMENTS

As always, huge thanks to the team that helps me in this crazy business—my agent, Emily Sylvan Kim; my sister and my daughter for working the numbers, which I hate with a passion; Cassie at Weaver Way Author Servies, and Emily Carthum for stepping in to help so capably. Also many thanks to my author friends who keep me sane, I am so grateful for such a supportive and understanding community. Most of all, thank you to you—for reading this book and supporting me.

ABOUT THE AUTHOR

Kelly Jamieson is a best-selling author of over sixty romance novels and novellas. Her writing has been described as "emotionally complex," "sweet and satisfying," and "blisteringly sexy." She likes coffee (black), wine (mostly white), shoes (especially high heels) and hockey!

Kelly appreciates your help in spreading the word about her books, including sharing with friends! Please leave a review on your favorite book site! You can also join her Facebook group, Kelly Jamieson's Sweet Heat Reader Lounge, to hang out with her, and for exclusive giveaways and sneak peeks of future books.

Visit her website at www.kellyjamieson.com or contact her at info@kellyjamieson.com

WINDY CITY KINK

SWEET OBSESSION

ALL MESSED UP

PLAYING DIRTY

BREW CREW

LIMITED TIME OFFER

NO OBLIGATION REQUIRED

ACES HOCKEY

MAJOR MISCONDUCT

OFF LIMITS

ICING

TOP SHELF

BACK CHECK

SLAP SHOT

PLAYING HURT

BIG STICK

GAME ON

LAST SHOT

BODY SHOT

HOT SHOT

LONG SHOT

BAYARD HOCKEY

SHUT OUT

CROSS CHECK

WYNN HOCKEY

PLAY TO WIN

IN IT TO WIN IT

WIN BIG

FOR THE WIN

GAME CHANGER

BEARS HOCKEY

MUST LOVE DOGS…AND HOCKEY

YOU HAD ME AT HOCKEY

TALK HOCKEY TO ME

THE O ZONE

GOOD HANDS

SCORING BIG

MERRY PUCKING CHRISTMAS

LIGHT 'EM UP

STORM HOCKEY

CROSSING THE LINE

STANDALONES

THREE OF HEARTS

LOVING MADDIE FROM A TO Z

DANCING IN THE RAIN

LOVE ME

LOVE ME MORE

2 HOT 2 HANDLE

FRIENDS WITH BENEFITS

LOST AND FOUND

ONE WICKED NIGHT

SWEET DEAL

HOW SWEET IT IS

HOT RIDE

CRAZY EVER AFTER

ALL I WANT FOR CHRISTMAS

SEXPRESSO NIGHT

IRISH SEX FAIRY

CONFERENCE CALL

RIGGER

YOU REALLY GOT ME

SCREWED

FIRECRACKER

BIG WITCH ENERGY

HATE ME UNDER THE MISTLETOE

www.ingramcontent.com/pod-product-compliance
Lightning Source LLC
Chambersburg PA
CBHW020644120726
47906CB00001B/112